A Real Piece
of Work

A Real Piece of Work

A DAKOTA STEVENS MYSTERY

CHRIS ORCUTT

A Real Piece of Work

A Dakota Stevens Mystery Novel

by

Chris Orcutt

Second Print Edition: 2015

This is a work of fiction. Names, characters, places, and incidents either are the product of the author's imagination or are used fictitiously. Any resemblance to actual persons (living or dead), companies, institutions, events or locales is entirely coincidental and not intended by the author.

ISBN-13: 978-0692206379 (Have Pen, Will Travel)

The cover artist for this book is Elisabeth Pinio, a graphic designer based in the Silicon Valley. The photograph on the cover, "Paint Brushes Close-Up," is by photographer Tech109 on Flickr. The ebook formatter is EBook Converting|High Quality Ebook Conversion: ebookconverting.com

Also by Chris Orcutt:

The Rich Are Different (Dakota Stevens #2)
A Truth Stranger Than Fiction (Dakota Stevens #3)
The Man, The Myth, The Legend (A Collection of Short Stories)
One Hundred Miles from Manhattan (A Novel)

www.orcutt.net
www.dakotastevens.com

For Alexas:

My Véra, My Hadley, My Muse

"We're talking about a very, very clever scheme."

— A former Christie's modern-art specialist
on the alleged art fraud perpetrated by
New York Art Dealer Ely Sakhai

"I would always hesitate to recommend as a life's companion a young lady with quite such a vivid shade of red hair. Red hair, sir, in my opinion, is dangerous."

— Jeeves in *How Right You Are, Jeeves*
by P.G. Wodehouse

1

THE TEASER

Back in my FBI days, during soporific stakeouts when I dreamed about the life I might lead as a private detective, I never imagined the job would one day require me to scuba-dive across a half-mile of ocean brimming with sharks.

Basically, anything capable of eating me was absent from my business plan.

Right now, despite the Caribbean sun on my face and the piquant salt air in my nose, I wished I were back in snowy Manhattan, safe behind my desk, listening like Sam Spade to some elegant dame tell me her troubles. Instead I had a 20-year-old scuba bum and my bikini-clad associate, Svetlana Krüsh, all but shoving me into the water. They stood silently beside me as wave after wave spanked the hull. Under my wetsuit, the heat began to rise.

"You're positive they're both on there," I said, nodding at the 80-foot motor yacht in the distance.

"According to the chambermaid," Svetlana said, "they left together this morning."

"And we're sure they're, ah, busy?"

"I am told they never leave the room."

She adjusted her bikini strap. After three days down here, Svetlana had only a whisper of a tan, but the way the leopard print hugged her aristocratic curves, you didn't care. Kyle, our alleged guide, leered at her. I grabbed him by the mouth and pinched his cheeks together.

"How about it, *dude*?"

"Wha?"

"Our friend on the yacht."

"Already told you—guy runs their slip says they put out every morning, come back around one."

"What time we got?"

With a flourish, Svetlana held out her watch. High noon.

"How long to get over there?" I asked.

"Half an hour, tops." Kyle scratched in his ear. "Quit stalling, man. I've gotta meet somebody at Sloppy Joe's soon."

I looked over our stern. Key West was a purple mist on the horizon. I turned back to the yacht.

"Let me see, one more time."

Svetlana passed the binoculars. While the captain and his mate read newspapers on the bridge, three body-guards sunned themselves on the bow. Conover and his mistress had to be inside, doing what mistresses and CEOs of financial services companies did.

"*Moneta?*" Kyle said. "What the hell kind of name for a boat is that?"

"Goddess of money," I said. "Greek, I think."

"Roman," Svetlana said.

"There you go—Roman. We know what he worships anyway."

To the south dark clouds were creeping in, and the mounting wind flapped Svetlana's hair across my cheek. Between their boat and ours was a gulf of iridescent blue-green water that looked like it would take a week to cross. I wanted to call it off, but if I chickened-out now, in two weeks my business would shrivel up. Besides, Mrs. Conover was counting on us. I handed the binoculars back.

"Ready, Mr. Stevens?" Kyle said.

"Stop with the 'Mister' already. It's Dakota." I strapped on the flippers. "Why am I doing this again?"

Why? Because Mrs. Conover had made it sound so simple—snap a few photos, collect a big check. "I'll cover any expenses," she said. "Consider it a vacation...take a week, a month—I don't care. Just catch the bastard."

Svetlana nudged me. "Because you are sucker for jilted women. Especially when they are rich." She handed me a mask. "And don't forget, a blizzard is starting in New York, so we must catch six o'clock out of Miami."

I spit in the mask, rubbed it around and put it on.

"Sharks?" I said to Kyle.

"Sure. Blacktips, a few bulls maybe. No big deal."

I squatted down and slipped into the vest with the scuba tank. Kyle showed me the buttons for the buoyancy compensator.

"So, Miss Krüsh," I said, "while I'm risking life and *limb*, what will you be doing?"

She donned a pair of Dolce & Gabbana sunglasses and tied a mocha sarong around her waist so it hung fetchingly off one hip.

"Wave when you finish, and I swoop in like cavalry." She plopped down behind the wheel, crossed her runway legs and rubbed sunblock on her shoulders. Kyle jammed the regulator in my mouth.

"Remember what Nietzsche said, man—the shit that doesn't kill you makes you stronger. Trust me, you're gonna love it." He tipped backwards into the deep.

I patted the vest's waterproof pouch to check for the camera and plunged in. By the time the bubbles cleared, Kyle was already 50 yards ahead and paddling fast along the reef. A school of blue and yellow fish darted around him. I pumped furiously to catch up, my ears shrieking. By the time my Eustachian tubes kicked in and balanced the pressure, I had caught up to Kyle. He was treading water in a shaft of sunlight.

"Slow down," I tried to say.

He gave me a thumbs-up, and we were off again, hovering over the craggy surface of the reef. Bent and slender growths of coral jutted up like cacti, and red and green plant life swayed in the current. I almost began to relax and enjoy this undersea desert. That is, until the reef vanished.

Before leaving Key West, Kyle had told me that just beyond the reef the seabed descends from fifty to a thousand feet. Little by little the friendly coral disappeared along with the ocean floor. Even in the cool water I felt the hot pulse of adrenaline down my back and legs. I couldn't see the bottom anymore. The water was a ghastly deep blue. My sight was hazy at the fringes and swimming beasts seemed to materialize like ships out of the fog. A barracuda bigger than my leg drifted past me, its fanged jaw hanging open, its cruel eye sizing me up. I turned and a pair of hammerheads crossed our path. My instincts screamed for me to turn around, but my legs refused to listen. They kept pushing me forward.

I had long believed that mingling with creatures in the open sea was a bad idea. This was their turf. No matter how nimble you were with your stupid flippers, they were always going to be better at it than you. My shin muscles burned from all the kicking. I shouldn't be down here. But this was my last chance before Conover jetted off for Zurich, and I wasn't following him to Zurich. The Hilton in Key West, the Pierre in New York, the estate in Greenwich when the wife was away—in all three cases he'd been too well-guarded. Mrs. Conover needed ironclad proof of her husband's infidelity, and I was going to get it.

Gradually a spectral shadow of the yacht appeared, its edges glowing like the corona of an eclipse, its two shiny anchor chains plummeting into the gloom. I punched Kyle in the arm, pointed up. Silhouetted by the sun, dozens of sharks swam in erratic loops around the bow. The damn bodyguards were feeding them. We crawled up toward the ladder at the stern.

On deck, we crouched next to a vile-smelling bait box and shed the scuba gear.

"Five minutes." I checked the camera. "Second you hear me, wave for Svetlana."

Kyle stared at the water. I slapped his arm.

"Didn't count on so many, did you, smart guy?"

"There's a Tiger down there, man. Those things are vicious."

"Well, we won't have to go in again. Hang tight till I get back."

I padded up the stairs and entered a beige-carpeted living room with cushioned seats under the windows. I continued forward, down a passageway of dark wood. Faint at first, the walls resonated with a woman's moaning. Much too enthusiastic to be real. Reveling in my first bit of luck in a month, I smiled and switched on the camera.

At their door, I pushed, but it wouldn't open. I pushed harder.

Locked. Well, I hadn't come a thousand miles and through my personal hell on earth to give up. I kicked the door in.

Conover and a striking Latina sprang up in the bed. I let the camera absorb the full range of their emotions— from shock to embarrassment to outrage to anger—and all the while they did nothing to cover up. Mrs. Conover was going to be pleased.

"What the fuck is this?" Conover blurted out.

"Wait, hold that pose," I said. "Nice."

As they finally scrambled out of bed, I ejected the camera's memory card and sealed it in a Ziploc bag. Hustling down the hall, I tucked the bag under my suit, against my skin, and ran out on deck.

"All right, Kyle, let's—"

The three bodyguards stood between Kyle and me with their arms crossed. They wore nothing but Speedos, and their bare chests glistened with sweat. This was disturbing on many levels. Above us, Conover rushed onto the balcony tying his bathrobe. A gust of wind grabbed his comb-over and flapped it from the side of his head like a windsock.

"Get that fucking camera," he said, mashing the hair back against his skull, "and throw their asses overboard."

With no effort they seized Kyle and pitched him into the drink. I was cornered at the rail. They moved in. I dropped the one closest to me with an elbow to the throat, but the other two grabbed my legs and heaved me so hard that I did a backwards somersault in mid-air. The camera flew out of my hand. I kicked to the surface and heard our boat in the distance, humming toward us.

Conover galumphed down the stairs and hurled buckets of chum into the water.

"Nothing like a good feeding frenzy!"

"Mother," Kyle said.

We raced away from the yacht. Sharks swirled around the stern, their fins slicing the water everywhere. Every wave was sinister. Something brushed my leg. It was Kyle, thrashing.

"Calm down," I said. "Just get ready to grab the ladder when she comes."

As Svetlana rolled in, I grabbed Kyle and hooked the ladder with my free arm. The boat dragged us until we pulled ourselves out.

We were safe on the deck, speeding for Key West. Kyle took the wheel.

"All that equipment," he said. "I'm screwed."

"Relax, we'll expense it." I handed Svetlana the Ziploc with the memory card. "Email these to her lawyer the second we get to the hotel. I want somebody to meet us with the money when we land."

"I just hope we can get back before they close LaGuardia," she said.

"I just hope they serve martinis on the plane."

2

CALLING CARDS

For a guy, few things are more humbling than getting your ass kicked in chess by a woman. In the current game I'd lasted forty-five minutes by taking a painfully long time between moves. My strategy? Simple—bore Svetlana to the point that she would make mistakes. So far, it hadn't worked.

Snug in our office at 82½ East 10th Street, I hadn't heard a single car outside for hours. Last I checked, it was a textbook blizzard out there. We'd been cooped up since 11:00 a.m. waiting for our new client, and to pass the time I was helping Svetlana prepare for a 20-board simultaneous exhibition next month. Building her confidence by losing.

"So this guy," I said. "He didn't say what this was about?"

Her wide-set, almond-shaped eyes devoured the board.

"Nothing. I don't even know his name."

I considered my pieces. The best word to describe my situation? *Grim.* Svetlana laced her fingers together on the edge of my desk.

"Your bishop is exposed."

"Uh-oh." I checked the fly on my pants.

She smiled faintly and tapped the board with a clear-polished fingernail.

"He is defenseless. Every piece must be supported."

"Maybe I'm planning a sacrifice before my big attack." I sipped some Pellegrino.

"It would be a stupid sacrifice. You should give up material only when there is a definite advantage to be gained in position or tactics."

"Fine." I moved my bishop back two squares. The move seemed innocuous until I noticed it cleared the way for Svetlana's rook. She used it to capture my remaining knight.

"Thanks for the tip," I said.

The end was near. Her pieces converged around my king like personal injury lawyers around an accident victim. I moved him a square closer to some pawns, but they wouldn't be much help; they had their own problems.

"Mate in six," she announced.

Svetlana wore a white silk blouse with turn-back French cuffs. The top two buttons were undone, and as she leaned over the board I used my skills of observation to ascertain a nude lace bra and a lick of cleavage. She rapped her queen down in the center.

"Check."

I studied the board. Svetlana had skewered my rook behind my king. I thought you only saw moves like this in chess books. Then again, Svetlana had written a chess book. The second I pushed my king out of check, she shot her queen down the diagonal and snagged the rook.

I nodded, sipped some water. Play enough chess against a bona fide International Grandmaster and you tend to develop a fatalistic view of the game.

I was planning a retaliatory strike when the bell on the outer office door jingled.

"Ah...saved by—"

"I didn't think he was coming," she said.

Our office and the conference room across the way were glass fishbowls. I stood up and opened the blinds so we could see out in the reception area. A man clomped snow off a pair of hand-tooled cowboy boots. Dark complexion, Middle Eastern features and a Clark Gable mustache. No hat, no scarf, no gloves. Hardly dressed for the weather.

The man's overcoat was glazed with ice. A leather briefcase, dark from melted snow, dangled at his side. He opened his mouth as if to call out, then wobbled and collapsed on the rug.

"Not good," I said.

We ran out to the reception area and lifted him up. His pulse was strong and he was breathing. I removed his icy coat and dragged him to the couch.

"He'll come around, give him a sec."

We watched him breathe for a moment.

"This is where I wish we had some brandy," I said.

"Brandy?"

"Yeah, anytime this happened in a Sherlock Holmes story, Holmes would say, 'Quick, Watson, the brandy!' and the guy would recover instantly."

"We do not have brandy," she said. "I will make tea."

"Good. And get him a blanket."

As Svetlana grabbed the man's coat, a packet of hundred dollar bills fell out. She pursed her lips and laid the money on the coffee table. In the meantime, I pried the briefcase out of his frigid fingers. I was looking for something with his name on it. The briefcase contained photos of a painting, a printout of our agency's home page, and a case of calling cards:

Nadir Serif
1020 Park Avenue
New York, NY

"Nadir?" I handed the card to Svetlana. "Who names their kid *Nadir?*"

"Yes, Dakota is so much better."

"Give me a break, will you? Somebody just annihilated me at chess."

As Svetlana left for the kitchen, our client stirred. Two cups of Earl Grey later, Mr. Serif had regained composure enough to follow us into the conference room. I pushed a pad and pen at him.

"Write something, please."

"Why?"

"I need a sample of your handwriting."

He did—with his right hand.

"Thank you," I said.

Svetlana took notes at the head of the table, while I sat opposite Serif so I could watch his eyes. In my ten years as an FBI field agent I had interviewed hundreds of witnesses, and one thing I had learned was that the eyes—especially the direction they looked when you asked a question—told you far more than the words alone.

"Forgive me," Serif said. "I didn't think it was so far down here. Out of shape, I suppose." He glanced at Svetlana. "I know who you are, Mr. Stevens, but Ms. Krüsh, she is your—what is it?—Gal Friday?"

I looked at her. "She's indispensable is what she is."

The photos from Serif's briefcase were on the table. I waved at them. "Let me guess. This painting is missing and you want us to find it."

"Stolen, to be exact," Serif said. "From my very apartment. And I know who did it."

"Who?"

"David DeAngelis, an expert I hired to examine it. Runs the Met's Provenance Research Department and does consulting on the side. The work is from Marcel Duchamp's early period."

Not being an art historian, I had no idea what a work from Marcel Duchamp's early period looked like, but this one had a group of peasants with absurdly large heads working wheat fields. Svetlana would research the painting for us later.

"Its name?"

"*Harvest Toil*," he said.

That didn't explain the big heads, but I let it go.

"And why did you hire DeAngelis?" Svetlana asked.

"I wanted an accurate appraisal for auction next month."

"Which house?" I asked. "Christie's, Sotheby's…?"

He shook his head. "Certain things must remain confidential."

The use of visual accessing cues had its merits. In Serif's case, his eyes kept moving to his right. Since he was right-handed, this meant he was using the creative side of his brain to construct elements in his story.

"Okay," I said, "what's the painting worth?"

"Slightly over a million."

Svetlana looked at him over her glasses. "Has your insurance company investigated?"

"Well, actually…it wasn't insured."

"Oh?"

Serif's eyes shifted right again.

"I've only had it for a few months, and…well…the insuring process is so damned intrusive." He scratched his nose. "I wanted to get it appraised and dump it at auction."

There was a rumbling noise outside as a city sanitation truck plowed the street. It was shaping up to be one of the worst blizzards in the city's history. I turned to Serif.

"So, did you get your appraisal?"

He put down his mug. "You must understand, there's more to it than just looking at the painting and saying it's worth such-and-such dollars. A true appraisal requires corroboration of the work's provenance."

"The paperwork that says who bought and sold it," I said.

"You're grossly oversimplifying it, but yes." He sipped some tea. His eyes drifted to the right again and stayed there. "Anyway, I kept the painting at my apartment and loaned him a key for the days my housekeeper wasn't there. Most of the time he did research in his office, but occasionally he dropped by to examine a detail or two. I went to Hong Kong on business for two weeks, and when I returned, the painting was gone."

"The painting," Svetlana said, "it is quite large, yes?"

"About three by four."

She wagged her pen. "The housekeeper, how could she miss such a large empty space on the wall?"

"Because…he hung another painting exactly the same size with a similar frame."

I nodded. "So it wouldn't be obvious something was missing—clever." I picked up the cash and zipped through the bills. "Lot to be walking around in a snow-storm with. Cab fare?"

"An advance on your fee," he said. "I'm paying fifty thousand for the return of that painting, Mr. Stevens. The ten thousand there is all I had in my safe, but it should be sufficient to cover your expenses."

"For now." I put down the money. "Why not a check?"

"I realize how this looks, however I assure you it is all on the up-and-up. I simply can't have the entire New York art world gossiping about the painting's disappearance."

"But you realize I *will* have to question people. His coworkers at the Met, for starters. You're not married, I take it."

"No."

"Any scorned lovers?"

"No."

"Well, I'll have to poke around your building a bit, talk to the doorman, your housekeeper, et cetera."

"I understand you will have to make inquiries, just don't mention the painting. I know he has the painting. What you're really looking for is him."

My instincts didn't like it. Any of it. Unfortunately, my instincts didn't pay the bills. I stood up, paced to the other side of the room and leaned against the glass.

"Look," I said, "if you know DeAngelis stole your painting, why not go to the police?"

Serif sneered. "Idiots. I want personal attention on this. I want my painting *found*."

"First of all," I said, "some very smart people work on the NYPD, and I happen to know a few of them. Second, they have fingerprint records and mug shots, information I can get but not easily. Third, they deal with stolen artwork all the time. In fact, they have a squad that specializes in art burglaries and jewel thefts. All I'm saying is we might want to get in touch with someone—someone discreet—when the time is right."

"Absolutely not," Serif said. "No outside interference. I don't want a bunch of cops stirring up rumors among the dealers and gallery owners. It could ruin my chances of a strong showing at auction. You're on your own. I want *you* to find my painting, are we clear?"

This wasn't the first time I'd taken a case where I didn't trust the client, and it surely wouldn't be the last. I turned to Svetlana, who had been studying Serif's face.

"Any thoughts?"

Without a word, Svetlana dragged the cash off the table and left the room. I took that to mean we were on the case.

3

Blizzard in Manhattan

Svetlana took pity on Serif and put him up in the guest room of her apartment upstairs. Then we bundled up and went out for a walk. After being trapped inside all day, I needed to clear my head in the cold air. Serif's labored account and near heart attack had left me drained.

The sidewalks were impassable, so we had to walk in the road. We tramped down 10th toward the West Village. Meandering south through the hushed city streets, we ended up at Washington Square Park. The giant triumphal arch glowed in the lights, and we gazed up at the snow swirling around it. I nudged Svetlana.

"You're considering how we should spend the money."

"He is lying," she said.

"You caught that, too."

"He is lying or holding something back."

"Gosh, a client that lies. What's this world coming to?"

We cut through the square, turned down Thompson and passed two of Svetlana's chess haunts on our way to Bleecker. Aside from a few pedestrians and the occasional plow, the streets were deserted. The wind howled, whipped snow into our faces.

"The Weather Channel was right," I said. "This *is* a blizzard."

Up ahead, at the intersection of Cornelia and 4th, lights blazed inside a Greek diner.

"Bring any of that ten thousand with you?" I asked.

"Enough."

We weren't the only New Yorkers who'd braved the elements. People in heavy coats jammed the restaurant. We thawed out and got a booth against the steamed-up windows. I had hot chocolate and two grilled cheese sandwiches, Svetlana got herbal tea and Spanikopita.

"Spinach pie at midnight?" I said. "What are you, with child?"

"The iron is good for me."

The waitress brought our drinks.

"I just realized something," I said.

"That you don't pay me enough?" She added a packet of Splenda to her tea and stirred with deft precision.

"No, he didn't do what every client does—insist on where we should start. Don't you find that odd?"

"I find it more odd that he walked all that way to see us—tonight. This could have waited until morning."

I sipped some hot chocolate. "Yeah, and that bit about not going to the police because he doesn't want to ruin the painting's 'showing at auction.' I'm not buying it."

"Where *should* we start?"

"The Met," I said. "Talk to DeAngelis's colleagues, find out where the guy lives."

Our food arrived. We savored every bite as if we were going to the gallows, then trudged back into the storm. It was a whiteout now, and we had to stop at the street corners to read the signs. At one point I turned around and Svetlana wasn't there. When she caught up, I held out my arm for her.

"So we don't get separated."

"Of course."

Her gloved fingers squeezed my bicep. It was like getting a mild electric shock.

"Let's rouse Serif good and early," I said. "I want to talk to him again before we start the hunt."

With her free hand, Svetlana held down her fur hat against the wind.

"That may prove difficult. I gave him a sleeping pill before I left."

"Drugging the clients," I said. "Lovely."

We turned onto 10th Street. Through the blinding snow, I made out the headlights of a big SUV idling a hundred yards away. We were in the middle of the road when it roared to life and accelerated straight at us.

4

A Two-for-One Deal

Svetlana clutched my arm. Instantly the road became a hundred feet wide. The truck bore down on us, much faster than I could pull us across, and our boots slipped in the loosely packed snow. Ahead, the snowbank was heaped over the parked cars. So was the one behind. Someone had chosen the perfect place to take us out.

With the SUV speeding straight at us and no time to pull my gun, our only chance was to make the truck oversteer in the wrong direction. Holding Svetlana's arm, I feinted backwards. The truck swerved. I grabbed her around the waist, and with everything I had, flung us into the snowbank. The snow buried us.

The SUV bumped against the opposite bank. A car alarm wailed. The engine roared and faded down the street.

We dug out, brushed each other off and rested on a stoop.

"Svetlana, you've got to start paying your credit cards on time."

She looked at me. "I did not sign on for this."

"You know what? Neither did I."

Still in a daze we slogged through the deep snow and crossed Fourth Avenue. I watched the street, in case they came around for a second pass. At our building, a three-story brick townhouse, Svetlana let go of my arm and went up the steps to the first floor. I stood at the stairs leading down to the basement office.

"I'll just use the fold-out. There's no way I'm getting uptown tonight." I kicked the snow off my boots. "Let's have breakfast, ask him some more questions."

"I will research the painting," she said.

"Check him out, too. You're right about his hiding something."

She went upstairs, I went downstairs. At the office door, I had the pleasant surprise of finding it open and the glass with my name on it shattered. There were tool marks along the doorjamb where the burglar had tried to pry it open. I drew my gun, a Smith & Wesson 9mm, jacked one into the chamber and eased inside.

The place was dark. I took a deep breath and moved forward in a low crouch. Reception area, clear. So was the office. No drawers were tossed, nothing was missing. Except in the conference room. Serif's briefcase and the photos of the painting were gone.

My cell phone rang. I answered it.

"Yeah?"

"We have a development," Svetlana said. "Get up here."

I ran upstairs. Her apartment door was already open.

"Svetlana?"

"In here."

The apartment was a floor-through. I found her in the guest bedroom, sitting at the desk. Untouched on the nightstand were a sleeping pill and a glass of water. The bed was empty. I felt under the blankets. Not warm, but not ice-cold either.

I checked the rest of the apartment for stray bad guys and, finding none, holstered my gun. I went back to the bedroom.

"Any of his clothes still here?"

She nodded at the bureau. Just a belt and a pair of socks.

"Overcoat?"

"I hung it up earlier," she said. "It's gone now."

"Well, look on the bright side. Wherever he is, he's warm."

We went out to the kitchen. I made us some hot apple cider, sat next to her at the kitchen island and held up my mug.

"Well, here's to us. Hired by a client for a total of two hours, and then somebody kidnaps the client." We clinked mugs. "Now it's a two-for-one deal. Find DeAngelis *and* Serif."

"It is not our fault," Svetlana said. "If there was danger, he should have told us."

"If it's the same people—and I'm guessing it is—they broke in downstairs, too. Got the briefcase and the photos."

I put down my cider and paced around the room.

"Okay, his belt and socks are still here, which suggests he was taken by force. If he'd left voluntarily, he would've put them on. But there are no signs of a struggle, so it's possible he knew them. Then again, they could have pointed a gun at him and told him to simmer down."

"Simmer down?" She cupped her mug.

"Something my grandfather used to say when I acted up."

"Ah," she said.

"So the one with the gun goes, 'Okay, Serif, where are the photos?' At this point, Serif is scared shitless. He throws on his clothes, except the socks and belt because they're rushing him, and leads them downstairs. They break in, but clearly they aren't pros at B&E because they used a tire iron—the impressions are rounded, not flat like a crowbar. Anyway, it doesn't work, so one of them smashes the window and grabs the stuff. Then they wait for us in the SUV."

I sat down and sipped my cider. "What do you think?"

"It is wild speculation," Svetlana said. "But I enjoy watching you flail."

"One thing's for sure. You were right about his holding something back."

"Like you, I am good at reading opponents."

Outside, another plow rumbled by.

"So," she said, "do we report him as missing?"

"If he doesn't turn up by morning, yeah—call and report it with the SUV incident. But hopefully we'll find him ourselves."

"And we have *so* much to go on."

"Swell, right? At least they didn't get the cash. Where'd you hide it, anyway?"

Narrowing her eyes, Svetlana reached into her blouse and produced the bundle of hundreds. She flapped it.

"All ten thousand?" I said. "Concealed in your modest décolletage?"

"I wanted a place no one would look. Especially you."

"Well, if you don't want me looking, you better give me some of it."

With a smirk, she peeled off an eighth-inch and handed it to me—reluctantly.

"Okay," I said. "Tomorrow, we start."

5

Park Avenue

Late the next morning, I caught the express up to 86th Street and trudged over to Serif's building on Park Avenue. Two 20-something men loitered across the street. They wore red ski jackets and were just standing there, trying not to look like they were just standing there, which only made their presence more obvious. I went through the revolving door.

The doorman, a muscular African-American with insightful eyes, stood erect at his desk. He wore a crisp navy and gold uniform with a name tag that read, "James."

"Dexter Price to see Mr. Serif," I said.

James eyed me for a moment. He was a shade taller than my six feet, and his posture told me he was either ex-military or ballet. I doubted ballet though; guys like him used prima ballerinas for toothpicks.

While James picked up a phone and dialed, I glanced outside at the redcoats. Still there. James hung up.

"No answer, sir."

"Is the housekeeper in?"

"What is your business, Mister, ah…?"

"Price," I said. "Dexter Price. I'm a dealer from downtown."

"You're no art dealer."

"Excuse me?"

"Way you're dressed." He considered me as one would a statue. "Dealers I seen, bunch of wusses. Wouldn't be caught dead in boots like that."

"Hmm. What else?"

"Way you move."

"Yeah? How do dealers move?"

"Sneaky," he said. "But you don't need to sneak. You've had training, I can tell."

"FBI. And you? Marines?"

"Yup."

I offered him a stick of gum. He accepted.

"Alright, you got me." I tossed him a business card. He squinted down at it.

"Dakota? That your real name?"

I nodded. We worked on our gum.

"So," I said, "nobody's home up there. Where's that leave us?"

"Gonna take more than a stick of Big Red."

I pulled a pair of hundreds from my wallet and slid them across the counter.

"I may need to come back. Will these cover me?"

"We'll put 'em on your tab." He snapped up the bills. "Don't have a key, but I 'spect with you being F-B-I and all, you'll have no trouble with that."

"Course not. And the super?"

"All over the place. Better work fast. Comes out of nowhere, that guy."

"Gotcha." I leaned on the desk. "By the way, those two clowns across the street—ever seen them before?"

He didn't look out the door, which surprised me.

"Dudes in the red jackets? Here when I came in this morning, six thirty. First time I seen 'em."

A gangly, silver-haired man and his great dane loped off the elevator. James hopped out from behind his desk and opened the door for them.

"Cold out there, Mr. Crawford." He tipped his cap. "Good day, sir." He resumed his post.

"Serif had any visitors lately?" I asked.

"Nope," James said. "Just the housekeeper. Here Tuesdays and Fridays. Nice lady."

"How about Serif himself?"

"Cheap bastard."

"No—when did you see him last?"

"Left yesterday afternoon. Hasn't been back that I seen." He took off his cap, scratched his head. "'Course, it's possible he went on one of his trips."

"Trips?"

"Shit, yeah. Dude's gone like nine months out of the year. Goes away four, five weeks at a time."

"Where?"

He shrugged. "Europe, Japan—all over."

"Guy named David DeAngelis," I said, "doing some work for Serif. Know the last time he came by?"

"Never heard of him," he said.

"You're sure?"

"Man, I say I don't know somebody—"

"Okay, okay. Do me a favor. If anybody tries getting into his place—like our pals over there—let me know. Cell number's on the card. What's your number here?"

With a wink, he handed me a card of his own. Nowadays, everybody's got one. As I turned to go, James jutted his chin at me.

"Hey, how I know you won't go up there and rob the guy blind?"

"You don't," I said. "But it looks like Serif might have been kidnapped. That's why I need to see his place."

"All right, 18A. But anybody asks, you slipped by when I was putting one of the old ladies in a cab."

I saluted him and jumped in the elevator.

Upstairs, Serif had five neighbors on his floor. So much for covert. I put away my winter gloves and slipped on a pair of latex ones. Then I took out my lock-picking set.

I hated this part of the job. I especially hated how in the movies they made it seem like a two-minute process. Let me tell you, it's more like ten, minimum, and an uncomfortable ten at that, because you've got little metal sticks jutting out of the lock like acupuncture needles, and you have to hurry because if you're caught, people assume you're up to no good. Nobody picks locks for fun.

Fifteen minutes later, I was in. I paused in a dark foyer, closed my eyes and listened. A clock was ticking somewhere. I sniffed. There was the sharp scent of urine. I clicked on my Mini-Maglite and waved it inside the foyer closet. There were expensive overcoats, umbrellas and a shelf of hats and gloves. On the floor a cardboard box brimmed with shopping bags from Zabar's and Barneys. A forlorn pair of squash rackets leaned against the back wall. I moved on.

The hallway opened into a living room with high ceilings. Portraits, landscapes and abstracts filled every square inch of wall space. The furniture was all modern, expensive stuff, and the entire southern wall was windows, with an unobstructed view of Park Avenue down to the MetLife building. Apparently, Serif didn't have to clip coupons.

Neither the living room nor the kitchen contained anything clue-like, but in the utility room, I *did* find the source of the pungent ammonia smell: a litter box. The bathroom was a bust. Next came the bedroom, where I found the ticking clock. Checking the walk-in closet, I noticed an empty space between two suitcases, and gaps among the hanging clothes. Several hangers were askew. Someone had packed in a hurry. *Serif? Or somebody else?*

As I entered the office, there was a bookcase full of antique typewriters—Remington, Smith-Corona, Olivetti and a few foreign models I'd never heard of. The answering machine was empty, so I turned my attention to the computer. While waiting for it to boot up, I rummaged through the desk drawers. There were old boxes of linen paper and trays of rubber stamps, but no planner or address book.

Serif's computer didn't have a single web site bookmarked, and his settings didn't allow cookies or a page history, so I couldn't learn what sites he frequented. Searching the hard drive, I discovered it was practically empty. The folders in his email program were also empty, along with the bin of deleted mail. Serif seemed to be covering his tracks. But why?

All of the new mail was junk, except one message from the day before. It was a *Yahoo!* email address and the subject read, "We need to talk." I opened it:

I KNOW WHAT YOU TWO ARE DOING

No signature, no "have a nice day," nothing. The email address began with "dd," which gave me the sense that David DeAngelis had sent this email. I took out my cell phone and called Svetlana. Something rubbed against my leg.

"Jesus!" A plump calico cat squinted up at me, meowed, did its figure-eight routine through my legs.

"Hello?" Svetlana said.

"A cat just scared the crap out of me."

"You, the big, strong detective?"

"I'm in Serif's place. There's an email. I think it's from DeAngelis."

"Send it to me as an attachment," she said.

"But it doesn't say anything."

"There is more to an email than what you see on the screen."

She walked me through the process of attaching the "We need to talk" email to a new email, and sending it.

"On its way," I said. "Now, lunch—Benihana, two hours. Think you could have something by then?"

"You and that foolish restaurant. Okay, I will work on the email while the glass people finish."

"Right, the office door. That'll give me time to drop by the Met and talk with DeAngelis's coworkers. No word on Serif, I take it."

"None."

I petted the cat. "Listen, there's a couple of hoods outside this place, and there might be others, so keep a sharp eye."

"Yes, boss."

We hung up. I deleted the email I sent, reset the "We need to talk" email to Unread, emptied the email trash bin, and shut down the computer.

The cat rubbed against me again. My conscience wasn't going to let me leave without feeding the thing and cleaning its litter box.

I always was a sucker for defenseless creatures.

6

HALF A MILLION VOLTS

I told James about the cat and went straight out of the building. He offered to show me a back door to the alley, but I wanted the two redcoats to see me.

I sauntered down Park Avenue toward 81st, where I'd cut over to the Met and hopefully find DeAngelis at his office. When I reached the corner of 85th, I saw them in my periphery, plodding along behind me. After standing around in the cold for hours, their sudden urge to stroll couldn't be a coincidence.

I had a half-block head start. The moment I turned the corner, I sprinted along the buried cars until I came to an opening. Shielded by a high snowbank at the mouth of an alley, it was the perfect spot for an ambush. I pulled out my new toy—a 500,000-volt stun gun. I held it in one hand, picked up a big chunk of ice in the other, and waited.

Crouching against the snowbank, I strained my ears. A taxi whisked by. Children shouted. A snowblower ran in the distance. And then I heard them, their footfalls quick on the snow. I unlocked the safety on the stun gun and poised the ice chunk for a catapult launch.

The swishing of their ski jackets grew louder. Then they appeared. I hurled the ice at the closest one, hitting him behind the knee. His leg buckled and he toppled to the sidewalk. His buddy lunged at me. I slid sideways, threw a knee into his belly. He skidded into the snowbank. I zapped him in the leg with the stun gun, and when I turned around, his pal punched me in the ribs. It was hardly worth noting on my blog. I swatted him in the face. He reached inside his coat, and I unloaded the stun gun into his neck, the jolt crackling in the cold air. He collapsed. Groaning, the first one tried to push himself up. I zapped him again.

They were breathing, but otherwise lay motionless in the snow, glaring at me. The sour scent of ozone hung in the air. Across the street, a woman stared. I pocketed the stun gun.

"Muggers. It's okay, miss. I took care of them."

"Should I call the police?"

"No, I'm a cop."

The woman nodded and set off toward Madison Avenue. I squatted to get a better look at my new friends. One was in his early twenties, his buddy closer to thirty. They both had Middle Eastern features and failed attempts at beards. A siren wailed in the distance. It probably wasn't for me, but I needed to make this quick anyway.

"All right, who sent you?"

No answer. I kicked the older one in the ribs. He grunted.

"Where's Serif?" I asked.

Usually with a stun gun, the perp comes to in about a minute. Then again, I'd never hit one with half a million volts before. *Ouch.*

I fished through their pockets. Neither had a wallet or ID. Just some loose cash and subway passes. The younger one carried a map of Manhattan. Serif's address was circled on it, as well as my office. Next I pulled out a brass coat check marker. It looked like one from an upscale restaurant. Inside the older one's jacket was the item he'd been reaching for—a .22 auto. Cute, but it'd still put a hole in you. The serial numbers had been filed off.

"Sorry, boys, mine now." I pocketed it. "I don't know if you understand me or not, but tell whoever you work for that I don't scare easily." I studied their faces again. Their jaws were still clenched shut. They began to stir, their muscles twitching, building to jerky spasms of their arms and legs. "Well, you guys look busy, so I'm going to let you do your thing here. Have a nice day."

Softie that I am, I made sure their limbs weren't dangling in the street before I walked away.

7

BLONDE AT THE MET, BRUNETTE AT BENIHANA

Deep in the marble bowels of the Metropolitan Museum of Art is a library that houses the Provenance Research Department. After checking my parka and hanging a visitor's pass around my neck, I followed a security guard down an interminable hallway. At the door, he waved me in and left without a word.

The room was dim. The only light came from the other side of the stacks somewhere, and the stillness was so absolute you could hear dust motes settling. Through a hole in the stacks, I saw a long table with a lamp switched on. A closed laptop sat among some folio-sized books. At the end of the row I found a door with a nameplate: Dr. David DeAngelis, Director. The office was dark, the door locked.

There was a wooden creak from the other side of the stack. Through another gap in the books I made out the well-shaped calf of a woman. She wore a knee-length tweed skirt and lace-up pumps and stood on a ladder with her feet pinched together. A guy could go his whole life without seeing such a sight.

But not this guy. I whistled to myself and crept around the stack.

She stood high on the ladder, resting a book on the top shelf, licking her forefinger each time she flipped a page. I watched until the urge to say something was irresistible.

"If you run out of saliva, let me know."

She spun around, a swoop of hair concealing half her face. It reminded me of an old Veronica Lake movie. She scrutinized me like I was a painting of questionable provenance, then snapped her book closed and proffered a hand. I helped her down. Her blouse was cream silk, her hand cool and slender. In the heels, she was almost as tall as me. She glided over to the table and shoved some photos in a book.

"I didn't hear you come in, Mr...."

I was transfixed by her hair. Even in the dim light, it glistened like wet straw in the sun. I sat down across from her.

"Dakota Stevens, private detective."

"Devon Trevelyan, senior researcher." Her British accent was faint. "How may I be of assistance?"

"Actually, I'm looking for Dr. DeAngelis."

She opened the laptop. Her eyes were profoundly blue, and as she typed, the computer screen reflected in them.

"David hasn't been here for a couple of weeks."

"Vacation?" I asked.

"No, not on holiday. Unfortunately for some of us, David has a habit of dashing off without a word to anybody."

Dashing off. I loved the English, especially the women. Well, at least the ones with nice teeth, like Ms. Trevelyan here.

"Any way to reach him?"

"How do I know you're legitimate?"

I showed her my license. "It's important."

"I'm not sure I can help."

"You'd be surprised," I said. "Let's start with something easy. Where's he live?"

"Afraid I can't tell you that."

"How about you let me in his office to look around?"

"Sorry." She crossed her arms. A wall of large, heavy volumes towered behind her.

"Well," I said, "so far this is going swimmingly."

She closed her laptop and offered me a pitiful half-smile as a consolation prize.

"Okay, new category," I said. "Ever heard of a Nadir Serif?"

She frowned. "What is that, a font?"

"My client, actually. He's gone missing."

"Not having much luck, are you?"

"So, does it—"

"Ring a bell? Not really."

"Short man, thin mustache. Middle Eastern, Turkish maybe."

"This is New York, Mr. Stevens. I've met dozens of men in the art world by that description."

"Where?"

"Galas, openings, one-man shows…"

"Any events coming up where I might look for him?"

"Your guess is as good as mine," she said. "Get a copy of *Art News* and pick a function. But it's impossible to know who will attend." She cradled her chin in her palm. "What does this Serif fellow have to do with David?"

"It seems Dr. DeAngelis was appraising one of Serif's paintings for auction. *Harvest Toil* by Marcel Duchamp. Heard of it?"

"No, but that doesn't mean anything," she said. "Most major artists have dozens, in some cases hundreds, of lesser-known works floating around."

"You wouldn't have a picture of David by any chance, would you?"

"Afraid not."

"Well, that about does it then."

We stood up at the same time. She walked around the table.

"I fear I haven't been much help."

"You haven't. But you've been very gracious." I handed her my card. "If you hear anything about David, call me?"

"I shall." She reached across the table, pulled a card from her purse and gave it to me. I sneezed.

"*Gesundheit*," she said.

"Thanks. Good luck with the provenance stuff."

We shook hands. Her grip was steely.

"And good luck to you. Hopefully you will find this painting"—she smiled—"and your client, soon."

Inside Benihana I paused at the wall of photos of Rocky Aoki, the restaurant's founder, with movie stars, politicos and other celebrities. Secretly, I hoped one day to solve a case for Rock and have my own photo up here with him. I checked my parka, but kept my fleece on and zipped up to conceal my gun. The hostess led me to a hibachi grill in the back, where Svetlana waited. A club soda with lemon sat in front of my chair.

"Thanks."

"I am in a good mood," she said.

Ironically, we were seated with a group of Japanese tourists. They snapped photos and laughed. Once the waitress took our orders, I told Svetlana about my altercation with the two young men.

"They looked Middle Eastern," I said. "'Dumb and Dumber.' How would you say that in French?"

"*L'idiot et le con.*"

The waitress brought our soup.

"Seriously," I said, taking a sip, "they were just young punks. It's like somebody hired them off the street."

"Why were they watching Serif's?"

"Didn't get that out of them. But I did get this." I showed her the map.

"Why our place?" she asked.

"Given the timing, it appears somebody isn't happy Serif hired us. Dumb and Dumber might have been the ones in the SUV last night. Oh, I also got this." I placed the coat check marker on the table. "You've been to all the chichi places in town. Recognize it?"

She glanced at it while spooning her soup. "Yes, the River Café."

"Don't tease me."

"I am going to Brooklyn." She slipped it in her pocket. "I will claim it, whatever it is."

The sushi chef approached with a copy of Svetlana's book, *Krüsh Your Opponents.*

"Please, Miss Krush—you sign?"

"Certainly." She took out a Sharpie and scribbled her signature across the cover—a close-up of her staring across a chessboard at you.

"*Domo arigato*." He backed away from her, bowing.

"Damn," I said, "it must be nice being you."

She shrugged coyly and put away the pen. The chef walked in pushing his cooking cart. He opened with some spatula flipping, then laid onions and zucchini on the grill. Smoke curled up into the ventilation hood. I ribbed Svetlana.

"So, why the good mood?"

"The email you sent me," she said. "I traced it."

My cell phone rang. I bowed in apology to our Japanese visitors. It was Devon Trevelyan.

"Mr. Stevens," she said, "I called David's building. According to the doorman, he left a few days ago with several pieces of luggage. The building superintendent checked the apartment, and everything seems in order."

"Any indications where he went?"

"Such as?"

"An itinerary? Credit card statement? A jotting on a calendar? How about you tell me where he lives so I can check it out myself?"

"That would make me an accomplice, Mr. Stevens. I rather like my job, and want to keep it."

"Well, you're still a doll. Appreciate the help. Bye."

I put the phone away. Nobuhiro sliced the shrimp, flipping the tails up into his chef's hat. Svetlana squinted at me. "Who was that?"

"Spinster from the Met," I said. "Looks like DeAngelis skipped town."

"Mmm-hmm. Did she tell you anything about the painting?"

"Never heard of it."

"Well, I couldn't find anything on it either."

"You, the research queen?"

"Based on what I saw of Duchamp's work, it doesn't look like something he painted."

The chef dished shrimp onto my plate and nearly raw steak onto Svetlana's.

"Anyway," she said, "I traced the email."

"Great. Who sent it?"

"It is not that simple. In most cases, the email source code will tell you the sender's IP address, and from that you can find the general location of the sender."

"So, you were able to find out where the email came from?"

"No," she said. "I was able to trace it as far as his service provider—The Catskill Connection, in Cobleskill, New York. We will need to ask *them* for DeAngelis's address."

"The Catskills, interesting." I popped a shrimp in my mouth. "Think I'll go up to Millbrook in the morning. I need to plow the driveway, among other things. Why don't you come up on the train? We can follow this lead together."

"Why, is your *doll* not available?"

"She might be," I said. "But she's not the mysterious, loyal, brilliant and beautiful Svetlana Krüsh, and *that's* who I want by my side on this. Come on, play country mouse with me. Whaddaya say?"

Svetlana stabbed a piece of beef with her fork. She gave me a sidelong glance.

"I will think about it."

8

SANCTUM SANCTORUM

When my maternal grandparents died, they left me a rent-controlled apartment in Manhattan and a modest estate in Millbrook, NY, about ninety miles north of the city. The apartment was a blessing from day one, but the property brought complications like taxes, oil bills, electric bills and more taxes. I finally understood what Thoreau meant by our possessions owning us. Even so, I didn't have the heart to sell it. I could still feel my grandparents around the place, and part of me hoped I'd meet someone special to share it with. So far, she had eluded me.

When I got there at six thirty, the driveway was blocked by the county's handiwork: a mountain of plowed snow. I parked at the Quinns' up the road and hiked back. Traversing the property was grueling. Two feet of powder covered everything—the driveway, the bridge over the brook, the pond, the pool, the tennis court. The only thing reminding me I wasn't in the Yukon was the house itself, a comforting citadel up on the hill.

Sweat was building beneath my clothes, along with my frustration over the case. Where was Serif? Did he take off or was he snatched? And if somebody did grab him, who the hell was it, and what did it have to do with the painting? Also, if Harvest Toil was so valuable, why wasn't it insured? I didn't like Serif's answer to that one: *"The insuring process is so damned intrusive."* Nothing in his story rang true. I'd let my subconscious chew on it for a while. In the meantime, I had a steep hill to deal with.

I hadn't anticipated this spate of Arctic weather before I left, and the house was cold when I got inside. With my coat still on, I turned up the furnace and started a fire in the big living room fireplace. I warmed myself for a few minutes, then went to work. I shoveled a path from the back door to the garage, started the pickup and plowed out the driveway. Finished, I hiked over to the Quinns' and got the car. As an agent, I'd spent way too many nights in cheap government vehicles and had promised myself something luxurious one day, when I could afford it. A raven black Cadillac STS. With all the time I spent in the car, it was well worth it.

The house was cozy when I returned. I poked the fire, showered and shaved. Dressed in my L.L. Bean best, I made flapjacks and bacon with homemade maple syrup and ate at the big slab coffee table in the living room. I sifted through the mail while I ate, tossing the junk straight into the fire. After breakfast I wound the grandfather clock, then went into the office to make some calls.

The first was to Serif's home number. Instead of him, I got the housekeeper. She wondered when Mr. Serif was coming home. Maybe mañana? He owed her dinero. I apologized in fractured Spanish and hung up. Somehow I doubted her involvement in Serif's disappearance.

Next I called James, who said the red-jacketed nitwits were still around, but not Serif. Recalling the squash racquets in Serif's closet, I asked James how often he played.

"Not much," he said, "case you couldn't tell."

A couple times a year Serif went to a club on Central Park South. Buoyed by this new intel, I phoned the membership office.

"Maybe you can help me," I said. "I found a racket belonging to one of your members—a Nadir Serif. There's a hundred-dollar reward mentioned. Could you tell me when he comes in so I can collect?"

The woman sighed. "I'm not supposed to do this, but..."

There was the click of computer keys in the background. I bit my lip. Maybe this would work. She came back on the line.

"His membership has lapsed, sir."

"Thanks." I hung up. So much for that line of inquiry.

Finally I called Devon and got her voicemail. I asked if her boss had come back yet, and if he had, to call me. No sense trekking into the boondocks if he'd already returned to Manhattan. I hung up and stared at my blank notepad.

Out in the living room, the clock gonged. I still had time before I had to pick up Svetlana, so I went over to the pool table and racked them up for 9-ball.

I called this room the "office," but with a pool table six feet from my desk, very little work got done in here. Svetlana had chess, but pool was my game. I sunk the 2 and 7 balls on the break and put the 1-ball to bed next. I scanned the table and called the shot.

"Three-four in the corner."

It was a long shot that called for a bridge, but I never used one. A player always looked self-conscious with the thing, like if he didn't make the shot he had to go outside and rake with it.

Holding the cue by my fingertips, I exhaled softly and sent the cue ball rolling with a smooth but solid tunk. The 3 connected with the 4, which banked off the first cushion, then the second, and dropped in the pocket beside me. I smiled as I chalked my cue. You wished other people were around when you made shots like that.

I sighed in the empty room. *Where was Serif?* As far as I could see, there were three possibilities. One, he was dead. Two, he took off and was holed up someplace. Three, somebody abducted him. I bounced the fat end of the cue on the floor. Until I found Serif, I was stuck with this case. I might not trust him, but he had given us ten grand to find his painting, and looking out for him was part of the deal. I groaned and put away my cue stick. There was a knock at the back door. I went out and answered it. A small man in a ski mask stared at me.

"See 'em yet?" he said.

It was Johnny Quinn, my 16-year-old neighbor and part-time caretaker.

"See what?" I asked.

"Footprints. C'mon."

I put on my coat and boots and met him behind the greenhouse, near the bird feeder. Sure enough, a ragged trail of footprints emerged from the woods and went window to window until they disappeared around the corner of the house.

"Bumped into him yesterday afternoon," Johnny said. "I was gonna call you, but I lost your card and—"

"Wait, you saw him?"

"That's what I'm saying."

A sharp wind rattled the bare trees. I regretted not wearing a hat and gloves.

"What'd he look like?"

"Thin guy, dark skin—I don't know—took off soon as I said something."

"What color was his coat?"

"Couldn't tell. Sun was going down."

"A red ski jacket maybe?"

"No, long," Johnny said, "like an overcoat."

Bizarre. Only Svetlana knew about this place, and last I checked, the property was still listed on the tax rolls as belonging to my grandparents. Johnny pointed at the stone wall bordering the woods.

"Took off down there. I followed him out to the road."

"Catch what he was driving?"

"Had a driver. Town Car, I think. All I know is, guy's lucky I didn't have the 12-gauge with me."

I grabbed Johnny by the arm and shook him.

"Don't even think of doing that. The people I get mixed up with—these are bad people, Johnny. I'm surprised he didn't shoot when you startled him. From now on, if you see people wandering around the property, call the state police."

"All right, all right. I get it."

"But...I do appreciate your looking out for me, buddy." I pulled a business card and $100 bill from my wallet and slapped them in his glove. "Now, let's get this bird feeder filled, and then I'm going to show you how to drive the pickup."

"Yeah!"

"So you can plow the driveway, Mr. Quinn, not pick up girls."

He nodded soberly and started toward the garage.

"I'll get the seed," he said.

I tried not to show my apprehension in front of Johnny, but this recent development bothered me. Between the Bureau and private practice, I'd been around criminals for fourteen years, and not once had one of them come up here. Not even Jehovah's Witnesses came up here. Millbrook had always been my *sanctum sanctorum*. And now somebody had invaded it.

9

A SNOWBOARDING JAMES BOND

After Johnny's snowplowing lesson, I swung over to the Dover train station. Svetlana had just taken a two-hour train ride, and as she came down the ramp her sunglasses and black baseball cap warned me she was in a foul mood. Without a word, I handed her a large latte and put her bags in the back seat. A pair of taxis pulled out with us.

I waited until we were on the Taconic State Parkway heading north before breaking the silence. Svetlana sipped her coffee.

"So," I said. "Miss me?"

"Yes, I missed you. I missed you when somebody followed me to the train this morning."

"Followed? You're sure?"

"I get in cab at my apartment and a car pulls away at the same time," she said. "It stays with us all the way to Grand Central. When I get out, somebody walks in behind me. I call that being followed."

"Get a look at him?"

"Average height, slim. Dark skin. Middle Eastern, perhaps. Wearing a leather trench coat and sunglasses."

"How cloak-and-dagger of him."

Slim and dark, like the guy Johnny saw. *Interesting.*
Instinctively I checked the rear-view and wasn't surprised
by what I saw: one of the taxis from the train station.
Svetlana plopped a scarf and gloves in my lap.

"What are these?" I asked.

"Items from the River Café coat check."

"Great." I tossed them in the back seat. "I take it the
person's name and address aren't sewn inside."

"That is correct." Svetlana put her coffee in the cup
holder and eased her seat back. "I take nap now. Wake
me in one hour."

I set the cruise control to 65 and enjoyed the Currier
& Ives scenery for a while. The taxi stayed in sight, half a
mile back. I frowned. There were several ways to handle
this new development including shooting their tires out,
but only one appealed to me—a showdown.

At the exit for Route 23, I stopped at the end of the
ramp. Left went across the river into the Catskills; right,
the Berkshires. I turned right. When we reached Great
Barrington, a town near Butternut Ski Resort, I roused
Svetlana and explained the situation.

"I did not see him get on the train," she said.

"Probably waited until you boarded and took a seat
in the next car. Relax, we'll have answers soon enough."

I turned on the car's GPS and pointed at the screen.

"Here's Butternut. When we pull in, I'll get out and
laughing boy will follow. Then you take the car and meet
me on this road over here. Got it?"

"You mean I actually get to drive the precious Dako-
tamobile?" she said.

"Don't get used to it."

I whipped into the turn so our tail would think we were trying to lose him. The taxi followed my lead, fishtailing ridiculously in the packed snow. At the main lodge I stopped, unclipped the mini-compass from my keychain and patted Svetlana on the arm.

"Twenty minutes," I said, and jumped out.

I bounded up the steps and was already at the doors when the taxi pulled up. A slim man in sunglasses and a black leather trench coat got out. He said something to the cab driver and slammed the door. Once Svetlana had pulled safely away, I went inside.

A giant chalet fireplace burned in the center of the lodge. Skiers crowded the couches with their boots stretched out toward the fire. They sipped coffee and laughed. When Slim entered, I let him see me and headed down the back stairs to a narrow corridor with guest rooms on one side and a view of the bunny slope on the other. Skiers crowded past me with their equipment. Others stood chatting about the slopes. I was looking for an isolated place where I could jump Slim, but before I knew it, the hallway had ended and we were outside again, crossing a level area between the slopes.

Casually, I took a reading on the compass. Svetlana would be waiting to the southwest, which put me in line with a distant equipment shed. If I could lead him there…

I glanced over my shoulder. Slim was headed back toward the lodge. I took a shortcut to the front and waited behind a big pine. The cab idled near the steps. A minute later Slim emerged from the building and started down the stairs. I stepped out from my hiding place between him and the vehicle.

"Howdy."

Slim's eyebrows jumped. He spun around and sprinted back up the stairs. I chased him into the lodge and out a side door. He was heading toward the chair lift for the main slope. I jogged after him.

There's nowhere to hide, Slim. Might as well face the inevitable.

But I'd underestimated him. At the chair lift, he spoke to the attendant as he reached for his wallet, and boarded the next chair. Bypassing the corral of skiers, I went directly to the punk Slim had bought off. He weighed in at a buck-oh-five—a buck-ten with the eyebrow rings—and spoke with a sneer that used to be reserved for genuine tough guys.

"*Dude*, there's a line."

I reached in my pocket, whipped out my PI license. I've discovered if you do this with panache, people don't question you.

"Look, I'm a detective, and the guy you just let up there is my suspect. So unless you want to get hauled in for aiding and abetting, put me in a chair—right now."

The kid snorted, rolled his eyes at his buddies.

"Whatever. Get on."

I was squeezed into a quad-chair with a trio of 12-year-old girls. One chair had gone up empty between mine and Slim's, which gave him about a minute head start. But where could he go? Up ahead, Slim talked to the snowboarders on the chair with him. One of the girls next to me tapped my arm.

"Hey, where are your skis?" She chomped on a wad of gum.

"Skis? What are those?"

The girls beside me giggled, but the one on the far end of the chair—a wavy-haired redhead in a sleek powder blue ensemble—sulked with her chin in her hand as the treetops passed below.

"She okay?" I asked.

The gum-chomper spoke up. "Tallulah's upset 'cause—"

"Wow, great name."

"Yeah," Gum said. "Anyway, Jimmy Haskell found out she likes him, but Jimmy said redheads are ugly and that he wouldn't go out with her in like a million years or something."

I glanced at Tallulah. She wore earmuffs without a hat, showing the full glory of her mane. Here was a girl who in the near future would need a stun gun to keep the boys away. Maybe I should give her mine now.

"Jimmy's a dumbass," I said.

More giggling.

"You know him?" Gum asked.

"Nope." Ahead, Slim's chair reached the summit. "Tallulah?"

She leaned forward so I could see her.

"Lots of boys love red hair. Some of them are crazy for it. Heck, if you were twenty years older, I'd be asking you out myself."

"Really?" Her eyes opened wide.

"Yup. You're beautiful—all three of you."

The chair clanked up to the platform, the attendant scowling when he saw I didn't have skis. Fifty feet away, Slim chatted with the snowboarders.

"Don't break too many hearts, girls," I said.

"We won't."

I headed straight for Slim. He saw me but wasn't running. Something was different. A board lay flat on the snow. One of the boys was kneeling beside it and... strapping him in. I sprinted and dove to tackle him just as the boys pushed him over the edge. Staring down the slope, I hoped he'd fall so I'd get another chance, but to my amazement Slim bent his knees and launched off a mogul, his trench coat sailing behind him like Batman's cape. He slalomed cartoon-like down the mountain.

"Dude!" the boys said in unison. One of them clutched a fistful of hundred-dollar bills. I stood up and brushed myself off. The tallest one planted his board at my feet.

"Wanna buy?"

"How much?"

"Nine hundred, just like him."

"No thanks."

I trudged back to the chairlift and rode dejectedly down. *Who the hell was that guy?* Of all the tails in all the world, mine had to be a snowboarding James Bond.

At the bottom, I took a reading with the compass and hiked across the resort. When I reached the road, Svetlana was there with the car. I collapsed into the passenger seat.

"So?"

"Round one to the mystery man," I said. "But something tells me we'll meet again."

She put the car in drive. "You are not usually bested. He must be good."

"Yeah, he's dreamy."

"Where next?"

"DeAngelis's service provider. I'd like to regain some dignity before the day is through."

10

THIS NEVER HAPPENED TO MARLOWE

The farther we traveled from Cobleskill, NY and its slender foothold on civilization, the worse the driving became. Snowdrifts had covered the pavement everywhere, making the steep and winding roads even more treacherous. Since leaving The Catskill Connection, we'd driven the same stretch three times, trying to find the turnoff to DeAngelis's.

"Where is this place?" I said to Svetlana.

"We followed his directions exactly."

I didn't question Svetlana's memory for a second. Anyone who could memorize hundreds of chess games was more than capable of remembering how to get from A to B. Again we crossed a bridge that dated back to the Polk administration, and again its decrepitude gave me a bad feeling.

"Okay," I said, "I'm looking on the left, and there's no Gobbler's Nob Road. I say we go back and kick junior in the pants."

"You already broke his paddleball."

"And *you* broke his heart. Flirting with him like that, shame on you."

"Your threats failed to get results, so I—"

"Wait a second…"

Barely poking out of an eight-foot mound of snow was the sign for Gobbler's Nob Road. I pulled over and cut the engine.

"Doesn't look promising."

"Should I come with?" Svetlana asked.

"No sense both of us getting cold. Figure an hour. I assume you can entertain yourself for that long."

She unzipped her purse and pulled out a pocket chess set.

"Leave the keys. In case I decide to abandon you."

I glanced at the outside temperature: -2°F.

"Wish me luck?"

"What is luck to trained detective?" She nimbly set up pieces. "Now go."

I put on my parka, hat and gloves, and stepped into the balmy mountain air. *Gobbler's Nob*, I thought as I climbed over the glacier blocking the road. *What freak came up with that name?*

This was the second time in as many days that I was wallowing through snow up to my groin, and I didn't like it. This never happened to Marlowe. Then again, it didn't snow much in LA. I could have been one of those Polar explorers—Peary, Amundsen, Shackleton—except it would have occurred to them to bring snowshoes. I resolved to get a pair for next time, if there was a next time.

No one had been in or out since before the blizzard. The only sign of a road was a pristine river of white through the forest. Beautiful in the setting sun, but strenuous. Every few hundred feet I had to stop and catch my breath. My hip flexors burned.

About a half-mile in, the light began fading fast. Four o'clock. I wasn't crazy about doing this in the dark, but what choice did I have? The road wound through the woods and ran along a frozen lake. By now darkness had engulfed the trees, leaving the snow gray. Except for my breath and the soft swish of clothing, there was total stillness. Bitter cold. At least there wasn't any wind. All that was missing was the howling of wolves. Not that I was worried. I had my favorite gun—a .45 S&W revolver—and a pocketful of rounds. What *was* troubling me, though, was the possibility that, like a swimmer who goes out too far, I could get halfway in and have my muscles cramp up. Then I'd be screwed. Also, as the snow melted on my jeans and refroze, I became mildly concerned for my genitals. That's not a place you want to get frostbite. For the rest of the hike I cupped my hands over my groin, grateful no one was around to see it.

Small humiliations like this one were relatively new to me. Just a few years earlier, when I was with the Bureau, I had the force of the Law behind my every action. Not anymore. As a private detective I'd had to adopt more creative approaches, like hiking through deep snow in subzero weather to question a suspect instead of compelling him by subpoena to come to *you*. Besides access to overwhelming resources, FBI agents have the luxury of approaching every case legally and methodically. I used to have that luxury. Not anymore.

As I came over a rise, a light flashed on. I rolled over a drift and scrambled behind a tree, my thighs as nimble as two frozen hams. I drew my gun and peeked around the corner. The light came from the back of a building.

A motion detector. I stepped out from behind the tree. No one shot at me—yet. I put the gun away and dusted myself off. I was behind a garage. There was a 4x4 inside and around the corner was a mailbox half-buried in the snow. The letters on the side read, "DEANGELIS." I'd made it.

I waded up the driveway. High up on the house, a second light clicked on. The windows were dark. Before picking any locks, which in this cold could take until spring, I decided to look for an easier way in. I circled around to the front where it faced the lake and shone my flashlight in the sliding glass door. A living room. Decanters of liquor, art on the walls. Unfortunately, the door was locked and a stick lay in the track to prevent some jerk like me from bucking it open.

The snowdrifts on this side were too deep to walk through, so I backtracked and found the front door. It was shielded by thick evergreens, which explained why I hadn't seen it. Stealth be damned; I was freezing my ass off here. I pounded on the door and rang the bell like I was being chased in a slasher film. Nobody came.

I'd been avoiding picking any locks, but I was out of options. Heck, for all I knew, Serif's painting was right inside. I was pulling out the lock-picking set when the flashlight beam landed on something in the bushes: an old milk box. I opened it. Empty. Then I picked it up. Underneath were two keys in a Ziploc bag. I grinned into the night.

The second key opened the door. Once inside, I took a deep breath.

And immediately regretted it.

11

DAMN LIAR

There's no way to accurately describe what a dead body smells like. Knowing that a sack of rotting protoplasm awaits you tends to color your perception, making an already vile smell seem as bad as death itself. The house was dark and searing hot, intensifying the putrid odor. I pinched my nose and breathed through my mouth. To gauge whether I was getting close, I took a few short breaths through my nose. The smell wasn't as strong in the kitchen as it was by the staircase. I replaced my ski gloves with latex ones and went upstairs.

On the landing, I flicked on every light switch, and my growing urge to vomit told me the corpse lay nearby. I continued down the hall toward an open door, the stench so thick now, I could feel it on my face like fog. At the door, I reached inside and hit the lights, praying no animals were feeding on the corpse. What I found wasn't what I expected.

The body was in bed, tucked in for a long winter's nap. At least he looked peaceful. I picked up the phone to call it in, but the line was dead, and my cell wasn't getting reception.

I took a deep breath and walked toward the bed, but before I could reach it, a needle-like pain pierced my temples. I tried shaking it off. *Why was I here? Oh yeah, a painting.* I stumbled and smashed a clothes valet. Something was wrong. I staggered downstairs to the door. The knob wouldn't work. Kept slipping. Tired. All that walking. Grabbed the knob, wrenched it open. Refreshing outside. I crawled out into the snow, retched, collapsed on my back. Stars winked at me from an infinitely black sky. Great stargazing up here.

Lying in the snow, I sucked in the sharp air until my chest hurt. I must have lain on my back for twenty minutes before the stabbing sensation in my temples subsided. I wobbled to my feet.

Through the trees I made out a flashing yellow light. A giant plow truck rumbled up to the driveway and stopped. I squirmed behind a bush. A figure in a puffy white coat climbed down from the cab and waved. The truck honked and continued plowing up the road. Arms spread for balance, the white coat climbed over the mound of snow left by the plow.

It was Svetlana. Still woozy, I tottered out to meet her.

"What'd you do," I said, "flag him down?"

"Yes. You told me an hour. What have you been doing?"

"Oh, not much. Just inhaling carbon monoxide."

"What?"

"I was in there for all of five minutes and got sick. The CO level must be outrageous. Oh, and there's a dead guy"—I thumbed over my shoulder—"nice-'n-ripe."

"DeAngelis?"

"Not sure yet. Anyway, I need to poke around. I'm going back in and open up windows."

Svetlana shoved her hands in her pockets. "I wait here. I did not sign on for dead bodies."

"Fine," I said, "but if I collapse again, I'm expecting generous mouth-to-mouth."

I went in holding my breath and opened all the windows on the first floor. Then back outside for fresh air. On the next trip I checked the thermostat. It was set to 85 degrees. I repeated the in-and-out process until all of the doors and windows were wide open. While waiting for the CO to clear out, I pointed out constellations to Svetlana. When I showed her Orion, she scoffed.

"It looks nothing like a hunter."

"You have to use your imagination," I said. "All right, I'm going in. Holler if you hear anything."

I went upstairs and flung the blanket off the corpse. I was faced with a nude middle-aged man, on his side and very dead.

At least there were no insects. At the Bureau I'd come across bodies at outdoor crime scenes, and if the weather was warm there was always infestation. In this case there was *livor mortis* where the blood had been drawn down by gravity, a greenish hue around the lower abdomen and bloating throughout, but no bugs.

I coughed. Never mind carbon monoxide, if I didn't speed things up I was going to pass out from the stench. Taking an overview of the body, one thing struck me as odd: the *livor mortis* was uneven. Although darkest on the side against the bed, there was also a purplish area on the stomach. Wendy Hamilton, a forensic pathologist gal-pal of mine, once told me this could mean the body had been moved.

Thinking about the carbon monoxide, I examined the skin more closely. In cases of CO poisoning, the skin becomes suffused with a bright cherry color, where the CO molecules attach to the hemoglobin in the blood and won't let go. The color stays with a corpse indefinitely, until an autopsy or decomposition. The skin did have a pink tint, but this wasn't a fail-safe sign. Short of a blood sample, there was no way to know for certain.

Then I remembered something else Wendy had showed me. In cases where the cherry tint is hard to make out, look at the fingernails. I stooped down and studied the half-moons. Normally white, his were cherry red, which meant CO poisoning. But there was something else. His wrists and ankles were crossed, and *rigor mortis* had set in while in that position. I studied his wrists with a magnifying glass. They were hairless and covered with a gummy residue. There were also signs of bruising.

A theory that explained the facts was beginning to form. This person, presumably DeAngelis, had been bound with tape and killed by CO poisoning—but somewhere else, which would explain the uneven *livor mortis*. Then he was brought here, dumped on the bed and the furnace tampered with to pump out carbon monoxide. DeAngelis must have known something they didn't want him knowing. I had no idea who *they* were yet, but I had a hunch Serif's painting was involved.

I was able to confirm the body was DeAngelis from his driver's license photo, and after a fruitless search of the other upstairs rooms, I went down to the kitchen.

I began with the refrigerator. For some reason, we detectives tend to start here and never find anything. Maybe we're just hungry. In the wastebasket I uncovered a banana peel, a used coffee filter and crumpled aluminum foil. I dug deeper. Buried at the bottom were several strips of duct tape with hairs stuck on them. *Ah-ha*. My abduction hypothesis was getting stronger by the minute.

In the living room, I scanned the walls for Serif's painting. No luck. There were plenty of antiques, but nothing that resembled evidence. Overall, the place was immaculate.

I followed a short hallway to a cluttered studio/workshop. Atop a workbench stood an empty easel, and behind it leaned a painting. Once again hope fluttered in my chest, and once again my hope was dashed.

It wasn't *Harvest Toil*.

In the corner was a stack of electronics and appliance boxes, including one for a CO detector. The box was empty, which begged the question, *where was the detector, and why hadn't I heard it?* If somebody had wanted to make DeAngelis's death look like an accident, getting rid of the CO detector would be the first priority. Now I was almost certain DeAngelis had been murdered.

I turned my attention to the desk. A laptop power cable dangled from the desktop, but the computer was gone. The desk itself was a rat's nest of museum correspondence, magazines and gallery catalogs. I rummaged through the pile, found a fat envelope and opened it.

Inside was a handwritten description of a painting called *Autumn in the Fields* by Auguste Chavet, and darn it all if it didn't sound exactly like *Harvest Toil*. A set of

Polaroids, taken in this room, showed the painting I'd been searching for, with those big-headed peasants. As I shuffled through the photos, a business card slipped out: *Helene Bundt, Senior Vice President and Senior Specialist, Impressionist and Modern Art, Sotheby's New York.* There was also a cryptic list, written with a skipping ballpoint pen:

Notify Helene
Clear Title Pre-War
Jean René—Williamsburg?
Visit Gallery
Serif—China?
Watch Li

It was official: *My client, wherever he was, was a damn liar.*

"Dakota, someone's coming!" Svetlana called out.

I took the envelope and its contents, shut out the lights and went back outside. The drone of distant snowmobiles carried in the cold. I pulled Svetlana behind a shrub, handed her my latex gloves and the envelope.

"Hide these."

She tucked them in her boot. "So?"

I grinned and rubbed my hands together.

The droning grew louder until a band of snowmobiles launched over the hill out on the road. Their headlights sliced the darkness and disappeared into the woods.

"Let's move," I said.

12

EVENING GOWNS

The best thing about the dress salon at Saks, besides the cushy sofa and the chilled bottles of Perrier, is how perfectly quiet it is. The cream carpeted walls block out the din of Manhattan, letting you focus on the issue at hand: does she look nice in *this* dress?

Svetlana needed an evening gown for her charity tournament in a few weeks. So far, she had tried on six. The current contender, a wine red strapless gown, showed off her smooth shoulders. She stepped onto the lighted dais and looked herself up and down in the mirrors.

"Well?"

The saleswoman, a smiling grandmother type, stepped forward. "It's lovely. And did I mention it has inner boning for bust support?"

"Inner boning?" I said. "Sounds good to me."

Svetlana turned and looked at her back. "So, you reported DeAngelis. What next?"

"The *livor mortis*," I said.

"Yes, there were *two* examples of it on the body?"

"Yup. That's how I know something's rotten in Denmark. Somebody went to a lot of trouble to make his death look like an accident."

I caught a glimpse of the saleswoman. Her beaming smile had gone crooked. Svetlana smoothed out the fabric on her hip.

"And your state police friend? What did he say?"

"He spoke to the sheriff up there," I said. "Seems DeAngelis had a natural gas furnace. The things are notorious for carbon monoxide problems. They examined it and sure enough, it wasn't vented properly. I told him about the duct tape and how it looked like the body was moved, but he won't get involved. Doesn't want to start a turf war."

Svetlana sighed. "Betty, could I try the cashmere again?"

"Certainly."

I leaned back and laced my hands behind my head. You can do a lot worse than watch a beautiful woman try on dresses. From Svetlana's changing room came the squeak of a hanger.

"Hey," I said over my shoulder, "how about something shorter?"

"A cocktail dress? This is a formal event."

"I was thinking more like a babydoll. Pink chiffon maybe."

"In your dreams, Dakota Stevens."

Betty brought me a fresh Perrier. "So, you and Miss Krüsh...?"

"We work together," I said. "We're detectives."

"Oh?"

Svetlana strutted back in, the black cashmere gown eating up the room.

"I solve the crimes and handle the money," she said.

"Is this true?" Betty asked me.

"Pretty much."

Svetlana adjusted the spaghetti straps and swiveled her hips to take in the dress.

"So, Krüsh," I said, "if this were a chess match, what would you do?"

"Resign."

"Seriously."

"I would keep asking questions." She faced me, gestured at the dress. "Well?"

"Nice drape. Not as sexy as the red, but elegant. Are we going to work on the case at all?"

"You are good sport to come shopping with me. Talk it out the way you do, and I interrupt when you make mistakes."

"You're sweet," I said. "Okay, a guy named Nadir Serif staggers into our office in the middle of a blizzard and wants us to find a lost painting. But, as we just discovered, the names he gives us of the painting and the artist are bogus, so it's clear he doesn't want us knowing too much."

"By the way," Svetlana said, "I searched for *Autumn in the Fields* by Auguste Chavet this morning."

"Let me guess—nothing."

"You are correct."

"Must have special records, those appraisers."

"And what of our client?" she said. "Have you found *him?*"

I hadn't, of course, and Svetlana knew it. A more thorough search of Serif's apartment netted a 20-year-old photo of him, a matchbook from The Pierre Hotel, and a bathrobe from The Four Seasons. Knowing it was futile before I started, I showed the picture to hotel doormen and concierges and asked if they'd seen him. Nobody had. The problem was, Serif was fifty pounds lighter in the photo. Desperate, I took it to clothing stores Serif frequented. At Bally on Madison Avenue, a young salesman clammed up the moment I showed him the picture. It was obvious he'd seen Serif recently, but he looked too honest to bribe, and with customers around I couldn't beat it out of him with a shoe. I looked up. Svetlana was still scrutinizing herself in the mirror.

"I think you're obsessing about this," I said. "It's a dress."

"Perhaps, but you are not the one who has to wear it in front of three hundred people."

"Touché." I cleared my throat. "So the appraiser is found dead in the middle of nowhere. His death is made to look like an accident, and the painting is gone. Therefore, it makes sense that his death and the painting are connected."

"What about Serif?" Svetlana returned to the changing room.

"As the killer?" I said. "Maybe, but doubtful. Why give us DeAngelis as a lead if he'd just offed the guy? No, we need to work from the hypothesis that there's somebody else out there with just as strong a motive for getting that painting and shutting up DeAngelis. We have a list linking DeAngelis to a Jean René in Williamsburg and a Helene Bundt at Sotheby's. We'll look into them next." I sipped some Perrier.

Svetlana emerged from the changing room in her street clothes. "I am sorry, Betty. You will call me when the others come in?"

"Of course." Betty walked away.

"All right, Krüsh," I said, "what questions should we be asking?"

Svetlana took my Perrier, sipped and sat down beside me. "I am hungry, so I will be brief. First, where is Serif?"

"Let's skip that one for now."

"Second," she said, "what is the painting's significance? Perhaps more than money is at stake. Third, who is Jean René? And fourth, what is the connection to Sotheby's?"

I checked my watch. Five thirty.

"Well, it's too late to follow up with Sotheby's tonight, but I suppose we could go door-to-door in Williamsburg looking for the mysterious Jean René."

"We can do better than that," Svetlana said.

"Ah, your DMV contact."

"A good magician does not reveal her secrets. But now you take me to dinner. The Blue Water Grill."

"What about reservations?"

She flapped a hand that said, "*Pshaw.*"

"Right, silly me," I said.

13

FIFTY-THREE CALLS TO SHANGHAI

Jean René lived in a converted warehouse in the Williamsburg neighborhood of Brooklyn. I knew this area well. Francis Falcone, a "business associate" who provided services similar to mine for somewhat more nefarious clients, had a lair nearby. René's building, part of an abandoned factory complex, faced the East River. Even in the cold, I could smell the fetid water. A single streetlight struggled to keep the area lit, the dirty snow sucking up any brightness, leaving everything gray.

I had called René's number from the restaurant, and after getting his answering machine three times, concluded he wasn't home. Svetlana waited in the car while I picked the locks. Once inside, I called her on my cell phone. She came upstairs.

"Solve it yet?" she said brightly.

"Wiseass."

It was a giant loft, all open-concept, with rows of steel columns that divided the space into four areas. First, as you walked in, an office and a living room with a massive TV. Next, a kitchen-dining area. Then a painting studio, then a bedroom/bathroom suite walled off with frosted glass. Everything was decorated in ultra-modern style. And capping it off was a glittering view of Manhattan across the river.

"Soak it in, sister," I said. "Here's how the other half lives."

I tossed her some latex gloves and together we gave the living room and kitchen-dining area a cursory search.

"Okay, you take the office," I said. "I'm checking out the studio over there."

I cracked my knuckles and strode across the loft. Chrome utility shelves stored plastic jars of paints, and in the middle of the space was a stainless steel work surface, like the dissecting tables used in morgues. A pair of large, H-frame easels with magnifying lamps attached stood side-by-side near the windows. Both were empty. I went over and examined them.

The easel on the left was spotless. The one on the right had blotches of dried paint on its tray and on the floor beneath it. Meanwhile, there wasn't a single watercolor, sketch or cocktail-napkin doodle anywhere. Not even a blank canvas. I was on my haunches staring up at an empty painting rack when Svetlana tapped me on the shoulder.

"Anybody home?"

"Notice anything odd?" I said.

She crossed her arms and looked around. "It is surprisingly clean."

"I'm not talking about what you see. I'm talking about what you *don't* see. Like how there's not one painting here. Don't you find that strange?"

"Perhaps he sold them all."

"Maybe." I jumped to my feet. "Come here, let me show you something."

I pointed at the shelves on the two easels, where until recently canvases had stood.

"See the dust lines? The same on both easels. I'll bet there were two paintings here for quite a while." I went behind the easels and examined the crank mechanisms that raised and lowered the canvases.

"And, my dear Watson…"

She waved down her body. "Do I *look* like a Watson?"

"No, thank God." I tugged her arm. "Note the absence of dust on the screws. The dust-free sections are equal in length on both easels."

"Exciting," she said.

I loosened the top clamps on both easels and carefully lowered them until I saw dust lines on the wood. They were at the exact same height.

"So, what can we conclude from all of this?"

"That Jean René is out of Swiffers?" she said.

"Come on, I'm in my element here."

Svetlana gazed out at a glowing Manhattan. Her lips curled into a smile.

"Two paintings of identical size."

"Right. Now, I don't know much about painting, but it doesn't make sense that an artist would work on two paintings of the exact same size at the same time."

"Many artists work in series," she said.

"Maybe so, but then why is there no paint on the left easel? What if…"

I went to the left easel, positioned the magnifying lamp where a canvas would go, and looked through it. Then I stepped over to the right easel and pretended to make brushstrokes. Svetlana spoke up in a bizarre Ukrainian-British accent.

"By jove, Holmes, I think you've got it!"

"By jove?"

"If you can say 'simmer down,' I can say 'by jove.'"

"Fair enough," I said. "It looks like René was copying another painting, but we don't know what painting or where it's gone to. Hey, are there any Ziploc bags around?"

She snapped one out of her Gucci handbag.

"Impressive," I said. "What else you got in there?"

She shook her head. With a clean painting knife, I scraped up some paint beneath the right easel. I put the flakes in the bag and tucked it away.

"You never know," I said. "So, what did you find?"

"Not much." She yanked a stack of file folders out of her handbag and dropped them on the table with a gong. "Just a bunch of dossiers, one artist's obituary and a phone bill with fifty-three calls to Shanghai." She inspected her fingernails.

"What, no clues?" I sifted through the folders.

There were a dozen dossiers. One by one, I opened them under the warm overhead lights. Six were of Chinese painters and galleries based in Shanghai, with a few in Hong Kong. Inside were glossy photos of paintings and a few art catalogs in Chinese. I skipped ahead to the folders with Western names: Maia Gallant, David Birchfield, Cindy Bourassa, Jamal Carter and Shay Connolly. Paper-clipped to Jamal Carter's folder were his obituary, dated a week ago, and a clipping from *The Post* describing how he had been killed by a mugger in Tompkins Square Park. I skimmed the other folders—that is, until I got to Ms. Connolly's.

Besides a catalog, there was a postcard with a painting on the front—a nude portrait of a redheaded woman, rendered in such lifelike detail that it could have been a *Playboy* centerfold. I licked my eyeteeth. The description was on the back: "SHAY CONNOLLY, THE NUDE SELF-PORTRAITS — AN ONGOING SERIES." The show was at Mallorca Galleries on East 73rd.

"And this was next to the phone."

Svetlana handed me a Mallorca Galleries business card with an appointment written on it: "Contessina, 1:30 p.m." The appointment was in a few days.

"Day Planner?" I asked.

"No."

"Find Serif's name anywhere?"

"No." She pointed at the redhead. "They are your—how you say?—like the rock that destroys Superman?"

"*Kryptonite?* Nah." I studied the postcard for a moment then tucked it under the other stuff so it wouldn't distract me. I nodded at the pile of clues. "Nice score, by the way."

She shrugged and slipped the folders in her bag. "I just looked in the right places."

"What about the bedroom and bathroom?"

"Neat as pins," she said.

"Any photos we could use?"

"Not one."

"Odd," I said. "All right then, let's go."

At the door, I gazed across the loft at the easels.

"Curious about those paintings."

"But there are no paintings," Svetlana said.

"*That*, my dear, is what's curious."

14

The Loading Dock at Sotheby's

Helene Bundt had an office on the eighth floor of the Sotheby's building on York Avenue, but I never saw the inside of it.

Svetlana was doing research today, so I was alone. My plan was to ambush Ms. Bundt at precisely nine o'clock, and I'd even worn my favorite suit—a navy stripe Hickey Freeman—so I'd look debonair while doing it. I managed to reach Bundt's outer office before her assistant, a semi-adult Lolita, stopped me with a pout.

"Ms. Bundt is not in," she said. "Do you have appointment?"

Her French accent startled me. I considered saying I had a $50 million estate to auction off, but for once I had leads and didn't have time to fool around. I tossed a business card in front of her.

"I need to ask her a few questions."

She crossed her waifish legs under the glass desk and regarded me from behind half-open eyelids.

"What is this in reference to?"

"It's a private matter," I said.

"Her schedule, it is booked for two weeks."

"I was hoping for ten minutes. This morning."

"*Impossible!* Ms. Bundt cannot be disturbed. You must leave."

What this snippy tart needed was to be bent over my knee and spanked. Trouble is, she'd probably like it.

"Tell her this concerns Monsieur DeAngelis and *Autumn in the Fields*."

She huffed and went through a puddle of papers, plucked out a phone list and ran a finger down the page until she reached an entry for "P2 — RECEIVING." Turning her back to me, she spoke in low tones and after a string of yeses, hung up.

"She says you must speak to our legal department."

"This is important," I said.

"Leave, Mr. Stevens, or I call security."

She put a hand on the phone and taunted me with slitted eyes. I considered telling her, "I shall return," but I wasn't sure she'd get it. I nodded and went to the elevator. There was a button for P2. I waved to her as I punched it.

The car belched me out onto a loading dock. It was like Home Depot, but cleaner. Hordes of paintings, sculpture and antique furniture stood on pallets. Each pallet had a lot number and was protected by a foam barrier. Three men in aprons and gloves shuffled past me carrying a heavy piece of pottery. I followed them.

Ahead, daylight poured into the loading dock. It was cold enough to see your breath. At the end of the platform, a tractor-trailer was being unloaded. A woman with a haughty profile examined each painting as it came off the truck, and a man checked off items on a clipboard. The woman was the quintessential *grande dame*.

"Ms. Bundt, I presume?"

"You? I specifically told Brigitte—"

"Yeah, your legal department. Afraid this can't wait."

"Well, as you can see"—she gestured at the truck—"I am very busy. I do not have time for—"

She smiled at something behind me. I turned around. Four large men in suits were headed my way, led by the bitchy Brigitte.

"It appears your visit will be cut short, Mr. Stevens."

"That's okay," I said. "I'll just talk to NYPD about the dead art appraiser. Good day."

I turned around and strolled across the loading dock. The security team was almost on top of me.

"David? Dead?"

I kept walking.

The security men surrounded me. They turned to Ms. Bundt.

"Fine," she said, "let's talk."

I winked at Brigitte, and as she stomped back to the elevator, I followed Ms. Bundt into an office. A window looked out on the loading dock. We sat down at a table.

"How did David die?" she asked.

"Carbon monoxide poisoning, let's leave it at that. What I want to know is, what's your connection to him?"

"Why, I hired him, of course."

"*You* hired him?" I said. "What for?"

"To research the provenance on *Autumn in the Fields*."

"For Serif's auction?"

She glared. "Who is Serif? What are you talking about, young man? Aren't you from the insurance company?"

"No, let me explain."

I told her how I'd come into Serif's employ, how I'd found DeAngelis's body, and how her business card had been among photos of a painting that I knew as *Harvest Toil* but which really seemed to be *Autumn in the Fields*. To make sure we were talking about the same painting, I described it. She concurred. I mentioned René, but if she knew him, she didn't show it.

"Before we continue," I said, "could you clear up something for me? Who was the artist?"

"Auguste Chavet," she said off-handedly.

"Yeah, DeAngelis had that in his notes. My associate wasn't able to find anything about him."

"That isn't surprising," she said. "Chavet was a minor Parisian Dadaist and contemporary of Jean Crotti. He later joined with the Surrealists, but was fastidious about his work and destroyed most of it before it could be sold. Therefore, any painting of his that survived tends to have great value."

The man with the clipboard came inside. Ms. Bundt signed it and he went away.

"Now," she said, "this Nadir Serif—whoever he is— does not own the painting. Of that I can assure you."

"Then who does?"

Her shoulders stiffened. Clearly this was a problem she wished would disappear.

"The couple that brought us the painting emigrated from Shanghai two years ago."

I thought of René's calls to Shanghai, as well as DeAngelis's note to "*Watch Li.*"

"Either of them named Li?"

"No," she snapped.

"Sorry, please continue."

"According to the couple, the painting was a wedding gift, and when the husband lost his job on Wall Street, they contacted me about selling it. And that's when I hired David."

"Issues with the provenance?"

"Perhaps," she said, "but it's actually standard operating procedure now. You see, because it's an early 20th century European work and was unaccounted for between 1939 and 1945, we must be more circumspect than usual. Auction houses have been sued for selling works with sketchy wartime records. To protect ourselves, we have stepped up our provenance research. David was one of the top experts on European works from that period."

A pair of painting-bearers raced past the window carrying an Impressionist work. Might have been a Renoir, but what did I know? Ms. Bundt flew to the door and yelled at them.

"Gentlemen, that's six-point-two million you're carrying!"

They slowed to a crawl. I wanted to get the hell out of here before I bumped into something and the "You Break It, You Bought It" rule applied. Ms. Bundt returned to her chair and wagged a finger at me.

"There is something else," she said. "But it will sound strange."

"Try me. I'm used to strange."

"Well, the other reason I wanted David to examine the painting is that I had questions about its authenticity."

I thought of Jean René's easel setup.

"So," I said, "you're saying that not only was the painting's provenance questionable, the work might also be a forgery?"

"It's possible, but with David dead, we may never know for sure."

"But how could you know without another painting to compare it to?"

"Instinct," she said. "You spend a lifetime working with the real thing and you develop a second sense about what's genuine and what's not. Unfortunately, David has left me in quite a bind. The couple wants to know the status." She glanced out the window. "You said you found photos of the painting. What about the painting itself?"

"Gone."

She swore under her breath. Outside, the tractor-trailer started up and pulled out of the loading dock.

"Ms. Bundt," I said, "I'd like to speak with the Chinese couple to find out how the painting came into their possession."

"That I cannot help you with."

"Or, I could visit my buddies at NYPD…"

She pointed at me. "You…are an arrogant young man."

"I prefer to think of it as self-assured."

After a long moment, she nodded and led me out to the elevator. I got on with her.

"I will talk to our legal department," she said. "Perhaps we will retain your firm to find the painting." Her eyes twinkled with a bribe.

"That would present a conflict of interest, given that Serif hired me to do the same thing."

"Sotheby's is certain to pay you better. And we have other resources."

Considering that my first client was missing, it seemed like a good idea, but I wasn't keen on answering to a corporation right now. Just like the Bureau, they expected regular reports. And reports only slowed me down. Still, I needed to speak with the Chinese couple. The elevator opened at the lobby. I stepped off.

"Well?" she said, holding the door.

"Fax me the couple's contact info. Then I'll decide."

She nodded.

"Wait," I said. "There's something I'm dying to know."

"Yes?"

"Bundt," I said. "Any relation to the cake pan?"

She shook her head like she felt sorry for me, and the doors closed between us.

15

CONTESSINA MALLORCA

The gods must have been smiling on me when I went to question Contessina Mallorca, because I found something you almost never find on the Upper East Side—a parking spot on the street. And right across from her gallery no less.

Stepping out of the car, I slipped on a patch of ice. When I righted myself, I noticed the black SUV that had been following me all morning. It idled at the end of the block, as subtle as a brick through a store window. It looked like the one that had tried to run down Svetlana and me. My breath hung in the bitter air as I waited for someone to get out of it. Nobody got out of it. I crossed the street to Mallorca Galleries. There were framed portraits in the window and a placard that read, "Visions of the Artist: Self-Portraits of 10 New York Painters." Just as I grabbed the door handle, my cell phone rang. It was Devon Trevelyan.

"My condolences about your boss," I said.

"Thank you. The sheriff contacted the museum yesterday. Carbon monoxide, it's simply awful."

"Yeah," I said. "Actually, I have another theory on what happened."

"Really? That reminds me, Helene Bundt from Sotheby's just phoned. Said you could fill me in on what you found at David's place."

In the back of my mind, I'd been mulling over asking Devon out. Tall, blonde, smart and English, she was my kind of gal.

"About my theory. I'd love to discuss it with you over dinner."

It was getting cold out here, and colder still with her silence. Finally a long sigh whooshed out of my cell phone.

"I shouldn't. You're not my type."

"Oh? What type is that? Tall? Well-dressed? Educated? I went to MIT, you know."

"No," she said. "Cocky. American. And operating on the fringes."

"Most women like that about me. All right, it was worth a shot."

There was another epic pause during which four taxis sped by.

"Very well," she said. "Tomorrow night, seven o'clock sharp, on the steps of the Met. We shall see if you prove me right or wrong."

"Your confidence in me is staggering. Until then."

I snapped my cell phone shut and went inside. The noise of the city evaporated. I stood at the top of a short set of stairs, looking over an airy space festooned with portraits. Hardwood floors glowed from the warm lighting. Lots of exposed brick. As if to balance the refined atmosphere, a sullen young man sat at the reception desk clicking a computer mouse.

"Help you, sir?" He stared at the screen.

"Is the owner available?"

"She'll be out in a minute. Make yourself comfortable."

It was warm in here. I draped my overcoat over my arm and strolled around. Lots of paintings of painters, most of them at easels. Thrilling. Then I rounded a corner and ran into a massive self-portrait by the redhead, Shay Connolly, and for a few seconds, I left my body. I wanted to climb into the frame with her. After careful study of her technique, I read the placard beside the painting:

Morning Coffee at My Window

No. 7 in an ongoing series of nude self-portraits, Ms. Connolly's *Morning Coffee* depicts a moment of vulnerability and reflection at the start of an artist's day. The steaming coffee in a dainty china cup, poised precariously over her bare body, creates a unique, resonant sense of danger; however the hot beverage is not the source of the greatest tension in the painting. Rather, it is the artist's wanton facial expression, which places the work in a tenuous category somewhere between an aesthetically pleasing study of the female form and a sexually charged image of a beautiful woman. Shay Connolly lives in New York City. (Oil on canvas, 84"x48"). $11,950.00

Shay Connolly. With any luck, I'd get a chance to question *her* over morning coffee. In the meantime, I sensed there was a connection between her, Jean René and the gallery owner I was about to meet.

Like a drum-roll, the click of heels preceded Ms. Mallorca's entrance. She materialized out of a wide archway with tanned olive skin and black coffee hair. It was impossible to tell if she was 41 or a miraculously well-maintained 51. The woman gleamed with afternoons spent at Elizabeth Arden.

"Contessina Mallorca?"

"My-orca," she said. "Like the Mediterranean island."

We shook hands. It was the firm but sensual handshake of a successful businesswoman, a woman used to swaying men with her touch. Her nose was exquisitely slender and genteel. She appraised me with her eyes and pulled a curtain of hair over her shoulder.

"And what can I interest you in today?" she asked.

I pointed. "That self-portrait by Shay Connolly is rather nice."

"You will find that all of her work is excellent. Are you a collector?"

Dexter Price had failed me of late. I would stick with the truth. Mostly.

"Actually, I'm a detective. Dakota Stevens."

Her voice was instantly weary. "What has she done this time?"

"Is there someplace we can talk?"

Dangling in her cleavage was a crucifix on a string of pearls, the serenity on Christ's face as clear as a Maine summer night. She caught my not-so-subtle leer and craned her neck toward the front of the gallery.

"Raymond, I will be in back with Mr. Stevens."

We went into her office. She closed the door. There was a cherry desk with a banker's lamp and three chairs, but she waved me to a leather couch instead.

So this was what the den of a cougar looked like. I'd always wondered.

On the bookshelf behind us were several black and white photographs of an American soldier in uniform and a shadow box of medals, including a Purple Heart. I was about to ask her about the mementos when she crossed her legs. The side-slit of her skirt yawned, revealing a trim and eager thigh.

"So," she said, "what laws has Shay broken now?"

Our eyes collided. Contessina twirled the pearls around her finger. When I tried to break the tension, it backfired.

"That's a lovely necklace," I said.

"Thank you." She hoisted Christ out of that enviable place. "A gift from an ex-lover." She leaned forward. "But then, I never *could* turn down a pearl necklace from a handsome man."

When I encountered scenes like this as an FBI agent, I'd always been saved by the Bureau's policy of agents working in pairs. But now, with no one to answer to, and an alluring older woman two feet away, I wasn't passing up this windfall. As she fondled her pearls, I slid across the couch, took her by the hair and yanked her mouth into mine so hard our teeth clonked together. My suit jacket got tossed to the floor. Raking her nails over my back, she muttered something in Spanish or Italian. I couldn't tell which, and given the circumstances, didn't care. I smothered her to the cushions, breathed hotly in her ear. She had that rich woman smell—of spicy perfume and dry-cleaning. Twenty years older than me? No way. Ten, maybe.

The phone rang. It rang again. She opened her eyes, pecked me on the lips and squirmed out from beneath me. Her silk blouse was untucked, one shoe was off. She kicked off the second one and jumped to the phone.

"Hello?" She paused for a second and put down the receiver. Standing at the desk with her chest heaving, she smiled wryly at me. Her hair was askew. I sat up and fixed my tie.

"Forget the paintings," I said. "That *kiss* was a work of art."

"It was," she said. "We should leave it at that. For now."

"Agreed." I picked up my suit jacket and slipped it on. "Can we talk, Ms. Mallorca?"

She sat down again. "Please, Contessina. You said you were a detective. Shay is not in jail, I hope."

"Actually, I'm a private detective and—"

"Private?"

"Yes. I've been looking into a missing painting, and I came across a billing for a show she had here. I need to get in touch with her."

"Don't tell me Shay stole a *painting*."

"No, but her name showed up in a suspect's apartment."

"I am not in the habit of revealing personal information about my artists."

"*Your* artist? What is she, an indentured servant?"

"I act as her dealer," she said. "I find buyers for her work and offer her paintings here on consignment. I would need some idea of what this is all about before interrupting her work."

"How long has she been one of your artists?"

"A while." She went over to the desk, produced a cigarette from a box and lighted it. "With Shay, it seems like a lifetime."

"Do you know who her dealer was before you?"

"No."

She puffed out the match with a seductive grace that only Mediterranean women can bring to such an ordinary gesture. I stayed on message.

"Do you know a man named Jean René?"

Her eyes flickered in recognition, but she immediately composed herself.

"No, I think not."

I didn't bring up the business card with their appointment, or DeAngelis's death. I've learned you're better off keeping something in reserve and surprising them about it later on. Contessina reached for an ashtray and flicked her cigarette.

"And what exactly do you wish to ask her?"

"It seems he knows her," I said. "I need to find out what their relationship is or was."

Smoke filled the room. I coughed. She opened the door and waved some of it out.

"I must warn you, Mr. Stevens, Shay is a volatile personality. If I merely *ask* if I can bring you over, she will scream at me."

"She sounds like a real piece of work."

"Yes, she is." Contessina gazed at a portrait out in the gallery. "She certainly is."

"Well," I said, "I've brought in some pretty tough felons, so I'm willing to risk it. Besides, if she gets too uppity, I've got a gun."

"Fine, I will be in touch." She flicked an ash. "And bring that gun."

When I came out of the gallery, three men were leaning against my car. They had Teutonic features and wore matching leather jackets and watch caps. These were hardly the young punks I'd toyed with outside of Serif's. I could feel the adrenaline kicking in.

The one leaning against my bumper had scar tissue around his eyes and a nose that had been broken multiple times. I would call him Hans. Slouched at the other end, wearing steel-toed boots and concealing something in his hand, was Klaus. And then there was Gunter, tall and lean, standing on the sidewalk. He had chestnut hair slicked to the side and a cleft chin. Hans straightened up as I approached. The street was empty. I stopped in the road and nodded.

"Hans, Klaus, Gunter. How nice to see you."

They looked at each other.

"Gentlemen, I'd love to stay and chat, but I'm on a roll." I jingled my car keys. "So, if you wouldn't mind."

Hans stepped in front of the driver's door and crossed his arms. Down the street, a UPS truck waited at the light. I was trying to devise a plan when I noticed Hans was standing on a patch of ice—the same one I'd slipped on earlier. Walking toward him, I fake-tripped, dropping my keys at his feet. He watched me as I reached for the keys, but before he could react I grabbed his pant cuffs and yanked like a magician snapping out a tablecloth. His legs flew out from under him, whacking his head against the door.

I was still on the ground when Klaus moved toward me in a low crouch, waving a knife. I rolled away. A kick landed on my ribs and stabbed through me like a railroad spike. It knocked the wind out of me. Klaus stooped over, slashed with the knife, but like most bruisers, he left his knees undefended. Bracing myself on my elbow, I thrust my heel into the side of his knee. Something snapped, and he dropped to the ground screaming. I couldn't help wincing myself.

The UPS truck roared by blaring its horn. I grabbed my keys and stood up.

Hans had been knocked cold, but Klaus stared at me in pain and confusion. Gunter remained on the sidelines. They'd wanted to prove they were tough guys, and I'd cheated. But professionals didn't care who was tougher. Maybe Hans and Klaus *were* tougher than I was, but they were also the ones I was stepping over to get into my car.

I collapsed into the seat and started the engine. My ribs were on fire. My favorite suit had holes in the knees. At least Hans and Klaus were still down for the count. They were blocking my tires. I rolled down the window and stared out the side-view mirror at Gunter.

"Move your buddies, or I'll run them over."

He gave me a tight-lipped smile and dragged them out of the way.

"We see you soon," he said.

His voice had an emptiness that made me shiver. I considered just shooting him in reply, but it would be impossible to justify. As soon as they were clear, I zoomed over to Madison and headed uptown. My legs trembled.

The adrenaline. Training had conditioned me to manage its effects during a fight, but it was always there afterwards.

Turning onto 79th, I checked my rear-view. No sign of the SUV or any other vehicle tagging along. Small relief. One thing was clear: I was making somebody nervous. Those three were far from lightweights, even if I had out-witted them. Next time they wouldn't underestimate me. Hell, next time they might just shoot me.

16

NOT THE REDHEAD

Another snowstorm hit overnight, and Svetlana and I were shoveling out in front of her building. Actually, I was shoveling while she touched up with a broom. To my knowledge, Svetlana had never shoveled her own walk.

"You are good at this," she said. "Have you considered a career change?"

I heaved a load of snow at her legs. A jolt ran up my side. Klaus had managed to put a hairline fracture in one of my ribs, and the entire area was deeply bruised. Even so, I was glad to be outside doing something physical. My only exercise of late had been fighting bad guys and hiking through groin-deep snow.

"This woman at Sotheby's," Svetlana said. "*She* hired DeAngelis?"

"Yeah, unless she's also lying."

"But why would Serif want to hire us, if the painting wasn't his?"

"To steal it. Convince us he's the owner, then have us do his dirty work."

I leaned on the shovel to catch my breath. No wonder old guys had heart attacks doing this stuff.

"Here's what doesn't make sense to me," I said. "If Bundt's instincts are correct about *Autumn in the Fields*—"

"—which Serif claimed was *Harvest Toil.*"

"*If* the painting was a fake, why would Serif want it?"

I shoveled the office steps and leaned the shovel against the door.

"So now we have a list of people," I said. "Serif, Bundt, René and some person named Li." I picked up the bag of salt and tossed cupfuls onto the sidewalk. "We know that the owner of the list—DeAngelis—is connected to at least two of them: Serif and Bundt. What we don't know is whether any people *on* the list are connected to each other."

I tossed some salt down the office steps.

"And then there's DeAngelis's email to consider. He writes to Serif, 'I know what you two are doing.' But what two? Serif and who else? Could the someone else be a person on the list? And, what are they doing?"

I put down the bag and unzipped my coat.

"Something else that's bothering me. Why is everyone from a different country?"

"The global economy," Svetlana said. "The art world is international."

"I think there's more to it than that."

She broomed off the railing. "So, what next?"

"Keep going with your research," I said. "Find out what you can about René and the artists in those dossiers. Bundt is faxing us the contact info of the true owners of the painting. They're Chinese, so unless you've added Mandarin to your repertoire, you'll need a translator."

"There is a player at the club," she said. "I think I can convince him to help us—even though I routinely destroy him."

"Good. In the meantime, I'm going to follow up with Contessina Mallorca and that artist of hers that was in one of the dossiers."

"Not the redhead."

Her voice was tinged with alarm, like I was about to run into a burning building.

"Yeah, the redhead," I said. "So what?"

Svetlana put down the broom and applied some Chapstick. "Maybe I should come with."

"I'll be fine."

"Famous last words," she said.

17

She's a Brick...

Named for its lettered avenues of A through D, Alphabet City is a jumble of funky shops, walkups and nightspots on the fringes of the East Village. It was also where Shay Connolly lived.

Contessina was nervous about intruding on her temperamental artist, and as if to compensate, she wore a full-length mink coat and carried a Chanel purse with a gold chain handle. I sensed she always dressed this way, but that today her clothing was more armor than fashion.

"There it is." She tossed her cigarette in the gutter. "The one on the left."

It was a brick tenement between two vacant lots. Another open area stretched behind the building, and the deep snow added to the feeling of empty space. A clanging sound echoed from the back, but I didn't see any work trucks. Across the street loomed a brand-new co-op. Shay Connolly's hovel seemed to know its days were numbered.

"The little place has spirit," I said.

"Shay's living situation is fragile," Contessina said. "Please do not bring it up."

"No real estate talk, I promise."

The outside buzzer was torn out. Somehow I doubted a butler would be taking our calling cards. We went in.

"Top floor." She clutched the banister with resignation. "In the back."

As we neared the final landing, the hallway boomed with the Commodores' song, "Brick House." Contessina heaved out a sigh.

"What?" I said.

"The music. When she is playing it, I know she isn't painting the work I need her to paint."

Contessina hesitated at the door, took a deep breath and knocked. The music continued to blare. We waited. She knocked again and still no answer. I tried the knob. It was open. She grabbed my arm. "I wouldn't…"

I eased down a crumbling hallway until it opened into a large room with high ceilings. "Brick House" slammed me in the chest. I took another step, and there she was, Shay Connolly, dancing and painting. She was just like the song says—*Mmm, mmm, mmm.*

The hair was even more vibrant in person, despite being worn up in a pile. A few stray locks, wavy and flame-orange, spilled over the straps of her cutoff overalls. Under the bib was a simple white T-shirt. Late 20s, early 30s. Curvaceously svelte. Agonizingly gorgeous. Here was the kind of redhead that inspired songs—and hexes.

Oblivious to our presence, she dipped her brush and stroked a thick curve of violet across the canvas. Her arms were sheathed in opera gloves. She swiveled her hips to the music and spun around in a pair of red cowboy boots. Contessina smacked me on the arm.

"You might want to close your mouth." She walked forward, the mink coat wagging around her ankles. "Shay?"

Shay continued to dance.

"I'm here with—"

Shay glanced up from loading her brush with paint. "Hey, let yourself in why don't you?" She clicked the stereo off and tossed the remote aside. Without the music, I heard the clanging noise from outside. It sounded like somebody was pounding on pipes right beneath the windows. Shay dug into her ears and removed earplugs.

"I'm glad you're here." She leaned against a steel cabinet. The overalls hugged her posterior impossibly well. "I need a big roll of canvas. The really good Russian linen stuff, not that cotton duck crap. Could you have Raymond get some for me? I don't have time." She pointed at me with the paintbrush. "Contessina, who is this?"

I nodded. "Dakota Stevens, miss. Love your outfit by the way. Eclectic."

She turned to Contessina. "I asked you not to bring the buyers here. The last one was *stalking* me, for Christ's sake."

"He is not a buyer." Contessina waved at the abstract work-in-progress on the easel. "Your show is very soon. You should work on the portraits."

"I'm tired of them," Shay said. "Why can't I do work *I* like for a change?"

"Because you have no talent for abstracts," Contessina said. "And they don't sell."

Shay's eyes flashed. She grabbed a hatchet off the table and hacked away at it. Chips of melamine flew like hornets. Contessina, a look of pity on her face, didn't move, didn't even blink. Shay finished by chopping deep into the tabletop, then whipped around and glared at me.

"Now, who the hell are you?"

"Whoa, easy there." I flashed my PI license at her. A cigarette and a Fedora would have helped, but one makes do. "I'm a private eye, miss, and I need your help."

The corners of her mouth twitched with amusement. "Private eye, huh?"

"That's right."

She dropped the brush in a jar and put her hands in her back pockets. I envied those hands.

"I saw an old movie once where the guy said he was a private dick working on a case." She strutted towards me. There was a wicked glint in her eyes. "Is that you? Are you a private *dick*?"

"Well…" Contessina was across the room, flipping through canvases.

"Say it." She stepped closer. "Go on…say it."

"All right." I stood tall and swaggered. "Listen doll— I'm a private dick, working on a case."

"I love it!" She jumped up and down and clapped. As the contents of her overalls jiggled, I averted my eyes. Mostly.

"Glad I amuse you," I said. "Can we talk?"

"Just a sec." Shay ran into the bathroom with an empty bucket. A moment later she came out with it filled, went to the window and opened it. The clanging noise was deafening. She gave me a long, salacious wink and poured the water straight down. The air boiled with obscenities.

"Yeah?" She leaned out. "You tell that prick I'm *not* leaving. I've got a lease till November and I'm staying. Now piss off!"

She slammed the window shut and scaled the bucket into the kitchen.

"Landlord hires a crew of guys," she said. "Not to build anything, just to bang on scaffolding to drive me out. Messed up or what? Well, screw him. That jerkoff has no idea who he's dealing with."

I was beginning to get that impression myself.

Shay pulled a paintbrush from her hair. She shook it out, and it tumbled heavily down her shoulders. The sight of that fiery mane cinched my throat up like a mail sack.

"Sorry for the mess," she said. "My cleaning lady quit."

She waved a hand at the oversized studio—bare queen-sized mattress, paint-splotched floors, rolling clothes rack, kitchenette, bathroom. A minefield of coffee cans sprouting brushes littered the floor, and in the far corner, a purple bra hung from an empty easel. She nodded at me.

"Okay, talk."

I cleared my throat. "Do you know a man named Jean René?"

"Who?" She looked out the window.

"Lives in Williamsburg. Had a dossier on you."

"Never heard of him." She sat on a stool, crossed her legs. "Contessina, you?"

Her dealer was still examining paintings and putting some aside. So far there were three.

"He's a collector, I believe." Contessina dusted off her gloves and walked over to us. "He might have bought something of yours—I'd have to look it up—or he may have been keeping an eye on your work, waiting for the right piece."

"*Have been?*" I said. "Why past tense?"

"My English is not perfect, Mr. Stevens."

"So," I said to Shay, "you've never heard of the guy."

"Nope."

"How about Nadir Serif? Either of you."

They looked at each other.

"David DeAngelis?" I asked.

"Him I *have* heard of," Contessina said. "Director of the Met's provenance department, is he not?"

"How do you know him?"

"I don't." She pulled the leaves of her mink together. "His name is familiar, that's all."

Contessina opened her purse and took out a cigarette. She was about to light it when Shay snapped at her.

"Damn it, Contessina, no smoking in here! You know I'm allergic."

I grinned. Perhaps Shay and I had more in common than the fact that she was gorgeous and I thought so. Contessina pointed at the three canvases.

"Take those to Raymond this week. I'm going downstairs."

"Hey, leave me a check this time," Shay said. "I have *rent*, you know."

"You will be paid." Contessina shut the door behind her.

Now that the banging had stopped, I could hear the wind whistling in the window cracks. For the first time I noticed the heady smell of solvents. Shay looked sideways at her painting-in-progress.

"So," I said, "David DeAngelis. Know him?"

"Have to say no."

"How about Maia Gallant?"

She squinted one eye shut, wagged a boot. "Nope."

"David Birchfield?"

"Uh-uh."

"Cindy Bourassa? Jamal Carter?"

She swallowed when I mentioned Carter.

"Where do you know him from?"

"What am I, on trial?" She tucked some hair behind her ear, smearing violet paint on her cheek.

"This René had a folder on him, too." I said. "And know what else?"

She blinked in the light from the window.

"Jamal's dead," I said. "Killed not too far from here, as a matter of fact."

I neglected to mention it was the result of a mugging.

"Killed?"

"So you knew him," I said.

"I didn't say that." She crossed her arms. "You're telling me some weirdo has folders on a bunch of artists, including me, and that one of them was murdered. Naturally, I'm a little upset. Wouldn't you be?"

"Killed. I didn't say murdered. And I didn't say they were all artists."

"What? You said a dossier…oh, never mind, I have to get back to work."

She picked up a thin brush and twirled it restlessly through her fingers.

"How do you know Carter?" I asked.

"Goodbye."

"Not until I get some answers."

Gently, she put down the brush. Before I realized what was happening, she had yanked out the hatchet and spun around. I ducked, she hurled. The hatchet boomeranged across the room and sunk into the kitchen cabinet with a loud thump. I doubted it would have hit me, but it was a tad unsettling.

"Impressive," I said. "Do you practice?"

She stomped her boots. *"Get out!"*

I decided to leave before she pulled out a crossbow.

"It's been educational." On my way out, I flipped a business card at the mattress on the floor. It landed face-up on her pillow. "Call me when you're ready to talk."

"Wait, I'm—"

I slammed the door and started down the stairs.

18

RESISTANCE IS FUTILE

I was still buzzing from my encounter with the ravishing and radioactive Shay Connolly when I picked up my dinner date—Devon Trevelyan. We went to Ruby Foo's for the legendary wok-seared lobster, and since the restaurant was only a block away from my apartment at 201 West 77th, we walked over afterward for a nightcap. When I turned on the lights, Devon gasped.

"My goodness, it's like a time machine. Who's your decorator?"

"No decorator. This was all my grandparents' stuff. Late Eisenhower–early Kennedy period."

"It's so clean."

I took her coat. "My grandmother was a neat freak. Anytime they went away, she covered everything in plastic."

She walked around the living room like a factory inspector. "A two bedroom? And rent-controlled? Wonderful."

"Yeah, over the years I've sublet to Bureau guys down on their luck, so it evens out."

"That's quite generous of you."

I poured us two sparkling ciders at the bar. Devon completed her self-tour and leaned over the counter. I pushed a wine glass in her direction.

"I have a policy of not drinking when I'm on a case," I said.

"How quaint." She sipped. "So, now that we've eaten that fabulous meal, shall we talk about your case?"

"Sure." I walked around the bar and leaned next to her.

"Are you any closer to finding the painting?" she asked.

"No, and it seems the painting is just the tip of the iceberg."

Twelve floors down on Amsterdam, a fire truck blared its horn. She glanced at her watch.

"Relax," I said. "I'll have you home before curfew."

"Sorry, habit. An iceberg, you were saying?"

"Yeah, turns out my client—who I *still* haven't found, by the way—doesn't own the painting. Ms. Bundt said she hired your boss because she suspected the painting was a fake. And I think I've found evidence of somebody copying paintings, although I'm not sure it's connected to my case." I sipped. "So there it is."

"Sounds fascinating. If I can be of any help…"

"Thanks, I might need it." I pushed my glass aside and edged closer to her. "But enough about the case."

Devon put her glass down. "Then whatever shall we talk about?"

"Have I proven you right or wrong?" I asked.

"Excuse me?"

"That I'm not your type," I said. "Right or wrong?"

"I haven't enough data yet."

She flipped her hair over her shoulders and leaned in to kiss me. We embraced gently. I ran my hand along her dress where it stretched taut on her thigh. The woman had a body like a whetstone. As my hand instinctively strayed to her backside, I recalled Devon's stinging characterization of me: *"Cocky. American. And operating on the fringes."* She was an incredible kisser, but I was determined to defy her expectations. I uncoupled my lips from hers.

"I think we should save this." My throat was thick.

She gave me a sidelong glance. "Are you being a gentleman?"

"I'm trying. But if you keep standing there in that dress looking coy, I can't promise anything. Let me take you home."

Outside, we crossed the street to the parking garage where I kept the Cadillac. I helped Devon navigate a narrow path through a snowbank, and when we reached the garage entrance, Gunter and two men hopped out of an SUV with guns drawn. Hans and another man stepped out from behind a van, also pointing guns.

"Devon," I said, "I'd like you to meet Hans and Gunter."

"Get in the truck," Gunter said. "Now."

"The woman isn't part of this." I tugged on my coat lapel. "I'm giving her cab fare."

They poked out their guns. I pressed two twenties into Devon's palm.

"Should I call the police?" Her voice was calm. I admired her bravery and considered asking if she had any to spare.

"Not tonight. But if you don't hear from me by tomorrow, call Svetlana at my office and tell her what happened."

I nudged her toward Amsterdam. She walked away without looking back. Gunter stepped forward and pressed a Luger into my stomach. He took the S&W automatic off my hip and the stun gun from my pocket.

"Any chance of a receipt for those?" I said.

He waved his gun at the car door. My ego didn't like it, but when you're beat, you're beat. I tried looking on the bright side: this might net me a couple of fresh clues, maybe even reveal the people behind this mess. Then again, it could get me killed.

I slid into the Lincoln Navigator with a goon on either side, and two more in the seats behind me. Gunter sat up front with the driver.

"Blindfold him."

Somebody threw a cloth hood over my head.

"Sit on your hands," he said.

Any resistance now would be futile. Besides, if they planned on shooting me, they wouldn't have bothered with the blindfold.

19

THE DONKEY, THE ROOSTER, AND THE LION

At first I tried estimating our speed and memorizing the turns, but all I could tell for certain was that we left Manhattan over a bridge. Given there are about twenty of them, it didn't help. After a couple hours I lost all feeling in my hands, and toward the end the road went from pavement to gravel. The next thing I knew, they were hauling me out.

"Give him some air," Gunter said.

The hood was snapped off. My face was drenched with sweat, and the frosty air bit shrewdly. I caught a glimpse of movement from my side. A punch landed on my cheek. My knees went limp. As they steadied me, I tasted blood.

"I told you we would see you soon," Gunter said.

Observing things right now was more important than a clever comeback. I took in everything.

We were parked in a shallow dell surrounded by tall firs and spruce. The evergreen smell was strong in the cold. Spotlights on telephone poles made the snow glare. A gap in the snowbank revealed a side road up a moderate slope, and at the far end of the dell, a path disappeared into the woods. No road signs or unique geographic features. No sound but the wind. They seemed to have taken every precaution. Every precaution, that is, except the license plate.

Crusted snow blocked half the letters, but I was able to make out the first three.

"Okay, enough," Gunter said.

I repeated the letters in my head—7J3, 7J3, 7J3. The hood covered my head again. Two thugs grabbed me by the arms and we crunched forward.

A short hike brought us to a long set of stairs going down. The brutes assisted me, and at the bottom a metal door clanged open. We were on solid ground now. Cement. Our footsteps echoed. Dank, with the stale smell of diesel fuel. Accordion music, very faint, was playing someplace. Right turn, up another staircase, and through another door. The air turned hot and humid with the pungent scent of chlorine. The men holding me stopped short. After a long silence, a man with a soft voice spoke.

"On the chair," he said. "Bind him, but leave the hood."

The Voice had a whisper of an accent, but of what language I couldn't tell. Its unnerving softness sent a chill through me. They shoved me into a chair and taped my wrists. I remembered the sticky residue on DeAngelis's wrists and ankles. This was the same MO. Hopefully it wouldn't lead to the same end.

"Mr. Stevens," the Voice said, "there are a few matters we must discuss."

Water slapped against something and every couple of slaps there was a sucking sound. My guess? A pool filter trap. Somebody struck a match. A moment later, the tang of pipe tobacco filled my nose.

"I must commend you on your handling of my people thus far," the Voice said. "I understand you are well trained and resourceful. It is unfortunate not to have you in my employ."

"Well, give me an application and—"

"I am doing you a favor by bringing you here tonight. I was tempted to have my men shoot you and dump you off a bridge."

"Thanks for the favor. Your point?"

Footsteps approached and the smell of the pipe grew stronger.

"My *point*, Mr. Stevens, is this. You will drop your case involving Mr. Serif and Mr. René."

So, Serif and René *were* connected.

"Nah, it's like a pet now," I said. "Think I'll keep it."

A metal chair scraped toward me and stopped at my side. Pipe smoke wafted under my hood. As if I didn't have enough problems, now I had to worry about suffocating.

"Mr. Stevens," the Voice said, "are you familiar with the fables of Aesop?"

"'Slow but steady wins the race,'" I said. "That's me, the tortoise."

"I have another one in mind."

He puffed on the pipe for a moment, then began.

"A Donkey and a Rooster were in the barnyard when a famished Lion entered," he said. "The Rooster crowed, startling the Lion, and the Lion fled. The Donkey, puffed up with courage, went after the Lion, but the Lion turned around and tore the Donkey to pieces."

"Wait, you lost me," I said. "If I'm the Donkey and you're the Lion, who's the Rooster?"

His chair squeaked. I was struck on the jaw and rocked halfway out of my chair.

"Do not interrupt."

I straightened up. Again, blood filled my mouth. I swallowed it. The Voice grabbed the hood and jerked my head back.

"The moral, Mr. Stevens, is this: *False confidence invites danger.*' What you have dealt with so far is but a fraction of my resources. Do not concern yourself with finding Mr. Serif or the painting. Concern yourself with your own safety and the life of your most attractive assistant."

My shoulders stiffened, my throat went dry. "If anybody does anything to her—"

"Your loyalty is admirable, young man," the Voice said. "In my day, you would have done well for yourself. But do not mistake me. I have squashed bugs tougher than you."

One of the men coughed. Somewhere, the pool filter switched on. The Voice stood up and walked away, the pipe smell fading with his footsteps.

"Drop the case or Miss Krüsh dies. I give you until tomorrow night to decide. We will be in touch. And I assure you, this is no fable."

A door opened and clanked shut. The goons untaped me, ripping all the hair off my wrists, and led me back to the SUV. We drove for an hour and stopped.

"This is good," Gunter said.

"What's good?"

There was a horrible thump on the back of my head, and the pain, white for an instant, turned red before fading to black.

20

A SEXY WEATHERWOMAN

Spend enough time in this business, and sooner or later you get bonked on the head and wake up with the worst headache of your life. Ask Marlowe. This being my first time, I wanted to savor the experience.

I slit my eyes open. I was sitting upright in a bed surrounded by a blue-green partition. My hands stung like hell. They were soaking in water, the fingers swollen and blistered. The partition scraped open and a nurse walked in. She peered at my hands.

"Yes, a little better. Doctor'll be in soon to check."

"Check?" I said.

"The frostbite. A truck driver found you on the side of the road this morning. You're a very lucky man. You could have died of hypothermia."

"Nice to know. How about something—"

"There are people here to see you. Police officers and a woman with an accent."

Svetlana. Suddenly I didn't feel so alone.

"I'll send the police in first," the nurse said. "They've been waiting a while."

Two State Troopers took their time questioning me. I was getting into my car, I said, when somebody hit me from behind. The nurse must have shown them my PI license because they didn't believe a single word.

"And that's it?" one of them said.

"I had a gun. Smith and Wesson nine millimeter. It's licensed."

"We checked your things," the other one said. "It's gone. We'll put it in the report."

They walked out muttering to each other, probably hoping I'd lose a finger.

Svetlana brushed by them on her way in. Sporting a fur-collared overcoat and high-heeled boots, she just about gave the cops whiplash. At my bedside, she pulled off her sunglasses and frowned at me.

"I knew you'd do something foolish..." She pulled up a chair.

"Yeah, getting abducted—what a joker," I said. "Where am I?"

"You are in the Columbia-Greene emergency room with frostbitten fingers, stitches in your mouth and a possible concussion." She produced a can of ginger ale, dropped in a straw and held it for me while I sipped. "Tell me what happened."

I shared everything except my kiss with Contessina and my date with Devon. Then I had her call Devon and hold the cell phone to my ear while I left a reassuring message. Svetlana pretended to be oblivious, but I could tell she was listening. She gave me a final sip of ginger ale and put the can aside.

"I still have not heard from Ms. Bundt about the Chinese couple," she said.

"Probably forgot. Call her later, would you?"

She nodded, studied my hand in the water. "Any idea where they took you?"

"Nope. All I know is we drove for about three hours. But I did get a partial plate. Seven-jay-three, a black Lincoln Navigator."

"Like the one that tried to hit us." She jotted it down. "I will look into it."

She sat up tall in the chair. That good old Soviet system. Must have beaten them with rulers to get posture like that.

"Now," she said, "while you were getting in fights and being kidnapped and having hatchets thrown at you—"

"Hey, it wasn't all fun and games."

"I made a couple of interesting discoveries myself."

She held up a computer printout for me to read. It was another obituary. I blinked at her in disbelief until the doctor came in. He examined me, applied a salve to my hands and bandaged me up. For my skull he prescribed a precautionary X-ray and gave me codeine for the headache.

"And Mr. Stevens," the doctor said.

"Yeah?"

"Try to stay away from blackjacks for a while." He wagged his eyebrows and left.

While I got dressed, Svetlana retrieved my things. In addition to my pistol and the stun gun, Gunter and the boys had borrowed eighty bucks from my wallet. I was lucky to still have shoes. We went upstairs to radiology and waited in a lounge with a view of a parking lot. It was snowing again—fine flakes with a strong wind. Svetlana read a biography on Garry Kasparov. I gestured at the windows.

"What's with this?"

"Nor'easter." She licked a finger and turned a page. "Six to eight inches, with up to a foot in higher elevations."

"Anyone ever tell you you'd make a sexy weather-woman? You know, with the accent and all."

"Yes."

I waited for details, but none came. Staring out at the relentless snowfall, I thought about the obituary Svetlana had shown me.

"David Birchfield," I said. "Could just be a coincidence."

"Two artists from René's files dying within days of each other?" she said. "That is too much coincidence."

"How about the others? Anything on them?"

"There is a Cindy Bourassa showing in galleries in Montreal, but I am not sure she is the same person. On Ms. Gallant, I find nothing."

"Doesn't matter...René—he's the link. Last night the Voice said I should 'drop the case involving Mr. Serif and Mr. René.' At least now we know they're connected."

I tried flexing my hands, but in the thick bandages it was impossible. If I wanted to grip a gun, these would have to come off. I was observing how bulbous my hands were when Svetlana interrupted.

"So, Monsieur Poirot"—she grinned as she flipped a page—"what is your next move?"

"Well, until I can confront René in person, our next best lead is Shay Connolly."

She raised an eyebrow over her book.

"It's not like that," I said. "She knows something."

"Mmm-hmm."

"She does. You'll see."

I couldn't shake the image of running my fingers through Shay's hair. The nurse called my name. Besides finding out if my skull was broken, maybe they could look in there and tell me why redheads flustered me so.

21

THE UMLAUT

Svetlana's father, Oleksander Mykhailo Krush, owned a Ukrainian restaurant (one of several profitable enterprises) in the East Village, a few blocks from my office. Going to see him was touchy for two reasons: I only went there when I needed something, and because of the thorny relationship he had with Svetlana.

The two of them had long periods when they didn't speak, including the past year. I was pretty sure Svetlana blamed him for her mother's early death. There was also Oleksander's monomaniacal obsession with Svetlana's chess career, which had driven her to spitefully add an *umlaut* (ü) to her last name. At his restaurant door, I stopped, took a deep breath of cold air and went inside.

The hostess, 18-year-old Anya, recognized me immediately. All of the Krush daughters had glossy hair and intense eyes, and Anya was no exception. She stared up at me.

"My cousin," she said, "when do you marry her?"

"Hello, Anya. Is Oleksander around?"

"Ah, you ask for her hand like gentleman," she said. "Come, he is in back."

At a round, elevated booth near the kitchen doors, Oleksander sat reading a Ukrainian newspaper and smoking.

"Uncle Olek? Mr. Stevens to see you."

The moment Anya walked away, my mouth went dry. I wasn't afraid of the man, but I liked his daughter and wanted him to like me. This made me vulnerable, and he knew it. Oleksander put down his paper and eyed me coolly.

"Montana Stevens," he said.

"Dakota, sir."

He squashed out his cigarette and lit another. The smoke swirled around his steel-gray hair.

"Yes, sit." He waved his cigarette at my hands. "Not leprosy, I hope."

"Frostbite."

Oleksander nodded, as though he knew dozens of people with the affliction. He poured a splash of vodka into two glasses and pushed one toward me.

"No thanks," I said. "I'm on a case."

He studied me before draining both glasses. As a waitress walked by he snapped his fingers, said something in Ukrainian, and made a circular gesture at the table. It had only taken me three years to learn this meant food was on the way. Oleksander leaned back and exhaled smoke at the ceiling lights.

"I am reading in *Chess Life* that my daughter has twenty-board exhibition in nation's capital next week. She is practicing, yes?"

I didn't observe Svetlana practicing much, but I knew she did most of her work with her coach, Lazar, at the Marshall Chess Club.

"Of course," I said.

"I study her last tournament," he said. "Tell her she must work on endgame with Queen's Gambit Declined."

"I'll be sure to relay that."

The waitress arrived and placed two dishes in the center of the table. The first was a platter of varenyky, the Ukrainian version of perogies, stuffed with potato and cheddar cheese. The second was a steaming soup tureen filled with holubtsi—cabbage rolls stuffed with rice and hamburger and served in tomato sauce. A busboy brought me a place setting.

"Please," Oleksander said. "Unless you also do not *eat* while on case."

I helped myself to the food. My host squinted at me through the smoke.

"So, now you are comfortable, tell me why you come."

I ate a varenyky. Not my favorite fare, but I hadn't eaten since the day before, so it tasted better than usual.

"I need your help."

"I already rent you nice office cheap. Why should I do more?"

"Because Svetlana could be in danger," I said.

He stamped out his cigarette and didn't light another one. He poured himself half a glass of vodka. "Tell me."

I kept it brief, describing my abduction and the threat they'd made against Svetlana. When I finished, he sipped his drink and gazed at the customers in his restaurant.

"This is why I object to this foolishness of yours." He muttered something in Ukrainian. "She is trained chess champion. She could have been number one woman player in world." Oleksander flicked an ash on his plate.

"Well," I said, "she was number *two* in the world and number one in the United States. She's still in the U.S. top ten, and the top twenty internationally. That's amazing if you ask me."

"I did not ask."

I looked at the food. My appetite had disappeared. I pushed the plate away.

"Sir, I need your people to watch her for the next couple of weeks. Starting *tonight*. But I don't want her knowing."

He drummed his fingers on the table, then ate a varenyky and dusted off his hands.

"I will do this. Three good men, twenty-four hours day."

"Thank you, sir."

"But, Stevens…if any harm comes to Svetlana, you I hold responsible."

"Understood."

I shook his hand, gripping him forcefully enough so he would respect me, but not *so* forceful as to suggest I didn't respect him. Another one of Life's balancing acts. Then, without another word, I left.

I walked back to the office through the evening snowstorm. Svetlana was out. I made coffee and stood at the front window watching the snow fall. This had to be the most depressing winter on record.

The phone rang. The caller ID was blocked, but I knew who it was. I picked up the extension. It was the Voice.

"So, Mr. Stevens, do you drop the case, or do we kill the woman?"

"No deal."

He hung up before I could think of a better curtain line.

22

FOLLOWING A PERSON IS HARD WORK

With Oleksander's men protecting Svetlana, I was free to pursue other leads. This was my second day following Shay Connolly and so far I'd learned a few interesting facts about her.

First, the woman had a *great* ass. One that should be cast in bronze and put in the Whitney. Second, she was a speedy walker, even for a New York City gal, and I had to work to keep up. Third, Shay Connolly didn't like spending money on art supplies. In an art store near my office, I watched her snatch up a fistful of expensive brushes in every size and style, and stuff them in her jacket. At the register, she bought a $4 palette knife and left without a hint of remorse.

Following a person is hard work, especially when you're doing it on four hours' sleep. The night before, I had parked across from Jean René's building with an enlargement of his driver's license photo, waiting for a swarthy, middle-aged man to appear. At midnight the side door opened and a woman in a heavy parka disappeared down the street. The high point of my night. Not one man showed himself. At eleven this morning Shay emerged from her apartment in airbrushed-on jeans and a green down jacket, and aroused my curiosity with a transport tube strapped to her back. Wherever she was going with that cylinder might present a clue.

After the art store, Shay went around the corner to Grace Church. Once she was inside I waited a moment, then slipped in quietly. While Shay knelt up front, I sat in the back corner. I couldn't imagine why she was here, unless she was asking God to forgive her for shoplifting. She prayed for ten minutes, shoved some money in the donation box and went up the street to a liquor store.

This chick was full of surprises.

Lingering outside, I watched her buy a pint of something then go next door for a coffee and add a shot. While she paid I noticed Slim, from the ski resort, across the street. He still wore sunglasses, but had exchanged his trench coat for a ski jacket.

I was faced with a dilemma. Should I continue following Shay, or should I lead Slim into an alley and get creative on him? Assuming he was following *me*. Two artists had been killed already, and Slim could be gunning for Shay next. I chose to stick with her and see what developed. My cell phone rang. It was Svetlana.

"What's up?" I said.

"I have been watching René's for two hours. I'm going home."

"No activity?"

"Do seagulls count as activity?"

"No," I said.

"Then no."

"See you at the office later?"

"Maybe," she said. "Goodbye."

As I put the phone away, we passed Union Square and headed into the Gramercy Park neighborhood. I followed Shay, Slim followed me. Things got complicated when Shay went down into the subway. Metrocard in hand, I glided through the turnstile with Shay's hair still in sight. My tail had to stop at a vending machine. On the platform, Shay sipped her coffee and paced along the edge, tossing her hair over her jacket collar. With every swish of those tresses, my heart raced. Farther down the platform, my tail materialized. He peered into the tunnel, checked his watch.

When the subway whirred in, I boarded the car next to Shay's. I was peripherally aware of Slim, but I ignored him and watched Shay through the window at the end of the car. At Grand Central she took the tunnel to the 42nd Street shuttle. Shay and I wove expertly through the chaos, and so far Slim had impressed me by keeping up. But when Shay headed for the far shuttle track, Slim made a mistake.

The shuttle trains are three cars long. While Shay boarded the front car, and I boarded the rear car, Slim cut off his escape route by getting on the *middle* car. Now I had him. Passengers were still crowding inside when I shoved past them and bolted ahead to Slim's car. I plowed through a dozen straphangers before he spotted me.

He ran out the far door, I jumped out the middle one. He tried to flee down the platform, but the oncoming crush of passengers stopped him. I was closing in. Slim looked around frantically. Two tracks over, a new train rolled in. The track between our train and the new one was empty. There was only one problem: an eight-foot gap between the platforms with a 700-volt third rail below.

And then Slim did something no sane person would even *think* of doing.

He stuffed his billfold in his jeans and shed the jacket. Too far away to catch him, all I could do was watch, dumbstruck, as he timed a space in the crowd, sprinted and leaped across. Standing tall on the other side, he beckoned me with his hand. Twice this guy had made an ass out of me. The doors chimed on Shay's subway. I grabbed Slim's jacket and jumped on board.

While the shuttle clacked cross-town, I rifled through the jacket pockets. It was a blue Patagonia, and except for the color was similar to the ones Dumb and Dumber had worn. I found some Treasurer cigarettes in their signature aluminum case, a lighter and a cash receipt from Nat Sherman Tobacconist on 42nd and Fifth. Whoever this guy was, between the pricey smokes, the $900 to buy a kid's snowboard, and the nonchalance with which he dumped an expensive ski jacket, he clearly had resources.

At Times Square, Shay hustled down Broadway to 39th, where she turned west. A homeless man shivered in a doorway. I tossed him the jacket and cigarettes. At Ninth Avenue, Shay headed downtown until she came to *Galerie des Maîtres Contemporains*.

She cupped her hands on the front window. Satisfied with whatever she saw, she tucked her hair under a ski cap, put on sunglasses and went in. Considering she looked like she was about to rob the place, I decided to risk her seeing me. I crossed the street.

The gallery didn't live up to its snooty-sounding name. It had all the aesthetic charm of a bomb shelter. The walls were bare sheetrock, the floors white Linoleum. The gallery went from one building into the next, continuing down the block, as though when they filled one space, they just punched a hole in the wall and kept going. On my way in, I passed a heavyset man at a table reading a *Daily News*, and as I continued farther into the place, I heard Shay muttering.

"Fucker thinks he's smart," she said.

I peeked around the corner. Shay was standing in front of another nude self-portrait. In this one she was alone in a movie theater eating popcorn and wearing nothing but a pair of red high heels. Like *Morning Coffee*, the detail was riveting.

Shay pulled out a Buck folding knife, flicked it open. Her shoulders stiffened. With a deep breath and a glance over her shoulder, she pierced the canvas edge and cut the painting out of its frame. As she rolled up the canvas and slid it into the transport tube, I noticed a wire behind the frame. It was alarmed. Gingerly, with her fingernails, she took the description card off the wall. When she turned to leave, I ducked behind a partition and let her pass.

For the next hour I followed her back downtown to her neighborhood. In Tompkins Square Park, Shay threw away the painting. I rescued it (*Nudité de Shay au Ciné-ma*, the card read), rolling it up as I ran to catch her.

A few blocks from her apartment, Shay went into PS 63 William McKinley School. I considered following her inside, but having come this far without being noticed, I didn't want to chance it. Then she appeared in the first-floor windows. She was in a classroom of elementary school kids, and as she removed her coat, several of them flapped drawings at her. She hugged another woman and sat down with the children. I checked my watch. Three thirty—around the time they'd have an after-school art program.

I shook my head. This woman was impossible to peg. The detective side of me knew she was a suspect, but I couldn't help being intrigued by her. I waited until she finished, at five o'clock, and tailed her home. She didn't reemerge and I gave up at seven. I was starved. Besides, it was time to check on René again. Hiking back across the East Village to get my car, I wondered what to make of the day's events.

23

THE MALTESE PAINTING

The afternoon of Jean René's appointment with Contessina, Svetlana and I met for lunch at Soup Burg, a diner specializing in—you guessed it—soup and hamburgers. Sitting in a window booth on Madison Avenue, we had a clear view down 73rd Street to the entrance of Mallorca Galleries. I had my binoculars beside me and Svetlana had a new DSLR camera with a zoom lens. René was due in fifteen minutes.

"It'll be nice to finally catch this guy," I said.

Svetlana sipped some tea. We had eaten lunch and were waiting for dessert.

"How did you make out with the tobacconist?"

"Didn't." I drank some coffee. "Salesman was a rude little nebbish."

Milling around outside were three men with weathered Eastern European faces. Two stood at the bus stop while the third window-shopped in front of an electronics store across the street. They were the bodyguards Oleksander had assigned to Svetlana. I could breathe easier now, knowing she was well protected.

"So," she said, "I had Eric Chen speak with the Chinese couple from Sotheby's."

I trained the binoculars on Contessina's doorway. Just the awning flapping in the wind.

"This Chen," I said, "you have confidence in his translation?"

"Yes."

"And they said…?"

"That the painting was a wedding gift, purchased from a gallery in Hong Kong. I talked to the manager and persuaded her to look up where they got it. It was sold to her by a dealer from Malta."

I choked on my coffee. "A Maltese painting? You're kidding."

"What is funny?"

"Nothing."

"The seller's name was Malcolm Azzopardi," she said. "He has not been back since."

The waitress brought our desserts and refilled my coffee.

"At least the name's memorable." I ate some of my apple pie and mulled over this new discovery. "She didn't happen to get his picture?"

Svetlana plucked out the center of her cinnamon roll and ate it.

"You know," I said, "normal people start at the outside and work *in*."

She licked her fingers. Unlike most women, Svetlana ate with dignified abandon.

"The center is the most delicious part, so I eat it first. Then if I get full, I can throw away the rest without feeling guilty."

"I respect your logic."

One of the bodyguards came in and sat at the lunch counter. I checked Contessina's again. Still no action.

"Back to Azzopardi," I said. "Can we get a picture?"

"No, but I got a description. A vague one. The woman has not seen him in three years. Short, with dark skin and a beard. That is all."

"Sounds like someone we know."

"Serif?" she said.

"Minus the beard, yeah."

Svetlana gestured with a piece of cinnamon roll.

"There are many short, bearded men in the world."

"And aren't we lucky to have them," I said. "Anything else?"

"I have news on the partial license plate you gave me. There are four SUVs in New York with plates starting with 7J3. One is registered to an address in Buffalo. Two more are in Queens."

Svetlana sat up the way I'd seen her at chess tournaments, just before delivering the *coup de grace* to an opponent.

"The fourth one," she said. "Guess where it is registered."

I hated to steal her thunder, but sometimes I liked to remind Svetlana which of us was the detective.

"The Catskills," I said.

She scowled. "How—"

"The Catskills are the right distance from the city, and the place they took me was in the mountains."

"Very good," she said. "It is registered to a Terrence Young. I printed out directions." She handed me a manila envelope. "He lives on a rural route high in the mountains. It looks very remote, Dakota, so I included a topographical map. You may have some difficulty."

"I'll be fine."

It was quarter to two. I had another bite of pie and checked Contessina's again with the binoculars. Not a single person had gone in or out of the gallery.

"Will you go up tomorrow?" she said.

"Not yet. Remember that state business database you showed me?"

"Vaguely." She dropped the rest of her cinnamon roll and dusted off her hands.

"Well, last night after Shay stole the painting, I looked up the gallery owner. It's Jean René."

"What?"

"It all fits now," I said. "The gallery, the painting Shay stole, Serif, DeAngelis, the Voice, the dead artists—everybody and everything points to him."

René was an hour overdue. I checked Contessina's one last time. Nobody. He wasn't coming.

"Enough. He's the guy, I know it." I threw my coat on. "I'm going over."

"And if he's not there?"

I lowered my voice. "Then I break in and wait for him. And if he doesn't show, then I'll fly to Shanghai." I dropped two twenties on the table. "Anything's better than sitting around. You coming?"

"I have practice with Lazar."

"That's okay." I worked my hands into my gloves. "René might require some persuasion and I'd prefer you didn't see me like that."

24

LONG RED HAIRS

I raced over to Jean René's only to find the place empty. Did this guy *ever* come home? I was confident he'd just stepped out, though, because the TV was on and a bagel sat on the coffee table. I left the TV alone, put on latex gloves and got a Diet Coke. Then I sat down in a swivel recliner and did what we PIs spend most of our time doing: I waited.

Tilting back in the chair, I thought of the scene in *Dr. No* where Sean Connery passes the time waiting for an assassin by playing solitaire. Slick. Maybe I should start carrying a deck of cards. The window blinds glowed in the late afternoon sun. I finished my soda. Out in the hallway the elevator door clanked open and banged shut. I pricked up my ears. There were footsteps. They faded down the hall. Confident I'd hear him in time when he came back, I started looking for clues.

There was nothing new in the office, kitchen or studio, so I wandered into the bathroom. Modern, cold and spacious like the rest of the loft, it had glass bowl sinks and pewter fixtures, a marble shower stall, and a stainless steel double-seat Japanese bath with a dead body floating face-up in ice water.

I steadied myself on the counter. *Please let it be someone else.*

I went over for a look. The occipital region of the skull was crushed in, the bleeding stanched by the ice, but the face was distinct. A blue-faced Jean René stared blankly at the mirrored ceiling. There was a smear of blood against the tub wall, above the water line. The partially melted ice water explained why I hadn't smelled the body. Even right on top of it, the odor was faint. Whoever did this had wanted to confuse time of death. However, what the killer didn't realize was that medical examiners had formulae for decomposition in various environments, including ice.

Listen to yourself. Your prime suspect is dead and you're talking forensic crap.

Now what, smart guy?

René was dead, but maybe I could salvage a clue around here. I scanned the counters: folded towels and a liquid soap dispenser. Hardly incriminating. The tile floor, at first glance, appeared clean. I opened the linen closet and the gutted remains of two dozen 10 lb. ice bags ballooned into the room.

How had the killer gotten all of this ice up here without being noticed?

I went back to the tub. His and Hers robes lay on the wooden bath mat, with hers on *top* of his, suggesting he got in the tub first. I examined them. The man's was clean, but the woman's had a few long hairs on the collar. Long *red* hairs. My shoulders went limp. Now that I was looking for them, I spotted a few around the sink, a few more beneath it. I picked up every one I could find and wrapped them in a Kleenex.

While tampering with evidence, I might as well inspect René's skull. I took off my coat and rolled up my shirtsleeves. Cringing, I reached into the water, and even with the gloves on, my fingers stung from the recent frostbite. I raised the head out of the water, but the neck didn't bend. In fact, the entire body was stiffer than a frozen steak. I rotated the torso enough to see the wound. Something—a hammer claw, a cleaver, a *hatchet?*—had smashed in this area of the skull, leaving a cluster of deep, narrow lacerations. It had been a while since I'd seen these kinds of wounds. My stomach shuddered as I lowered René back into the water. My arms were numb.

The other night...the woman in the parka I'd seen leaving this building...could it have been Shay? Her behavior fit the profile of someone who had murdered or was planning to. She had acted out violently, denied she knew René and removed connections to him by stealing her painting from his gallery. Then again, I hadn't seen the person's face. For all I knew, it was a slender man. Maybe Slim.

But these red hairs. I scrutinized them under the bright lights of the vanity. Like Shay's, some were flame-orange, some coppery like Mars in the night sky. There was something odd about them, though: none of them had roots.

I went into the bedroom. The bed covers were disheveled. On one pillow I found two more red hairs (also without roots) and dozens of black ones with their roots attached. The scene suggested that a sexual tsunami had passed through, yet I couldn't find a single pubic hair.

On the floor, peeking out from under the bed skirt, was a frayed piece of rope. I pulled and out came a 100-foot coil. Standing up, I noticed rub marks on the windowsill. I opened the window and looked down. Parking spaces abutted the building wall. This seemed to explain how the ice got up here, but it also suggested the involvement of a second person.

This case just got better and better. I shut the window.

My gut told me this was a setup. But considering how smitten I was with Shay, how reliable was my gut? What if she *did* kill him and my removing evidence helped her get away with it? And if she was the killer, what was her connection to Serif and the Voice?

On the other hand, what if she was innocent? At first glance, the hairs looked like clippings. What if the only thing between her and a life sentence was what I chose to do right now?

I gazed out at the darkening East River. A garbage barge plowed downstream beneath the Williamsburg Bridge. It was spitting snow. I was already into this thing up to my eyebrows, so why not go all the way?

My scalp tingled with perspiration.

Of course if you're wrong, you could end up in Greenhaven.

I decided to double-down. I scoured the apartment, collecting every red hair I could find.

25

YOUR BASIC NIGHTMARE

It was six o'clock and dark. Normal people were home, sitting down to hot meals and TV shows after a tough day at the office. But not me. I was encamped in my car with an empty bag of cashews, preparing to confront an unstable and possibly murderous woman.

That's PI work for you. Glamorous.

My cell phone rang. For a moment, something—guilt, probably—made me think that it was the police, that I'd been seen leaving René's, and that his body had been discovered. I looked at the display. A 212 area code, but the number was unfamiliar. I took a deep breath and picked up.

"Hey," a woman said, "whatcha doin'?"

It took me a second to place the voice.

"Working, Miss Connolly." I peered in the direction of her building. *Was she watching me?*

"Could you come over? I might need your help." There were loud voices in the background.

"Might?" I said.

"I'll explain when you get here," she said. "How long?"

"You'll answer my questions?"

"Yeah, whatever. Just come."

"Ten minutes."

"Good, I'll meet you outside."

I snapped the phone shut. What was so important that she was willing to stand in the cold until I got there? Well, whatever she was about to spring on me, I wanted to be awake for it. I walked to the corner deli and bought a large black coffee.

When I reached Shay's decrepit building, three men were loitering in front beneath the streetlamp. Two of them held hammers at their sides. They didn't have tool belts, so I figured these were the clowns trying to drive her out. Shay stood in the doorway yelling at them. I unzipped my parka.

"What seems to be the problem, Miss Connolly?"

I got between her and them. They were in their mid-20s and had rugged builds, all of them. The one not holding a hammer, a Latino, shifted his feet into a boxing stance. I would watch him the closest. Behind him, a black man and a white man glowered at me. Their heads were shaved smooth.

"I'll tell you what the problem is, *detective*," Shay said. "I get home and these *assholes* are snooping around in my apartment." She jabbed a finger. "You better not've taken anything."

I took in my surroundings. A dimly lit 10' by 10' patch of icy ground surrounded by snowbanks. No escape routes, except into the building. A couple of broken bricks and a rusted-out barrel with lengths of pipe and scrap wood in it. Desolate street. In short, your basic nightmare if it's three against one.

"Mr. Talese wants you outta here, *puta*," the Latino said.

The white guy jerked his head at me. "You a real cop?"

"Why, would you like me to be?"

"Fuck you."

He brandished his hammer, expecting me to flinch. I didn't.

"Guys, just leave and we'll forget it."

"Like hell we will," Shay said.

"Quiet, Miss Connolly."

"And if we don't?" the black man said.

"Then I report you to the carpenters' union," I said. "I have a sneaking suspicion you guys aren't in the local."

"Hey, Jack," the Latino said, "you oughta try counting. There's three of us."

With my thumb, I loosened the cover on my coffee. The steam rose in the frigid air. I focused on my breathing. I was trying to control the adrenaline and keep my muscles from tightening up. Then the white guy broke the silence by addressing Shay.

"Sweetie, somethin' I been wondering about you..." He stared at her pelvis. "Does the carpet match the drapes?"

"Let's have a look," the Latino said.

He stepped toward her.

26

A Shapely Vixen Whose Hair Smells Like Mint

Before the Latino took another step, I threw my coffee in his face and kicked him in the balls. Shay gasped. He doubled over, his face contorting with anger and nausea. Knees bent, he shot out a jab with some horseradish on it. I tried slipping it, but it grazed the side of my head, his knuckles practically digging grooves in my scalp. Luckily his buddies stayed on the sidelines. Waiting until he was upright, I shuffled inside him and drove my elbow through his jaw. I felt the surprisingly soft crunch of bone, and he landed hard on the walkway.

Before I could take a defensive stance, the other two moved in swinging the hammers. I sprang backwards, but not enough. The claw of one gashed my parka across the chest. Half-running, half-skating to the rusty barrel, I grabbed a length of two-by-four and spun around. As they charged me I rammed the wood end-first into the white guy's bald head, which collided into the black guy's bald head. Dazed, they dropped their hammers and crumpled into the snowbank.

God forgive me, but it was the best 8-ball shot I'd ever made.

Meanwhile, I'd forgotten about the Latino. When I turned around, he pounded me on the thigh with a hammer, right on the muscle. I buckled to one knee. The wood clonked on the stoop. The pain was so intense that I wanted to scream, but couldn't.

Enough of this shit. I yanked my coat open, revealing the .45 revolver. The Latino smiled at me with a scalded face. He dropped the hammer. I got slowly to my feet, struggling to hide the pain. My eyes were tearing as I caught my breath.

"Look, I'm only saying this once. You go back to this Mr. Talese…you tell him Miss Connolly will be staying…till her lease is up. Got me?"

The Latino man mumbled an affirmative, but the other two were too stunned to answer. I limped past them, up the steps. "Now get lost."

Inside I stopped at the foot of the stairs and hung onto the banister.

"Damn that smarts." I wiped my eyes.

Shay sat on the stairs watching me. "You burned that guy with your coffee."

"You use whatever's available, Miss Connolly. Please, give me a moment."

"I feel bad. What can I do?"

"Go away."

"I'll be upstairs." She leaned over the railing. "Come up and we'll ice that leg."

I waited until the tears stopped, then climbed, one step at a time, up the stairs. When at last I staggered to her door, Shay was leaning against the jamb filing her nails. She had changed into red leather pants that made her derrière as crisp as a candied apple.

"I thought you'd abandoned me," she said.

I hobbled past her into the kitchen and leaned against the counter. She took a box of spinach out of the freezer.

"Drop the pants."

I sighed. "Just give me the box."

"Nope, pants first." She wrapped the box in a dishtowel.

I didn't have the energy to wrestle frozen foods away from her.

"Fine," I said.

With her help, I got my boots off and slipped out of the pants. Shay kneeled down, kissed the bruise and guided my hand to the makeshift ice pack. The bruise throbbed even worse when the cold hit it.

"Better?" She stood up.

"Yeah, you're Florence Nightingale."

She peered down at my shorts. "Funny, I pegged you for the other kind."

"I defy augury."

"And I defy sobriety." She yanked a bottle of Old Grand-Dad out of the cupboard and flipped it in her hand. "Drink?"

"No." I nodded at the side of the cupboard, where the hatchet was still embedded in the wood. "You could have killed me the other day."

"Believe me, if I'd wanted to hit you, you'd be dead."

She shook the Kentucky bourbon and stamped a foot. Her breasts quivered.

"Please? There's nothing sadder than a woman drinking alone."

Pant-less and pressing a frozen vegetable to my leg, I now understood Svetlana's rebuke about redheads being my Kryptonite. It didn't help matters when Shay swung out her hip and bounced the bottle against her pert backside.

"Don't worry, private eye. I won't corrupt you... *much*."

She rolled the bottle over her luscious contours. Clearly this torture was going to continue until I joined her.

"All right," I said. "One."

She loaded two glasses with ice, poured the liquor and handed me one.

"Cheers," I said.

"Wait, you have to toast something."

"What, world peace?"

"Screw world peace." She raised her glass. "To all the struggling artists and private dicks in the world. May they find happiness."

We drank. I lifted the ice pack off my leg. Despite the first aid, a lovely contusion was forming. Shay poured two more.

"Look, I'm working," I said.

She waved at the violet canvas across the room. "What do you think *that* is, paint-by-number? Now you make the toast."

Shay had crept up close enough for me to feel the heat from her downy arms. She tossed her hair and a whisper of mint wafted up my nose. I dug my fingernails into the cabinet wood. Regrettably I couldn't just plant her on the counter and break some dishes with her.

"To Formica." I patted the counter.

"A smooth, durable and *versatile* surface," she purred.

We tossed them back at the same time, and I was frozen as she refilled our glasses. Caught in her reality-distortion field, I was incapable of saying no. She stirred her drink with a finger and licked it off.

"So, this thing you're working on. Got any—you know—whatchamacallits?"

"Suspects?"

"Yeah, them."

"A couple."

The warmth of the whiskey seeped into my head. Shay now stood a hair's breadth away, so that when she breathed, two things became clear: that she wasn't wearing a bra, and that she was cold. I put my pants back on. In the presence of a shapely vixen whose hair smells like mint, a guy can stand idly by in his shorts for only so long. She downed another drink.

"Thanks for helping me with those guys," she said.

"Yeah, that was fun," I said. "Time to answer my questions now."

She dragged her fingertips down my sweater. "Soft."

"Cashmere," I said. "Stop changing the subject."

"Fine, ask your stupid questions." She poured herself another whiskey.

"Night before last, where were you?" I asked.

"A club."

"Which one?"

"Purgatory," she said. "Need directions?"

"Anybody see you?"

"The bartender."

"What about Nadir Serif?"

"No, he wasn't there." She grinned, jiggled the ice in her glass.

"Cute," I said. "How about a painting called *Autumn in the Fields*?"

"No clue."

Nothing in her eyes said she was lying. In fact, she looked genuinely confused.

"How do you know Jean René?"

"We've been through this." She looked away. "I don't."

It was bull. She knew it, I knew it, and she knew I knew it. But I didn't want to force the issue. Try to get too much too soon and they'll clam up on you. I took a long pull from my glass and savored the burn in my throat.

"You were pretty upset the other day when I told you Jamal Carter was killed."

"We went to school together, okay?" she said. "Parsons, then a special program at the Sorbonne. I was shocked, that's all. I felt guilty because we hadn't talked in a couple of years."

"Who's David Birchfield?"

"I don't—"

"Reason I ask"—I drained my glass and refilled it—"Birchfield's the second artist from René's files to turn up dead."

She pitched her ice into the sink and refilled her glass.

"Care to comment?" I said.

She ignored me. I had no doubt she was connected to René—heck, she might have *killed* him—and while I might not find the missing link tonight, I would find it eventually. Before I continued, though, there was something I needed to do.

"May I use your bathroom?"

She pointed with the half-empty bottle. "Help yourself."

I did and wished I hadn't. Shay was no Martha Stewart. To get her bathroom, start with a prison john, then subtract. I found a brush with a wad of her hair in it, wrapped the hair in a tissue and stuffed it in my pocket. On the way out, I used the old toilet-flush trick.

I returned to our makeshift bar and poured myself a fresh glass. She glanced at me with beseeching eyes.

"What?" I said.

"It's all your fault," she pouted. "Talking about painters being killed. Is it a serial thing?"

I shrugged. "Sorry, kiddo, but whatever you're into, it's serious."

She held her glass up to the light and stared through the whiskey.

"I think somebody's been following me."

"Who?"

"I don't know *who*. And it's not all the time. Just lately, like when I go out, I get the feeling somebody's watching me."

"Somebody on foot, or in a car?"

"I'm not sure."

"Okay," I said.

"You don't believe me."

I shrugged. "You haven't given me any details."

Shay poured herself another drink. I didn't know about her, but I had a buzz on that a beehive could envy.

"Hey, I've got an idea," she said cheerily. "What if *I* hired you? Like, to keep an eye on me."

"I already have a client. Lost him, in fact."

"Well, I'm right here." She bit her lip.

"You certainly are."

"Can't pay you though."

"Always encouraging," I said.

"Money anyway…"

It was a mistake and I knew it. But between the drink and the palpable temptation she presented, my willpower was waning. I rationalized my decision with some crap about keeping your friends close and your enemies closer.

"All right," I said, "but if I find out you're into anything illegal, it's over."

"Okay, now we're talking." She went to her finished paintings against the wall and snapped her fingers. "Your retainer, babe. Choose one."

I walked over and flipped through the canvases, careful not to act too casual about it, as though I didn't respect the work involved. Most of them were crazy abstracts, but then I fell upon *the* one: another of her nude self-portraits. In the painting Shay was stretched out on a dock with a quiet, wooded lake in the background. It would go well with the movie theater one I had recently salvaged.

"Nice choice," she said.

"Yeah, I really admire your brushwork in this one."

"Brushwork my ass." She nudged me. "You *admire* my tits."

"Just how accurate is it?"

"Wouldn't you love to know." She squeezed my earlobe. "Not that I'm bragging. Fact is, we're all just a lightning bolt away from hideousness."

I stood back from the canvas, swept my gaze across the painted image of her and kept on going, down her very real body.

"Well, it looks like you've done a good job of avoiding thunderstorms."

"You want it, it's yours. Keep in mind, if you were buying it from *her*"—she jutted her chin toward Uptown—"it'd run you six grand at least."

"And worth every penny. I'm sure I'll get hours of viewing pleasure from it."

"You bad boy." She patted my butt. "Just hang on to it. When I kick off someday, it could be worth ten times what it is now."

I checked my watch. I'd been here almost two hours. "I have to go." I rapped my glass down and wobbled away from her.

"Wait." She grabbed my bicep. "I—*oooh…not bad…* not bad at all."

"Is there a question in this, or do you plan on squeezing my arm all night?"

She let go smiling and paced around the room twirling her hair around a finger.

"I've got an opening at Contessina's night after tomorrow," she said over her shoulder. "Maybe you could

come along, keep the wolves at bay? They won't try anything with you around."

"What if *I* turn out to be a wolf?" I swayed when I
said it.

She walked straight up to me so her lips were inches
from mine, and whispered, "Let's burn that bridge when
we come to it."

I slapped my hand around the back of her neck and
hauled her in for a kiss that made my own knees weak. As
we eased apart, I raked my fingers through her glorious
hair. She handed me my painting.

"Now get a move on, private dick."

At her easel, Shay switched on the stereo. The room
swelled with sax, and as she picked up a brush and twirled
it through her fingers, I ceased to exist.

On my way out, I grabbed the hatchet and wrapped
it in my coat.

27

HEMASTIX & LUMINOL

I sprang awake to banging in my left ear and whacked my head against something hard. I swore, opened my eyes.

I was in the Cadillac. It was dark and the windows were iced over. There was a knot in my back and a welt on my leg the size of a trailer hitch. My entire body felt seasick.

I stumbled out of the car. The second my feet hit the pavement a newspaper delivery truck banged over a pothole, narrowly missing me. It was a wide street with stoplights fading into the distance. Pretty sure I was still in Manhattan. Looked like an avenue, but there were no signs or landmarks to tell me. I got back in the car.

The keys weren't in the ignition. I fumbled for the light switch, got it on and saw them on the passenger seat. I started the engine and turned on the GPS. After a moment the display showed me on First Avenue, between 6th and 7th Streets.

I must have left Shay's, gone a few blocks and decided I was too drunk to drive.

You might have hit another car. Or a person.

I grabbed a flashlight from the glove compartment, jumped out and inspected the car. Not a scratch. Even parked in a legal spot. Still, my heart pounded. To not remember what you did or said, and to have lost control—it made me angry.

I let the engine warm up and took my time scraping the windows. Once I knew I was sober, I headed over to FDR Drive. I couldn't stay in the city today. If I did, I'd see Svetlana and she'd find out what I'd done and be disgusted with me. Svetlana was the most disciplined person I'd ever known, and the idea of losing her respect was more than I could deal with.

As the sun rose on another day of this wretched investigation, I went north.

This time when I got there, the driveway was plowed. I parked in the garage and inspected the house perimeter for footprints. Deer had been poking at the fences, trying to eat the shrubs, but unless they were really *big* deer, they didn't worry me.

I took three aspirin and brewed some coffee. All I had for food in the place were patty sausages and tater-tots. Briefly I wished I were that other detective, Spenser, who could make a gourmet meal out of vitamin C tablets and an onion. I choked down the food, limped downstairs with my coffee and drew myself a bath. Placing my gun and cell phone on the bathmat at arm's reach, I lowered myself in. The hot water awoke every cramp and ache and injury, and at first I barely breathed.

Gradually, my muscles relaxed and I decided to do some detecting. I reached for my phone.

First I tried Svetlana and was grateful when she didn't answer. I left a message that I'd found Jean René dead and was staying in Millbrook before going up to the Catskills. I didn't mention the hairs or what had happened with Shay.

Next I spoke to James the doorman. There had been a development. Two men had come by and handed James a cell phone with Serif on the other end. Serif said the men had a key and permission to enter his apartment and were not to be molested. They left with four big suitcases.

"What'd they look like?" I asked.

"Suits," James said. "Looked like a couple of Secret Service dudes."

Maybe these were the additional resources the Voice had alluded to.

"Any idea where they went?"

"Sure, I ran after the cab," he said. "*C'mon, man.* Went down Park, I can tell you that."

"What'd they take?"

"Housekeeper said some clothes and a bunch of small paintings."

"Was he under duress?" I added hot water to the tub.

"Scared?" James said. "Maybe a little, now you mention it. But what was I supposed to do?"

"Nothing."

I thanked him and hung up. Well, at least Serif was still alive. The obvious explanation was that he was holed up somewhere and had sent two men to pick up personals for him. *But then why grab the paintings?* Sounded like a guy taking a long trip. Inspired, I called one of my contacts at FBI Headquarters.

Josephine Best was a supervisor in Research and Records who had lost her son to leukemia. Occasionally Jo helped me, and I think it was because I reminded her of him. After three rings, she picked up.

"Mr. Stevens." She said it like a schoolmarm who'd caught me doing something naughty.

"Hello, Jo. How's the Bureau treating you?"

"Oh, good days and bad. I've thought about retiring, but I don't know what I'd do with myself."

"You're too young to retire anyway," I said.

"You're a sweet liar, Dakota. What can I do for you?"

"I need flight manifests and credit card activity going back two weeks, for one Nadir Serif and his possible alias, Malcolm Azzopardi." I spelled out the names.

"You'll hear from me this afternoon, dear."

"Thank you, Jo."

After my bath, I wrapped my swollen leg in an Ace bandage and lay down for an hour. Feeling less hungover, I drove into Millbrook. It was quiet at the framing shop, so they were able to mount and frame both of Shay's self-portraits while I ran other errands. I had snow tires put on the car, ate lunch at the diner and claimed some packages at the post office—one from L.L. Bean and another from a military surplus outlet. Back at the house, there was a message on the answering machine.

"Sorry, dear," Jo said. "Serif, Azzopardi—no activity under either name. Be careful, Dakota Stevens."

The click echoed in the empty house.

Another lead to nowhere. More and more, it was looking like Serif had been abducted. But where to and why, I had no idea.

In the office I leaned Shay's cinema self-portrait, wrapped in brown paper, against my desk and hung up the one of her stretched out nude on a dock. Crisp and meticulous. The style, I believe, was called photorealism, but what did I know? The woman was as talented as she was gorgeous. Hopefully she wasn't also a killer.

In the living room I got the fireplace roaring and spent the rest of the afternoon on the couch, nursing my leg. I stared at the flames and dreamed about Shay, the case, and what I should do next, getting up to put new logs on the fire or make more hot chocolate. All day I'd avoided thinking about the hairs and the hatchet because I was afraid of what I might discover. But when the last log burned down, I couldn't put it off any longer.

After my grandmother's death, I converted her dark-room into a small laboratory: a couple of microscopes, basic chemistry apparatus, black light and some second-hand testing kits for blood and fingerprints. There was none of the expensive equipment I'd used during my brief time with the FBI lab, like a mass spectrometer, gas chromatograph, or electron scanning microscope. The purpose of this little lab was to confirm or deny hunches, not to perform official tests that could be sworn to in court. Besides, the physical evidence I collected during cases didn't exactly have a *rigorous* chain of custody.

To do a proper hair comparison, having 25 known and 25 suspect hairs is the ideal. I only had 10 of each, but they were better than nothing. I started with the ones from Jean René's loft. Checking each one under a low-power stereomicroscope, I made an interesting find: in addition to having no roots, all of the hairs from René's had been cut square with scissors at both ends. But the ones from Shay's had tapered tips with most of their roots intact. They were also considerably longer: about 50cm on average. It was a sizable discrepancy, but not enough to clear Shay.

Fortunately I knew someone who could help. I wrote a short note to my former supervisor at the FBI Crime Lab, Dr. Lily Wang, asking her to test the enclosed samples. I put the note in a FedEx envelope along with the bags of hairs and the paint chips from René's.

Finished with the hairs, I could avoid the hatchet no longer. I moistened a cotton swab with distilled water, swiped the edge of the hatchet and applied a Hemastix strip to the swab. If there was blood, it would turn green.

It stayed yellow.

The last test I had for blood was Luminol reagent. Luminol was the forensic serology equivalent of a jackhammer; while extremely sensitive, it tended to destroy any blood found, rendering the sample useless for further testing. Still, I had to know.

I mixed up a vial of reagent powder with water and put it in a spray bottle. Once sprayed with the solution, any bloodstains would glow blue in the dark. My throat was dry. For a long time I poised the bottle over the hatchet.

"Here's looking at you, Shay…"

I misted both sides of the blade and shut out the lights. What I saw came as both a disappointment and a relief.

28

RECONNAISSANCE

The next morning I drove up to the Catskills to find the home of Terrence Young, owner of the SUV that had abducted me. With last night's Luminol test coming back negative, I needed to make something happen. After breakfast in a café on the outskirts of town, I headed into the hills to find Young's place.

Svetlana had warned me it was remote, but it wasn't until I stopped seeing dwellings—not even a tarpaper shack—that I realized she wasn't exaggerating. Mile after mile of narrow roads snaked through the woods without a single landmark. My eyes flicked between Svetlana's directions, the odometer and the GPS. Heaping snowbanks closed in from both sides. At least it was well plowed. My car might have had all-wheel-drive, but it was no 4x4.

I'd been driving for an hour when the road suddenly stopped. Another road veered right, uphill into evergreens. A worn sign declared, *"Entering Old Growth Forest Area — No Recreational Vehicles — Authorized Personnel and Residents Only — NYSDEC."* I recalled the heady green smell from the night I was abducted. According to Svetlana's map and the GPS, this was the road. It was steep. I dropped the car into low and took the turn.

Snow-laden branches hung down, and I zigzagged beneath them. The lane was icy at the curves. It became steeper. No guardrail to keep me from plummeting to the bottom. The car slid. A hot pulse went through my limbs. Clutching the steering wheel, foot firmly on the gas, I climbed a switchback. Then another. The car started to slide again, but the studs dug in. The new snow tires had paid for themselves already. As the road leveled off, I noticed a placard jutting out from a tree ahead:

Wittenberg View
A Private Retirement Community

I glanced at the map again. *An old folks' home? Up here? Where was Young's house?*

Nailed to the trees at hundred-foot intervals were orange POSTED signs: "NO FISHING, HUNTING, OR TRESPASSING FOR ANY PURPOSE. VIOLATORS WILL BE PROSECUTED." I drove another half-mile before the road came to a dead end.

The only sign of habitation for miles had been the retirement home. The SUV had to be registered there. Maybe Terrence Young was one of the residents. It made no sense, but I was up here to get answers. And unlike my last foray in these parts, this time I'd come prepared.

Outside I changed into winter gear: long wool underwear, ski pants, gaiters and a pair of snowshoes with poles. No more wet legs for me. Over it all I slipped a Russian military snow camo suit. I strapped on a pair of ski goggles and put up the jacket hood. In the trunk I unlatched the case containing my long-range firepower:

a Remington 700 SPS with a 24-inch stainless barrel chambered in .308 Winchester. The rifle had a retractable bipod and a Leupold VX-III 6.5-20x50mm scope. Bottom line? If necessary, I could reach out and touch someone from 500 yards away.

I threw a white cover over the car to camouflage it and pushed snow around the tires. Next, I got out the topographical map and my compass. I oriented north on the map with north on the compass, accounting for the difference between true north and magnetic north. The GPS on my phone would have been simpler, but if the batteries ran out, or I lost the signal, the thing was useless. No, better to go old-school with a map and compass. With my snowshoes secure, I slung the gun strap over my shoulder, gripped the poles and faded into the trees.

The scene reminded me of how my great-uncle Henry, a member of the 101st Airborne, had described the Ardennes forest during the Battle of the Bulge: the endless fir trees, their boughs freighted with snow, trailing off in all directions and forming a gray haze at the fringes of sight; the green fragrance made sharp by the bitter cold; and the eerie silence, broken only by distant machine gun fire or the wind whistling in the treetops. With the lower branches trimmed, there was nothing to conceal me except a thin fog hovering a few feet off the ground. I moved cautiously forward.

The woods sloped downhill. Soon the road was out of sight, and I stopped to take a reading. Without any distinct landmarks to navigate by, I had to estimate my position. From the gate, I had driven northeast. This meant if I now headed southwest, I would be moving roughly parallel to the road. But since I wanted to move farther in from the road, I set a course of south-south-west. My watch read one o'clock. About 3½ hours of daylight left. I picked up the pace.

Soon I reached a barbed-wire fence, too high to climb over, too solid to knock down. I drank some water and got out my Leatherman. As I cut the wires, the wind shifted and I caught a whiff of wood smoke mixed with an acrid odor, like something you'd smell around a chemical factory. I ignored it and passed through the fence.

I emerged from another stand of firs onto the edge of a snow-covered pond. While this one looked frozen solid, some were fed by warm underground springs, making the ice unstable. I circled around to be safe.

On the other side, the woods pitched sharply uphill and I had to herringbone step to keep going. The bruise on my leg throbbed. Far off, a snowblower rattled the stillness. I stopped to catch my breath. According to the map, I was nearing a sharp drop. As the ground leveled off, I parted some branches—and quickly grabbed them.

I was at the edge of a cliff, looking out on a mountain a few miles away. *Wittenberg Mountain.* An impressive sight, but the sight across the gorge on *this* mountain was far more interesting.

29

THE UNBURNED BRIEFCASE

I took out the binoculars. Spread out along the hillside was an elaborate retirement community, its buildings so well integrated into the landscape that they were almost indistinguishable from the surrounding woods. I shook my head in awe. It must cost a fortune to live here.

Scanning the property, I first noticed a residential area. Twenty or so bungalows surrounded a large building with windows that looked out on Wittenberg Mountain. That explained the name of the place. Old men inside watched TV and played cards. Some were eating. The building reminded me of a multi-purpose hall at summer camp.

Near the gorge edge and obscured by trees was an enclosed fire tower. Inside, a shape read a newspaper. The tower's location was such that I couldn't tell if it belonged to Wittenberg View, making sure the residents didn't fall off the cliff, or the DEC, keeping an eye on its Old Growth forest.

The multi-purpose building was connected to a main house by a gently sloping, enclosed breezeway. Through the windows I watched a Hispanic woman push a man in a wheelchair toward the main house. A gigantic Swiss chalet, it had a wide glass front that looked out on the valley. Smoke curled out of its four chimneys. A roomy deck stretched along the edge of the cliff. On the side of the house, stairs descended from the woods and disappeared underground. I remembered the stairs Gunter and the boys had taken me down. At the other end of the chalet was an extension with steamed-up windows. *Could this be the pool where I was interrogated?* I continued my sweep, spotting a rectangular building encircled by a tall chain-link fence. The building was a couple hundred yards away from the chalet and obscured by trees. To see anything, I'd have to get closer. But first I wanted a peek inside the glass front of the chalet.

I snowshoed along the ridge until I found a good vantage point behind a fallen tree. Squatting behind it, I trained the binoculars on the massive windows. Inside was a great room with vaulted ceilings and a stone fireplace. Five or six figures stood in the shadows, facing somebody in a recliner. Peeking over the top of the chair was a head of thick white hair. Three big Huskies were curled at the man's feet. Then one of the figures stepped into the light. My pulse raced.

It was Gunter.

He looked at the white-haired man and nodded. A hand jabbed out from the chair. *Was this the Voice?* I watched their conversation for a few minutes, hoping to get a look at the old man's face, but even once the others left, he never got up from his chair.

Moving on, I trekked along the backside of the ridge until I had a clear view of the fenced-in building. I zoomed in. About 50' by 150', it looked like a large barracks, except its walls were higher and it didn't have any windows. The roof was clean, and a long snow rake leaned against the eaves. An oversized generator sat beneath a lean-to, and an industrial heating/AC unit hummed against the building.

As for the fence gate, it was secured with a brass padlock. The door into the building was steel and had *two* locks: a combination lock and one of those mechanical pushbutton doorknobs. No easy pickings here. Somebody had gone to a lot of trouble to protect the contents of that building. Or was it to keep whatever was inside from getting *out*? Serif perhaps?

I swept the binoculars over the entire area again. There was something unusual outside the fence. I focused the binoculars. A charred flap of canvas hung out of a burn barrel. It was a big-headed peasant. *Autumn in the Fields!* Somebody had smashed up and burned the painting, but they hadn't gotten rid of the evidence. Then the wind picked up and the canvas moved, revealing an unburned briefcase—identical to the one Serif had been carrying that first night.

I was bursting with discovery and wished Svetlana were here to share it with. I wanted to get that flap as proof, but I couldn't risk them finding my tracks. It would have to wait for a better time.

There was one last thing I wanted to check out. When they abducted me, they had parked the SUV in a nearby dell. Following the ridge, I came to the edge of the woods overlooking a parking area. A spry old man evened out the snowbank walls with a snowblower. Backed into their spots and uniformly spaced were a dozen black SUVs, and parked next to some stairs was the Lincoln Navigator, license plate 7J3SB1. This was the place.

I watched the old-timer for a moment. *What kind of retirement home made its residents do grounds work?* This expedition had raised several other questions, such as... the Voice who had warned me off the case, was he a resident or the owner? Who was Terrence Young? What did a retirement home have to do with a stolen, fraudulent painting? And since I'd located the painting up here, what was this place's connection to DeAngelis and Serif?

Sufficiently confused, I headed back for the car.

James reported that he'd spoken to Serif, so there was a chance Serif was still alive. Was he being held here against his will? My instincts said yes, and that he was locked inside the fenced-in, windowless building. The one with a separate generator and climate control system.

What I knew could fit in a thimble. The important thing was, I'd done my reconnaissance without being discovered and—

The woods shook with the sound of big, barking dogs.

The Huskies. They were out for a run. And by the sound of it, without leashes.

And they were getting closer.

30

FORCING A ZUGZWANG

Swaying on the balls of my feet, twirling my racquet in front of me, I waited for the next ball to shoot out of the machine.

"It's a good thing dogs like me," I said. "I was throwing sticks all the way back to the car. Just desperate for somebody to play with, I guess."

"Honor among wolves," Svetlana said.

I was working out at the prestigious Sutton East Tennis Club beneath the 59th Street Bridge. Outside a wind chill of 10 below gripped the city, but inside, under the bubble, it was like a spring day.

"Strangest retirement home I've ever seen." I hit a ball back. "I stayed over last night and dug into the land rolls this morning."

Svetlana strolled around the backcourt, plunking up balls with a ball hopper. Every time she stooped, the white pleated tennis skirt rode up her backside, making it tough for the retired bankers next door to concentrate. I tore my eyes away just in time to drill a forehand. She sat down on the courtside bench, crossed her legs and adjusted her pink headband. One of the bankers was still leering at her when his opponent's serve bounced up and got him in the gonads. He doubled over. I shook my racquet scoldingly at Svetlana.

"It ought to be illegal for you to wear skirts like that."

She shrugged. "The skirts are the only thing I like about this game."

I stroked a backhand down the line. Across the way, Svetlana's bodyguards sat in the spectator's window. They looked like a trio of gargoyles.

"Anyway, checked the property ledgers. Wasn't easy, *but*"—I swatted a ball back deep—"I found the parcel. Turns out, Terrence Young owns the place."

"That's it?" Svetlana said.

"No…" I kneeled and quickly tied my sneaker. "According to the deed on file, upon the deaths of all the residents, the property—all three hundred acres—reverts to the state. The Catskill Forest Preserve, to be specific."

"Bizarre." She sipped some water.

"Yeah, I asked the town clerk about it, and she says there are tax benefits." I chipped back a drop shot. "What I want to know is, what does an old folks' home in the Catskills have to do with a shady art dealer in Manhattan?"

"I will look into this Wittenberg View."

"And Terrence Young," I said.

"Yes."

I lobbed a ball from deep in the backcourt.

"It's that fenced-in building that interests me. They're holding Serif in there, I know it. Any ideas on how we get in?"

Svetlana picked up her racket and bounced a ball on it.

"I did some research on the lock you described. It sounds like a Simplex."

"Yeah? That mean it's simple to get into?"

"It is somewhat easier than most," she said.

"Please elaborate."

She continued to bounce the ball. "Simplex locks have a major weakness. Once you depress a button, you can't use it again in the same sequence. For example, one could set a combination of 1-2-3-4-5, but not 1-2-3-4-4. This drastically reduces the total number of combinations."

"How drastically?" I hit a scorching forehand that ricocheted off the machine and sailed over to the next court.

"If all five buttons are used," she said, "there are a total of one thousand eighty-two combinations."

"Whew, I was afraid you were going to say eleven hundred."

Who bothered with *five* digits? Unless it was the CIA, a five-number combination seemed excessive. Hell, the key codes to most areas of the old FBI lab were only four digits. The fenced-in building was incredibly isolated, so why would they make things complicated for themselves? Besides, they'd chosen a mechanical lock; if they'd wanted state of the art, they would have had an electronic system. There was a good chance it was four digits.

"Four digits," I said. "How many combinations?"

Svetlana stopped bouncing the tennis ball and stared at the ground. Behind those intense eyes I could see that elegant mind at work, a calculating machine that made her one of the most feared endgame players in the world. I was kidding when I challenged her to figure it out, but here she was, actually doing it.

"Three hundred seventy-five," she said.

"How the hell did you do that?" I plunked the ball over the net.

"Discrete mathematics," she said. "Is complicated. You would not understand."

"God, you're sexy when you're mathematical."

"That is nothing. You should see me when I'm forcing a *zugzwang*."

I smiled and moved in toward the net, skidding left, then right in the clay, volleying the balls back deep into the corners. I hopped over, switched off the machine and joined Svetlana on the bench. She handed me a towel and a bottle of water.

"There is one problem," she said. "In order to get the combination down to four digits, we would have to know which four numbers are used."

"Leave that to me." I wiped my face and drank some water.

"How can you—"

"*Is complicated.*" I mimicked her accent. "Involves ultraviolet ink and UV lamp. You would not understand."

She ribbed me. I ribbed her back. Next door, the silver-haired foursome packed up and left. I put my water in the gym bag.

"I'll need your help."

"Of course you will," she said. "When?"

"Next snowstorm."

"Impossible to predict."

"It's our best option," I said. "There's a lookout tower I think belongs to the DEC, but in a snowstorm they won't see much. We'll be exposed the entire time, and who knows the shape Serif'll be in. The ideal would be to go in at night, commando style."

"When nobody is outside…and the snow covers our tracks," she said. "Clever. Too bad you don't apply these skills to your chess."

Down on the far court, two Asian men played a lively game. I thought of the final entry on DeAngelis's note.

"Watch Li," I said. "We're missing something there."

Svetlana looked at the Asian tennis players. "I checked all of the Chinese galleries and artists from René's files. No Li."

We rose from the bench together and started picking up the balls. She plucked them off the ground with the ball hopper while I gathered them in my shirt.

"Tournament's this weekend, right?"

"Yes. And Lazar tells me there is a late entry who could pose a challenge."

"Bobby Fischer?"

She rolled her eyes. "A *sane* late entry. The CIA Deputy Director for Operations."

"You probably ought to let him win."

She looked at me like I'd just shot a dog. We picked up more balls.

"I saw something interesting on the news yesterday," she said.

"Yeah?"

"The report said the police learned about René from an anonymous tip."

"Look, that message I left"—I poured my shirt full of balls into her basket—"there are a few things I should have told you."

She stopped. "Oh?"

I confessed to finding the body and the hairs, calling in the tip, fighting the hoods, drinking with Shay, testing the hatchet. When I finished, her face was stoic.

"I thought you trusted me," she said.

"Of course I trust you. What are you talking about?"

Without a word she put down the basket of balls, walked over to the bench and got her coat and purse. On her way past me, she kicked over the basket. The balls scattered across the court, and when I looked up again, Svetlana was gone.

31

A One-Woman Show

I was at Shay's one-woman show in Contessina's gallery, standing next to one of Shay's less popular self-portraits (she was partially clothed). The place was packed through the doorjambs with artists, critics, museum reps, dealers and collectors, and when we first arrived, I watched Shay greet them. She had said somebody was following her, yet I'd tailed her three times and waited in front of her building for hours, and with the exception of Slim, who had been following *me*, not once had I spotted anybody remotely threatening.

A tray of hors d'oeuvres passed just out of my reach. I nursed my club soda and thought of Svetlana. The next time we saw each other, all would be forgiven. That's how it worked with us. Still, I hated myself for not trusting her. When it came down to it, Svetlana was the only person I *could* trust.

Crunching on an ice cube, I watched Shay across the gallery with an older man. Her head was thrown back and she was laughing hard enough to take paint off the walls. Even if she hadn't killed René, she was hiding something. I'd tolerated her caginess because I thought I'd learn more by staying close and being patient. But my patience was running out and proximity to this little firecracker was dangerous.

What if her interest in me was all an act? For all I knew, she was the killer's girlfriend, and, borrowing from predictable *film noir*, he had pimped her out to lead me off the scent. What if I was too much under her spell to notice? I looked around for her again, but saw nothing but artsy types swilling champagne. Then I rounded a corner and came face-to-face with one of her life-sized self-portraits: Shay at the clock in Grand Central in nothing but her birthday suit. She winked at me from the painting.

"Damn redheads," I muttered.

"Boy, she's somethin', huh?" said a man behind me.

"Yeah, she's something all right."

I finished my club soda and dropped it on a passing tray. Opening the show catalog to the bio page, I was surprised to learn that Shay had grown up in Chappaqua, NY. Her father was a retired Merrill Lynch fund manager and her mother was a potter. At the bottom was a short sidebar. It read, "In its annual watch list, *Art Market News* rates Shay Connolly as one of its undervalued artists to watch, noting strong sales in the New York market."

Watch list.

I took DeAngelis's note out of my wallet, snapped it open and held it up to the lights. The skipping ballpoint pen had made it look like "Watch Li" when in fact the impressions revealed it was "Watch List." This was both exciting and annoying. I hadn't read the list in such strong light before and wished I'd thought to do it sooner.

Contessina edged through the crowd with a group of couture-clad women, all of them glowing from lavish beauty treatments and divorce settlements. I needed to ask her about the "watch list" item.

"Contessina, can I borrow you for a second?" I guided her to an empty corner. "Have you seen Shay?"

"Mingling, last I saw." She waved at somebody behind me.

"Did you hear about Jean René?" I asked.

"I told you—"

"Look, the guy's dead, so if you had any kind of relationship with him, you'd better tell me now. It won't be long before NYPD pays you a visit."

She let out a breath and leaned into me. "We were lovers, many years ago. That is all."

"You're sure," I said.

"Very."

"Because I know he scheduled an appointment with you for the other day, and he never showed."

"There was no such appointment." Contessina grabbed a glass of champagne from a tray. "The last time I saw him was at an opening five years ago."

Either she was lying or somebody had planted that card.

"How does Shay know him?" I asked.

"I'm sure she doesn't."

"What makes you so certain?"

"Because"—she sipped her champagne—"despite our bickering, we are quite close. She tells me everything."

"So, what is your business relationship with Shay? I know you're her dealer, but is she allowed to sell in other people's galleries?"

"Of course not," she said. "I have an exclusive on her work. Why, is she showing somewhere else?"

"No, just asking," I said. "One more question and you can get back to your guests. Does the term 'watch list' mean anything to you? That is, besides Shay's mention in *Art Market News*."

"There are many watch lists. Too many to discuss here. Check the Internet." She pushed a stray comma of hair off my forehead and kissed me on the cheek. "Ciao, Dakota."

She faded into the throng. Once again, Contessina had been no help. Tomorrow I'd pay Devon a visit. Maybe she—

From the back of the gallery came a muffled cry. It was a man's voice. As though on cue, all of the attendees whipped around. Instinctively I reached for my gun, remembered where I was, and withdrew my hand. I moved through the crowd, easing people aside. Halfway through the gallery I heard another holler. It was coming from Contessina's office. Then Shay shouted, "You like that? Here's another!"

The office door was locked. I had to kick it four times before it gave and swung open.

A gray-haired man lay sprawled on the floor with blood coming from his mouth. Shay was slumped on the sofa, one leg tucked under the other, her black dress hiked partway up her thighs. One of the straps was torn. She clutched an empty wine bottle in her opera gloves and panted fiercely.

I went to the man and checked his pulse. He was unconscious, but breathing. Slowly he came to. There were welts on his jaw and forehead. I stood up and pried the bottle from Shay's hand.

"What happened?"

Shay got to her feet and straightened her dress. Her legs trembled. Seeing her, the man raised an arm as though to ward off another attack. When nothing happened, he groaned and lay down again.

"It's not what it looks like," she said. "He came on to me."

A skinny man in a monochromatic suit strode into the room. The moment he took in the scene, his hands jumped to his hips, like they were trained to go there in a crisis.

"Shay, what the *hell* did you do to him?"

"He wouldn't stop, so I…" Her eyes wandered to the wine bottle in my hand.

"Wonderful." The suit walked over and jabbed a finger. "You come on to every guy in town, and when one of them responds, you crack him in the skull. What a slut."

"Okay, Jack Sprat," I said. "Go take a time-out."

"Who are you, her pimp?" He poked me in the chest.

I had no idea who this guy was, but I wasn't in the mood. I snatched his hand and twisted, then applied an arm lock with pressure that forced him to the ground.

"You bastard, you're hurting me!"

"And deriving no pleasure from it." I turned to Shay. "Get your things, we're leaving. As for you"—I tweaked the man's arm—"shut your mouth or I'll report that suit you're wearing."

Shay threw on her coat and grabbed her purse. By now a crowd had gathered at the broken office door.

I took Shay's hand and walked straight at them. They moved aside. Shay's eyes were wet.

"Is there a back door to this place?" I asked.

She gestured to the right. I tugged her down the narrow hallway until we reached a door with an alarmed emergency handle.

"How badly do you want to get out of here?"

She looked behind us. The rubberneckers were following. She nodded. I banged the handle with my hip and we ran down the alley with the alarm shrieking behind us.

32

Never a Mast Around When You Need One

Shay marched into her apartment ahead of me, shucked off the opera gloves and examined herself in the bathroom mirror. She held the torn strap of her little black dress.

"That jerk. He better pray I can get it fixed or—"

"*You* better pray he doesn't have brain damage," I said.

"How could anybody tell? He's already retarded."

I tossed my coat over one of the few clean chairs.

"You were alone with the guy in a locked office. What did you think was going to happen?"

"I told you, it wasn't like that." She brushed past me to the kitchen cabinet and poured herself a shot. "He said he'd heard about my abstracts and wanted to discuss them in private. Contessina thinks they're shit, but I believe in them, and this guy's a major collector talking about buying a bunch of them. So we go into her office, and the guy pounces on me and he won't stop, so I brained him."

"And you did nothing to encourage him," I said.

She downed her shot and rapped the glass down on the counter.

"Look, you don't know the art business, so drop it."

"What's to know, let them cop a feel and they'll buy more of your work?"

"Actually, yes," she said. "A little fooling around with the right collectors and critics doesn't hurt. But that's not what happened tonight. I thought the guy just wanted to talk. You saw him, he's twice my age."

"But if he'd been young and good-looking...?"

She stormed into the bathroom and slammed the door.

Leaning against the counter I peered down the dark hallway that led to the way out. I was becoming emotionally involved with a suspect. I considered having a drink, or five, but that would only make things worse. I'd already done enough I wasn't proud of while under this woman's spell. The smart thing to do was to leave. Walk out and don't look back. Go back to my apartment and, like those guys in *The Odyssey*, lash myself to a mast so I couldn't be entranced by her song. I looked around the apartment. This wretched dive said it all: she was *trouble*. Every cell in my body knew it, so why couldn't I move my feet?

The bathroom door squeaked open. Shay walked out in an emerald silk kimono, her hair still piled high. A few wily strands cascaded down her cheeks and bounced on her shoulders. Her lipstick glistened. I relished the swish of the silk, envied the fabric's closeness to her skin.

In her painting area, Shay cleared a large space between the windows and the bed, shoving cans and crates out of the way with her bare feet. She dragged a heavy roll of canvas from the corner and unfurled it across the floor.

"I'm going to paint. Wanna help?"

"Just so you know," I said, "NYPD could show up any minute and arrest you for aggravated battery, and there's not a thing I can do for you."

Working intently, she placed plastic jars of paint on the edge of the canvas. When she had six containers lined up just right, she skipped over and kissed me.

"What's your favorite color?"

"Depends on my mood," I said. "At the moment, it's black."

She poked me in the ribs. "Favorite...color."

"Fine, purple."

She tugged me over to the canvas and without a word cast off the kimono. My throat cinched up like that mail sack again. I stood frozen and beheld her sparkling eyes and porcelain skin, her trim legs and optimistic breasts. I was admiring the sweep of her heavenly backside when she stooped and picked up one of the plastic jars. She unscrewed the lid and poured its grape contents over her chest.

My tongue swelled, like I was being hanged. Dripping paint, she reposed on the canvas, leaning back on her elbows with her knees together, the purple liquid coating her flat tummy, sliding down her ribs.

"Care to join me?" She rubbed the canvas with curled toes.

"I don't know," I said. "Is that paint non-toxic?"

"Shut up and get down here."

There's never a mast around when you need one. I started shedding clothes.

33

THE QUEDLINBURG HOARD

When I phoned Devon at the Met the next morning, she curtly explained she would be somewhere in the American Wing, giving a tour to friends of the German ambassador. Ever the astute detective, I inferred from her brusqueness that I'd done something to make her angry, and brought white roses as backup.

I started on the first floor and worked my way up. Zipping through an exhibition of Gilbert Stuart portraits, I passed one of my favorite paintings—Thomas Cole's *The Oxbow*—before catching up with Devon and her group in front of *George Washington Crossing the Delaware*. There was ole' George, standing up in the boat with cocked boot and determined jaw, going over to kick some Hessian ass. Devon spoke to a group of urbane men and women, and made sweeping gestures at the painting. When she looked in my direction, I smiled and revealed the roses. She signaled a male associate to take over. We met in the next room.

"Dakota, I'm rather busy just now." She checked her watch. Her hair was pulled back in a severe bun that robbed it of its golden sheen.

"Can you spare fifteen minutes?"

"Fine, you can buy me lunch. The café downstairs." She returned to her guests.

The Petrie Court Café is in an airy marble atrium with a wall of glass facing Cleopatra's Needle in Central Park. The captain ushered me past a Rodin torso to a table near the window, where I waited an hour and three Diet Cokes for Devon to arrive. She sat down across the table. I placed the roses in front of her.

"Sorry I never called. I kept meaning to, but things got weird after our date, and then other things came up."

"I should imagine they did."

"Oh," I said. "You've heard about Ms. Connolly."

"I have."

How did she know this? Was the art world that incestuous?

"Would it make any difference if I told you I have a documented obsession with redheads?"

"Not particularly."

The waiter came. I let Devon order for us. She requested the butternut squash soup and linguini with sun-dried tomatoes and prosciutto. Outside, a lone cross-country skier glided down a path. Leafless trees raked the sky. I turned to Devon.

"That was German you were speaking to the visitors, wasn't it?"

She shrugged. "Part of a European education, I suppose."

"Speak any other languages?"

"A couple." The waiter brought her a glass of wine. She took a sip and placed the glass down with unsettling softness. "You didn't come here to talk about my language skills. What is it you want?"

"I found this at your boss's house." I handed her DeAngelis's list. "At the bottom. I'm wondering what he meant by 'watch list' and if it has anything to do with the painting Serif hired us to find. What do you think?"

"Hmm, watch list." She handed back the paper and buttered a roll. "Could be referring to any number of lists. Galleries and museums have watch lists of works they want to acquire. There are also watch lists of stolen art—when a private collector or museum has a piece stolen, they often register it with a watch list so others can report its attempted resale."

"Can you think of any specific list that DeAngelis might have had in mind for Serif's painting?"

"Afraid I can't." Devon sipped her wine and gazed out at the park. "Unless he thought it belonged to a museum or a private collector. But even then there are so many lists, he'd have no idea where to start."

The soup arrived. I did my best to suavely shovel it in between questions.

"Could the provenance give us any clues?"

Her eyes widened. "Why, do you have it?"

"No, but one of DeAngelis's notations read 'clear title before war,' which suggests it became fuzzy afterwards."

"*If* he was referring to the same work." She added pepper to her soup.

"The lists," I said. "Are there any that deal exclusively with that time period?"

"There are, but even if you approach them judiciously, they won't be of much help."

"Why's that?"

"Well, during the time in Europe you're talking about, a great deal of art disappeared—lost, destroyed, burned or abandoned—and yes, some of it was stolen." She ate a spoonful of soup. "But there is no one culprit. So many people and institutions were looting at that time. Galleries and museums robbing from each other, collectors for the Nazis and the Italian fascists, the Russians and, as much as we don't want to believe it, British and American soldiers. It was just in the late eighties, I believe, that they discovered the Quedlinburg Hoard—down in Texas somewhere, if I recall."

"Quedlinburg Hoard?" I said.

"A collection of priceless German treasures taken by an American G.I. at the end of World War Two. A German investigator eventually caught him."

I recalled the photos of a soldier and the shadow box of medals in Contessina's office.

"Wait a second. You really think it's possible Serif's painting was smuggled out of Europe by an American or British soldier?"

"More than possible," she said. "I would say likely."

The pasta came. I twirled some on my fork.

"Sounds like I need to look deeper into these watch lists. Any ideas on where I should start?"

"You should know what you're getting into," she said. "It's like trying to find a needle in a haystack the size of Manhattan."

"I'm extremely persistent. I don't suppose you could spare some time to help me."

"I don't think that would work."

She checked her watch and ate some pasta. I leaned across the table.

"I'm hoping we can stay in touch. It would be nice to have an art expert I could call on for future cases."

"I may be going back to England. There's a post opening up at the British Museum. In the meantime, I need to be getting back to my guests." She stood up with her purse and the bouquet. "Thank you for the roses."

"My pleasure. Good luck."

I watched her cross the dining area and vanish back into the museum. Her coldness annoyed me. Had she refused to help me because of Shay? I handed the waiter a credit card and slipped on my coat. To hell with it. This wasn't the first time I'd had a woman angry with me, nor was it the first time I'd had to follow a lead without an expert's help. I had two legs, a brain and Svetlana. I didn't need Devon.

34

WATCH LISTS

Back at the office, I got on the computer and typed "watch list" into the Google Search box. It came back with 75 million results. I thought about Devon's haystack comment. There was an Audubon watch list, a nursing home watch list, a terrorism watch list and a World Monuments Fund watch list. There was even one for threatened lighthouses. But nothing about artwork. Next I tried "watch list" and "artwork." This winnowed the results list to an oh-so-manageable five million. I tried other search strings like "stolen art" and "watch list of stolen art" but there were still too many results, and the ones at the top weren't useful. Svetlana was better at the computer stuff. I threw on my coat and went to the florist.

When I got to her apartment, Svetlana was running on the treadmill with headphones on. When her eyes flicked in my direction, I presented two dozen yellow roses with a flourish. She nodded, which in Svetlana parlance meant both "Thank you" and "You are forgiven." I put them in a vase with water and sat down at the kitchen island.

The apartment was a shambles. Empty water bottles and frozen yogurt cups littered the kitchen island.

Roll-up chessboards and plastic pieces covered the dining table. Autographed KrüshMaster 5000s (the advanced chess computer she endorsed) were fanned out on the floor. Books, printouts, pens and notebooks were strewn everywhere. Not that I was surprised; her place always looked like this before a tournament. While Svetlana finished her workout, I straightened up, mostly by collecting the garbage.

She stepped off the machine faintly perspiring. I handed her a bottle of water and a towel, and lounged on the sofa while she stretched on the floor.

"So," I said, "when do you go?"

"Tomorrow."

"And the tournament?"

"Day after."

Clearly, she was eager to leave; her bags were already packed and lined up by the door like the kids in *The Sound of Music.*

"Listen," I said, "are you up for a little detecting? Your research skills would prove invaluable at this juncture."

"A new lead?" Svetlana leaned forward and held her ankle as she stretched.

"It seems DeAngelis was looking into some sort of watch *list*. Not watching a guy named Li."

Svetlana stood up. She patted her forehead and nodded at the cleaner apartment.

"Thank you. I have been very distracted lately."

"No problem, Champ."

"Let me shower, and I meet you downstairs."

"I'll order Chinese. Chicken Moo Shu, right?"

"With extra plum sauce," she said, and walked down the hall.

Two hours later, Svetlana had found a dozen websites dealing with watch lists of stolen art, as well as museum watch lists of art with questionable provenance. She still hadn't found Serif's painting—the one that started this whole mess—but she did locate better resources to aid us in our search. The two that offered the most promise were the National Gallery of Art Library, with its collection of over 200,000 books and documents, and the National Archives, which had thousands of records related to art provenance and claims. Both were in Washington, D.C. I patted Svetlana on the back.

"Good job. Looks like I'll be joining you down there." I slipped on my coat and headed for the door.

"Where are you going?" she asked.

"Just getting some air."

"I will call the hotel and make a reservation for you," she said.

"And get the weather forecast for the Catskills."

Outside, it was snowy, dark and cold. I went to the BMW where Svetlana's bodyguards were and told them about Svetlana's trip. Then, feeling guilty, I bought them pizza. When I returned to the office, there was an unexpected guest.

"Don't touch that," Svetlana said.

"Trust me, he won't mind," Shay said.

I stood still for a second, clenching my teeth.

"That's Dakota's chair," Svetlana said.

I decided to get in there before the bickering turned violent. As I walked in, Svetlana gave me a tight smile that said, *"You sure can pick 'em."* She turned back to her computer. Shay's eyes twinkled and she jumped up and hugged me. I shivered from the warmth of it.

"What are you doing here?"

"Had your business card. Wanted to see what a real private eye's office looks like." She jerked her head at Svetlana. "I thought you worked alone."

"Nope. I couldn't do this without Svetlana."

Across the room, our dusty fax machine whirred to life, spitting out a copy of Terrence Young's driver's license.

"Well, looky here," I said.

"It's about time," Svetlana said. "I asked him for that days ago."

Terrence Young was an old man with a head of thick white hair. It resembled the hair I'd seen through my binoculars at Wittenberg View. The phone rang. Svetlana answered it, listened for a moment and hung up.

"Bad news, Dakota," she said. "That was the concierge at the Mandarin Oriental. Everyone is booked solid. Mayoral convention."

"Damn mayors," I said.

"They don't have any rooms"—she glanced at Shay— "but the suite they're giving me has a sofa bed. You could stay with me."

"You wouldn't mind?"

"No," Svetlana said, "but perhaps Ms. Connolly…"

"It's fine." Shay smirked. "He could probably use the sleep."

I turned to Svetlana. "And the Catskills weather report?"

"Clear and cold, with a seventy percent chance of heavy snow next week."

"What's in the Catskills?" Shay said.

As much as I wanted to trust Shay, I couldn't until she told me about René.

"That is privileged information," Svetlana said.

Shay zipped up her jacket, whipped her hair over the collar. "Fine, have your little secrets." She stormed out, leaving the reception door wide open.

"Pick you up tomorrow at eight?" I said.

"I was planning to take the Acela," Svetlana said.

"But the train doesn't have dual climate control," I said. "Or me."

She considered the point, then snapped her laptop closed. "Very well, nine o'clock."

"Eight thirty. Let me catch her."

"She is trouble, Dakota."

"Yeah, I know."

I jogged down 10th and caught up with Shay just across Third Avenue.

"Go away," she said. "Go back to *her*."

I grabbed her by the jacket and shoved her against a car.

"Let go of me," she said.

"We work together," I said, "that's all."

"I'm going home, I have work to do."

She tried to move, but I held her down by the shoulders.

"Listen, I have a place upstate. When I get back, we can spend some time together." *That, and I'll get you on unfamiliar turf so I can grill you about René.*

She looked down and kicked a chunk of ice.

"Can we go sledding?"

"I have a toboggan, sure."

"Only if we can make out in the snow," she said, "then take a hot bath and dry each other off. And have hot chocolate."

"We can do all of that. And there's a big fireplace. *And* I'll brush your hair in front of it."

"Mmm." She put her arms around me. "Careful, Dakota Stevens. An offer like that could get you laid."

"I'll take my chances. But this time"—I showed her my fingernails, where the purple acrylic was likely to remain until after my death—"no paint."

"Too bad," she said. "You should see me in orange."

35

Z. ZELLARS AND THE INFORMATION MAFIA

While Svetlana unpacked in the bedroom, I stood at the window of her Ambassador Suite gazing out at Jefferson Memorial. Across the Tidal Basin, Tom kept his eyes on the White House. I wondered if he'd seen anything that could help me. Somehow, I doubted it.

I called Lily Wang and left a message that I was staying at the Mandarin Oriental and was eager to hear what clues she'd garnered from the hairs and the paint chips. Then, with a Diet Coke from the bar, I sat down on one of the plush sofas. In the center of the living area they'd set up two chairs and a rolling marble-topped table with a hand-carved chess set. I'd already read the note from the concierge wishing her luck in the tournament.

As the belle of the chess world, Svetlana was unmatched in her ability to draw crowds, and in the case of tomorrow's 20-board simultaneous exhibition, all 300 seats had been sold out for months. And since it was a charity event for the area's schools, every chess-playing dignitary in the capitol district had challenged Svetlana, including the Governor of Maryland, the Mayor of D.C., two ambassadors, one Congressman, a Federal District

Court judge, a Georgetown Law professor, and the CIA Deputy Director for Operations.

Eighteen men and two women against *her*. And they didn't stand a chance.

In the bathroom, the tub ran. Svetlana walked in wearing a hotel robe. She got herself a Pellegrino and sat on the sofa opposite mine with her legs curled beneath her.

"So," I said, nodding at the digs, "this is all gratis from the hotel?"

"Yes."

"They must like you."

"I bring them business. You would like me, too." She tipped her bottle toward me. "What will you do this afternoon?"

"I take it staying here and watching porn isn't an option."

"That is correct," she said. "I am taking bath, then nap, then Lazar and I will do conference call to work on last-minute strategy."

"Too bad he couldn't be here. He's a riot."

Stocky, bald and brooding, Lazar was about as fun to have around as an IRS auditor.

"Afterward, you can take me to dinner," she said. "We can discuss what you learn today. Assuming you learn something. It will help me forget about tomorrow."

"I made an appointment with a librarian at the National Gallery. Afterwards, I'll be ready to distract you."

"I would prefer to be amused," she said, "but with you, I take what I can get."

With Svetlana, it was easy to forget who was the boss and who was the employee. I made sure I had my room key and left.

The National Gallery of Art Library was less than a mile from the hotel, so I decided to walk. There wasn't much snow, but with the wind up and the temperature in the low teens, it was unpleasant. Dusk was settling in as I crossed the Mall—that long stretch of ground between the Capitol and Washington Monument—and the few of us braving the cold were exposed in the naked landscape.

Two couples strolled along Constitution Avenue, and a pair of men stood at a bus stop in front of the Natural History Museum. I didn't think Gunter's gang had followed us, but they'd surprised me before. Unfortunately, I'd had to leave my gun back in the room safe. Security at both the Gallery and the Archives would be tight, and I couldn't afford to get caught entering a Federal building with a firearm. Technically, I wasn't supposed to have a gun in D.C. at all.

Like most libraries, the one at the National Gallery seemed designed to make you feel insignificant. In a vast atrium, massive granite columns supported balconied levels of endless stacks. I wound through a maze of researchers hunched over tables to a reference desk.

A woman in her mid-20s looked up from her computer screen. She was thin and nerdly pale. Her hair, pulled back in a ponytail, was tied with a red ribbon that matched her sweater. I smiled.

"Yes?" she said tiredly.

Clearly, every man tried the smile thing first.

"I have an appointment with Z. Zellars."

"Speaking. You are, let me see…" She typed on the computer. "Stevens, first name Dakota. Is that your real name?"

"Yes. Is your first initial really 'Z'?"

"It is, and I'm not telling you what it stands for," she said. "Now, what can I do for you?"

I showed her my license. "I'm a private investigator from New York, looking for information about a painting."

"May I ask why?"

"It's disappeared. I was hoping to learn about its history, maybe figure out who would be interested in it."

"Name of the painting?" she asked.

"*Autumn in the Fields* by Auguste Chavet."

She started to type. I continued.

"Let me warn you," I continued, "I don't think we're going to find anything. There's also the possibility that the one I'm looking for is a fake, so—"

"I've got it," she said.

"*What?*"

"A record of it anyway. Here." She swiveled the computer monitor. "According to this, the painting you're talking about was recovered and restituted at the Munich Central Collecting Point after the war."

"Restituted? To whom?"

"There's a microfilm," she said. "We'll have to check it. Come on."

She led me to a microfilm reader and pulled out two chairs. "Take a seat. I'll be right back." She scurried into the stacks somewhere.

Since talking with Devon, I'd been pursuing the idea that the painting had been smuggled out of Europe by an Allied soldier. But if the painting had been restituted back to its rightful owner, what did that mean? Was it re-stolen later on? I had my head in my hands when Ms. Zellars returned with two small boxes.

"Chin up, Mr. Stevens. We'll have answers in a jif."

She loaded the first roll, zipped it ahead to an index and ran her finger down the screen.

"Ah," she said.

As the reader whirred, the screen was a blur of text and pictures. Then the scrolling images slowed until she stopped the machine. A large photo of a painting covered the screen.

"Is this it?" she said.

There they were, those beautiful, big-headed peasants.

"Sure is."

She printed out the page, then rewound the first film and loaded the second. "This one has images of the property cards."

"Which are…?"

"Individual records for every item collected."

As she scanned the second film, Ms. Zellars explained how the recovery process had worked after the war. A group of museum officials and art historians assisted the U.S. military in the collection, inventory and restitution of all stolen art. Known as the Monuments, Fine Arts, and Archives (MFA&A) officers, or Monuments Men for short, they oversaw all recovery activities at several central points, including Munich. The Monuments Men identified, numbered and photographed every piece that came into a collecting point. And if the owner was located, they recorded restitution of the item. The reader stopped. Ms. Zellars tugged on my sleeve.

"Here, *Autumn in the Fields*. Recovered and cataloged in 1945. Restituted in 1951 to the O.B.I.P. Paris. I'll print this one for you, too."

"*O.B.I.P.?* What the hell is that?"

"The Office of Private Goods and Interests."

"What would *they* have done with the painting?"

"Returned it to the owners," she said, "if they were still alive. If not, maybe they put it in the Louvre, I don't know."

She gave me the printouts and boxed up the microfilm rolls. I looked around at the scholars, wilted over their tables and clutching their hair. I was in no better shape, even though, strictly speaking, I knew more now than when I came in here. All of this Munich-Monuments Men-restitution stuff had muddied the waters again.

Ms. Zellars held the boxes of microfilm like they were robin's eggs. "What is your next move, detective?" She blinked rapidly, the way a lot of sharp, eager women do.

"Thought I'd try the Archives next," I said. "I'd like to find out how the painting came into the military's possession."

She nodded crisply. "Excellent idea. I'll call ahead for you. Go to the microfilm reading room, ask for Mark. That's my boyfriend. He'll have the relevant materials set aside."

I tucked the printouts in my coat pocket. "What are you guys, anyway? The information Mafia?"

"That's exactly what we are, Mr. Stevens." She squinted at me without a hint of a smile. "And don't you forget it."

36

THE ESCALATOR

In the microfilm reading room at the National Archives, I felt like a head of state. Not only had Mark pulled two microfilm rolls for me, he had pre-loaded them. I put twenty dollars on a card for printing, sat down at the first reader and spooled through as much of the material as I could.

The first roll had the complete report of the Art Looting Investigation Unit (ALIU), a group established by the forerunner of the CIA—the Office of Strategic Services (OSS). The ALIU's mission statement, like that of all government agencies, made no sense, but with some digging I found the core of their work: *"To collect and disseminate such information bearing on the looting, confiscation and transfer by the enemy of art properties in Europe, and on the individuals or organizations involved in such operations or transactions...."*

Nicknamed "Project Orion" because unit members considered themselves "hunters" of art thieves and collaborators, the ALIU traced the theft of artwork and interrogated the major players. There was way too much material to read here. I printed the entire report for later.

By the time I got through the second roll, I'd had enough. My head swam with terms and acronyms like collecting points, Monuments Men, ALIU and OSS. I jammed the still-warm printouts in my coat, dropped the rolls on Mark's desk and got the hell out of there.

I hadn't gone down two steps in front of the Archives when Svetlana called, asking to be taken to dinner. As I put my phone away, I glanced over my shoulder and spotted Slim—Slim the Snowboarder, Slim the Train Track Leaper—slouching against one of the giant columns, smoking a cigarette. I skipped down the stairs to the sidewalk. He followed, his footsteps echoing in the cold, still air.

Pennsylvania Avenue teemed with cabs this time of night, but I stayed on foot. Having worked across the street for a few years, I had a distinct advantage over my tail. I turned down 7th Street, back toward the Mall, and stopped at the corner for one of the oldest tricks in the book: I tied my shoe and looked behind me. Slim was a hundred yards back. Without a weapon I would need stealth and guile to get the upper hand.

Halfway across the Mall I looked overtly over my shoulder, spotted him and feigned panic. I broke into a run down the snowy path, heading for the Smithsonian Metro station.

I went down the escalator steps two at a time to stay ahead of him. When I reached the bottom, he still hadn't appeared at the top. I dropped to all fours and crawled onto the Up escalator.

Lying flat on my stomach, scraping the inside wall, I heard the metallic click of hurried footsteps. My shoulders tightened in anticipation. I'd been burned twice before; it wasn't happening again. The steps grew louder. I slowly rose, and when I predicted he was about to pass me on the Down escalator, I sprang to my feet.

It was him, all right—sunglasses and all. His eyebrows arched in disbelief. Before he could move I cracked him in the jaw with a sharp left hook, putting plenty of shoulder behind it. He rocked on his heels and groped for the rubber railing. Reaching across, I grabbed his coat lapels and hauled him onto the Up escalator with me. I pinned him against the metal steps and dug a knee between his shoulder blades. He flailed his hands.

"I mean no harm, I mean no harm." There was a hint of a British accent. Commuters were beginning to stare. I pressed harder on his back.

"Shut up."

Still on the Up escalator, I frisked him. No weapon, but he did have a billfold loaded with hundred-dollar bills and a passport from Qatar. His name, printed in Arabic with English beneath it, was Mohammed Yahya Hasan Abedi. Maybe Dakota wasn't so bad. I put his things back. When we reached the top, I shoved him onto a bench.

"All right," I said, "you've got one minute to explain yourself. After that, you start losing teeth."

Mr. Abedi rubbed his jaw. Mid-30s, dark complexion, thin mustache. His hands were manicured, his overcoat hand-tailored. I pulled my gloves tight for effect and bunched them into fists.

"I'm waiting."

He took out a cigarette and lighted it. He held out the pack. I shook my head.

"I am looking for Nadir Serif," he said.

"I'm not him."

"This I know." He adjusted his sunglasses. "But...I also know he hired you to find a certain painting..."

I snatched the sunglasses off his face, wrenched them in my hands and threw them in the bushes. Underneath he had raccoon eyes. He blinked in the harsh light of the subway entrance.

"That was unnecessary."

"Enough with the mysterioso act," I said. "Get to the point."

Abedi took a deep drag of the cigarette and exhaled through his nose. He held the cigarette in that pretentious Continental way, pinched between his forefinger and thumb.

"I am Mohammed Yahya Hasan Abedi," he said, "special assistant to Sheik Mohammed Ahmad Qattan al-Thani, who is himself chairman of the National Council for Culture, Arts and Heritage for the Emir of Qatar."

"Nice to meet you, Mr. Abedi. Or may I call you Yahya?"

He held his overcoat closed with one hand and smoked with the other. A wave of people got off the escalator and rushed past us. Abedi didn't cry for help. Perhaps I was making progress.

"A few weeks ago," Abedi said, "it came to the Sheik's attention that a painting Mr. Serif had sold him was being appraised by Sotheby's. Naturally—"

"Wait a second. How did he know about Sotheby's?"

Abedi snorted. Now that he wasn't getting punched in the face, the snootiness was coming out.

"*Really*," he said. "The Sheik is one of the most prominent collectors of Western art in the world. He has contacts in all of the major art centers, including the auction houses. Often he knows a year in advance if a piece will be coming up for sale."

I shook my head. For the umpteenth time during this case, I'd been dealt a zinger. Serif had been peddling art to the Far East *and* the Middle East.

"Okay, he knew about the painting," I said. "Go on."

"When he heard the painting was being appraised by Sotheby's, the Sheik was quite upset." Abedi stomped out the first cigarette and lit a second one. "I understand his anger. The exact same painting has been hanging in his private gallery since Mr. Serif sold it to him five years ago. One of them is clearly counterfeit. Of deeper concern is that over the past fifteen years, the Sheik has purchased perhaps one hundred works from Mr. Serif. Now he must wonder how many of *them* are counterfeit."

The courtyard bustled with commuters as Abedi's story sank in. Serif, knowing the Sheik would hear about the painting, must have panicked and hired me to find it. Abedi leaned back on the bench, smoking. I tapped him in the shin with my boot.

"So, why follow me?"

"I know Mr. Serif hired you. It seemed logical he would meet with you again."

"Who told you about me?"

"One of the Sheik's contacts. It is not important."

I batted the cigarette out of his mouth. Abedi cowered.

"I don't know who," he said. "The Sheik gave me instructions to follow you. That is all."

"And those two punks camped up at Serif's?"

"I hired them."

"And while I was zapping them, you were poking around my place upstate. How'd you know about it?"

"Again, Mr. Stevens, it was part of a file I was given." Abedi lit a third cigarette. "I do not know where the information came from. I went there merely to see if you were hiding Serif."

"I haven't seen him since he hired me," I said. "Look, where are you staying?"

"The Hay-Adams."

"All right, I'll walk you back."

Abedi stood up and smoothed out his overcoat.

"Sorry about the sunglasses," I said.

He shrugged. "I will buy another pair at the hotel."

"Tell me something. How the hell does a guy from the desert learn to snowboard like you?"

Abedi smiled. "The Sheik spends his winter holidays in the Alps. I've had eight seasons to practice."

We headed up the Mall, toward the Washington Monument. The street lamps threw long shadows across the snow. I walked ahead of Abedi, upwind from his cigarette smoke.

"Listen, I think we can help each other. Tell me more about Serif's dealings with the Sheik and anybody else you know he's sold work to."

"I cannot compromise the Sheik's—"

"I'm not interested in getting your boss in trouble," I said, "but I need to know how it worked with Serif and who else was involved. If you help me, I'll help you find him."

He gave me a long look. Then he nodded.

"This is what I know…"

37

INSCRUTABLE PROVENANCE

By the time I left Abedi at the Hay-Adams, we weren't on our way to a beautiful friendship, but we *had* joined forces to locate Serif. We exchanged cards and shook on it beneath the heated porte-cochère.

I had missed dinner with Svetlana, so to make up for it I took her to the Lincoln Memorial. This was her first visit, and she marveled at the great man in his chair. Abe looked even better at night in the soft lighting, and with only a park ranger there in the cold with us, we were able to admire him in peace for a long time.

"Lincoln is the one president we were not poisoned against," Svetlana said dreamily. "It was his humble origins the party liked."

"Patriotic, for a former Communist." I was wary of the columns, behind which bad guys may be lurking.

"*Komsomol*, actually," she said. "First, Young Pioneer, then *komsomol* for teenagers, then member of Communist Party. We defected before I became Communist."

"Whatever, Commie."

We strolled down a shadowy path away from Lincoln and found ourselves in the middle of the Korean War

Veterans Memorial. Uneasy soldier statues looked for the enemy as spotlights on the ground gave them a spectral glow.

"Spooky," Svetlana said.

"Except for the being shot at," I said, "it feels like we're right on the battlefield with them. Speaking of battlefield, would you like to hear about my afternoon?"

She crossed her arms. "I knew you couldn't do some simple research without getting into trouble. What did you do?"

I described my run-in with Abedi and how he worked for a Sheik in Qatar.

"You punched him on an *escalator*?" she said.

"Cool, huh? I always wanted to do that."

"And what else did you learn, besides what escalator-punching is like?"

"That Abedi has been looking for Serif ever since the painting showed up at Sotheby's, because—get this—Serif sold the Sheik the *exact same* painting."

"Uh-oh."

"Yeah, uh-oh," I said. "Turns out Serif has sold the Sheik about a hundred paintings. They're all part of the Sheik's secret collection—ones acquired through crooked dealers. He has a second collection of ones with inscrutable provenance."

"And the Sheik. He is Serif's only client?"

"Nope. According to Abedi, Serif's done business with at least three other Sheiks in Qatar, and five or six in Saudi Arabia. He's probably had some dealings with Kuwaitis as well, but Abedi isn't sure."

We sauntered down the path. The clip-clop of Svetlana's high-heeled boots echoed across the empty space.

"So…" She put her hands in her pockets. "We traced one painting to Hong Kong, and now a second one to the Middle East. That is significant."

"And, we know one of them is a fake."

"But what is the connection to Terrence Young and the Voice who warned you off the case?" She looked at me with veiled lids. "And to Ms. Connolly?"

I'd been mulling over this problem since earlier in the evening, when I found out the painting had been restituted to the O.B.I.P. in Paris back in 1951. I put up my coat collar against the cold.

"How about this scenario? The Voice acquires the painting after the restitution…then Serif steals it from him. Serif has a copy made, sells one painting to the Sheik and the other to a gallery in Hong Kong under an assumed name. A name like Malcolm Azzopardi from Malta."

"It sounds reasonable," she said.

I looked behind us. It felt like we were being followed, but I was probably just keyed up from the statues.

"Maybe that's what DeAngelis meant in that email to Serif," I said. "'I know what you two are doing.' Maybe he knew Serif and René were making forgeries. And when the Voice found out his painting had been forged, he kidnapped Serif."

"I think you are on the right track."

"What, you're not going to shoot down my theory?"

"I sense it has many holes," she said, "but I must reserve my brainpower for tomorrow. After tournament I will be more than willing to dismantle it."

"I can't wait."

38

TRACE EVIDENCE

My early-rising New England genes came in handy with PI work, because while other detectives were still sleeping, I was getting things done. The next morning before dawn I swam twenty laps in the hotel pool, worked out on the Nautilus, read some of the research material and ate a delectable breakfast of poached eggs and Chesapeake crab cakes. Then, while the sun rose over the Potomac, I took a taxi over to FBI Headquarters.

The J. Edgar Hoover building is a monstrous, sandy-brown structure with a slanting, overhanging top floor that looks as if it will shear away at any moment and collapse onto Pennsylvania Avenue. Besides serving as the mother ship for field agents, the building once housed the FBI Laboratory. In 2003 the Bureau built a new, state-of-the-art lab facility at Quantico, yet in typical bureaucratic fashion they hadn't entirely abandoned the one here at headquarters, which explained why Lily Wang was meeting me here on a Saturday. At the security desk, a heavily armed guard took my driver's license and called the lab.

As my first mentor at the Bureau, it was Lily who recognized I wasn't suited for the insular, repetitive nature of lab work and encouraged me to transfer to the field. I'd never forget her looking out for me. She stepped off the escalator wearing a white lab coat, black slacks and flats.

"We'll have to make this quick," she said, signing me in. "I have a training session to give at Quantico later this morning."

"I appreciate any time you can give me, Lily. I know you're taking a risk using Bureau resources."

"Not so much," she said. "Ever since I made the Director look good to the Oversight Committee, the two of us have been what my daughter calls 'BFF.'"

"Best friends *forever*? I doubt it."

We passed the photos of past FBI directors and the rogue's gallery of the "10 Most Wanted." The air still had that odd smell—a combination of paper, cleaning solution and gunpowder. We took the escalator down.

"Of all the little problems you've sent me," she said, "this one has proven rather interesting. I don't often see artist's paint."

We walked along the fishbowl behind which I had once tested evidence while schoolchildren on field trips smeared their faces against the glass. Lily swiped her badge at the door, punched in a four-digit code and led me into the trace evidence examination room.

Spread out on a stainless steel table were the FedEx envelope and Ziploc bags I had sent, and a sectioned ceramic tray with the paint chips grouped by color. There was a scroll taped to the tabletop that I recognized as a gas chromatograph/mass spectrometer report, with its telltale readout of sharp peaks. Beneath it was a comparative readout.

"They're chromatograms on the yellow chips." She bellied up to the table. "The top one is of the chips you sent me, and the other one—our control—is a sample of standard oil-based chromium yellow you'd pick up at an art store. In this case, I used Windsor brand, but it doesn't really matter—there's not much variance. Now, what do you make of this spike here?"

It had been a long time since I'd had to decipher one of these, but I remembered enough of my analytic chemistry to know it indicated the presence a compound.

"There's a compound in the control that isn't in the paint chips I sent you."

"Correct. Any guesses what it might be?"

"No idea. You're the trace evidence expert."

"That I am."

She handed me two photographs. They were views from a scanning electron microscope.

"The left one is of the chrome yellow pigment you sent me. Notice anything?"

They were pictures of individual grains of pigment, each about two microns in diameter. I flicked my eyes between the two pictures, and then I saw it.

"There's a coating on the right one."

"Yes, yes, but why?" she said. "Think."

"Something to do with the brand of paint?"

She shook her head. "All chrome-yellow paint produced in the last thirty years has a coating on the pigment to prevent the color from oxidizing. The paint particles in the sample you sent me are not coated—"

"So they're much older," I said. "They predate the switchover of thirty years ago."

"No, it is more interesting than that. The pigment from your paint chips shows very little oxidation. Yet, the particles don't have the coating. This means that the pigment was produced recently without the coating, as though—"

"Whoever produced the paint wanted it to possess the characteristics of a much older paint."

"Right," she said. "But since there isn't much oxidation, we know the chips aren't from an old painting." She took off her glasses and cleaned them. "There is a remote possibility the paint chips are from a very old mixture of chrome-yellow, one only recently opened and therefore not exposed to air…but I think that unlikely."

I sat down on a stool and mused out loud.

"All right…somebody produces this special type of chrome-yellow…a pigment that is indistinguishable from chrome-yellow of decades ago. This person—I'm going to assume Jean René, since it was his loft I found the chips in—he knows that modern chrome-yellow paint has the coating. So, if he wants to create paintings that can stand up to scrutiny, he has to use new chrome-yellow pigment that doesn't have the coating…"

"Yes," Lily said.

"He wouldn't go to all this trouble for one painting, but if he planned on making copies of a lot of paintings…"

"Go on…"

"He would need a *lot* of this special paint. And he'd have to have it made someplace where the labor isn't…" I remembered the fifty-odd phone calls to Shanghai. "He was having the paint made in China. Thank you, Lily."

"You're welcome. Now, regarding the hairs…"

Lily led me to the next station, where two sets of red hairs sat under magnifying lamps. There were photo printouts from a comparison microscope.

"As you know," she said, "it's impossible to declare a definitive match or non-match without follicular tissue from both sets. But regarding the set of hairs with no roots, I believe they were cut from a natural hair wig."

"Makes sense."

"However...there's another side to this," she said. "I can't declare with one-hundred percent certainty that there is no intersection between the two sets of hairs. In other words, it *is* possible that some of the hairs with follicular tissue were among the cut ones. This could happen if the suspect had just had a haircut and some of the cut hairs fell from the suspect's clothing at the crime scene. What I am certain of is that the second set of hairs came from a female suspect."

"How do you know?"

"For starters, they're long, red, and have a thin coating of conditioner," Lily said. "Those three qualities alone make it ten times more likely that they belong to a Caucasian female. And since most of them had roots, I was able to stain the sex chromatin in the follicular tissue to positively ID the sex. Medium pigment density and excellent thickness of the shaft. The woman has a healthy head of hair. Oh, and there's no evidence of coloring or bleaching, so it's almost definitely natural."

"I've already established that," I said.

Lily rolled her eyes. We went into the other room. Beside the door was a shelf of forensic field kits, including ones for latent prints, entomology and blood spatter.

The one that really caught my eye, however, had "Scene-Scope" written in fluorescent green across the case.

"Say," I said, pointing at it, "mind if I borrow that?"

"What do you need reflected UV for?"

"Latent print experiment."

Lily looked around, as though seeking approval from someone who wasn't there. She groaned.

"Fine, take it."

"I'll send it back as soon as I'm done."

"Make sure you do," she said. "Someone *important* might want to use it."

I swiped my finger across the case and showed her the dust.

"I doubt it."

39

STORM FRONT

Svetlana didn't just win at chess, she trounced—with style. During the exhibition, I watched from the front row as she circled the pit in a blue sequin evening gown, pausing to consider each board and make her move before continuing to the next player. When it was over, she had carried the day with nineteen wins and one draw. Afterwards she stood for photos and autographed copies of her book.

During dinner I sat at Svetlana's table between the Congressman and the one person who had managed to draw against her: the CIA Deputy Director for Operations, Marty Paulsen. A small, bespectacled man in his late 50s, Paulsen radiated confidence and a keen awareness of his surroundings. According to an MSNBC profile, his father and grandfather had also held key roles in U.S. government. Two burly and intense men stood against the wall behind his seat. I was about to introduce myself when he thrust out his hand.

"Marty Paulsen."

"Dakota—"

"Stevens," he said. "Yes, I'm aware of your connection to Ms. Krüsh."

"Great, could you tell me what it is then? Because I'm a little fuzzy."

Paulsen chuckled. "You know…" He leaned in my direction and lowered his voice. "I thought she'd be a lot tougher. Not many draw against her."

"Well, you know how it is," I said, "playing nineteen other people and all."

He chuckled again and sipped his cocktail. "Interesting background."

"What do you mean?"

"Oh, you know…born in Odessa, Ukraine. In the late 80s, the parents use one of her U.S. tournaments as a ploy to defect. State Department grants the family political asylum. Father now in New York real estate with ties to the Ukrainian and Russian mob."

"For the record," I said, "she doesn't have much contact with her father."

"Then who's got those thugs watching her?"

"You've been following her?"

"No, my advance men picked them up. Based on what I know of her background, I figured Oleksander."

I pivoted in my chair. "Boy, you've got all the angles covered, don't you? Next time you ought to play her the way I have to—without the full intelligence workup."

More chuckling. "How's the PI business these days?"

As he motioned to the waiter for another drink, dinner arrived. Filet mignon and asparagus tips. Not bad.

"With all due respect, deputy director, isn't it illegal for CIA personnel to conduct operations within the United States?"

"Who said anything about ops? I happen to know you're ex-FBI, and I'm curious what private practice is like. Might want to consult in a few years myself."

"I'd stick to the lecture circuit if I were you."

Paulsen's new drink came. He sipped it.

"Understand you're originally from Maine," he said. "The coast."

"Yup. There and New York."

"Spent a couple summers in Bar Harbor as a kid. Honest, hardworking people up there."

"It's those hard winters," I said. "Cleans out all the wimpy liars."

Paulsen swirled his drink. "You know, we're rooting for you over at Langley."

"*Rooting* for me? What for?" My steak sliced like a poached egg. It was delectable.

"Serif," he said. "Man's a cold sore. Been selling artwork to those terrorist-funding oil peddlers for years."

"Is Sheik al-Thani one of them?"

"He is suspected of having supported certain Muslim extremists, yes."

I turned to face him. "The CIA's been watching me?"

"No," he said. "We were watching *Abedi*. When he came stateside, we handed off to the Bureau."

"Let me guess. That new information-sharing program."

Paulsen grinned like a wolf.

"Look," I said, "I want to be clear about something. Abedi was following *me*. He said the Sheik is looking for Serif. That's it."

"I know. The Bureau shared their intel."

My head shook involuntarily. "And this tournament?"

"A late entry. So imagine my surprise when I found out you'd be here tonight."

"Yeah, imagine."

After dinner I retired to the room, showered and changed into pajamas. In my bathrobe and slippers, I was feeling very Cary Grant—in a put-upon, *North by Northwest* sort of way. By the time I poured myself a root beer and put my feet up, Svetlana had walked in, her blue dress sparkling in the foyer lights.

"Order up food, would you?" she said. "I'm ravenous."

I grabbed the phone. "Didn't you eat at the banquet?"

"Absolutely not. I would never let them see me eat." She went to her bedroom. "A chicken Caesar would be nice."

After a bath, Svetlana joined me in the sitting room. I gave her a bottle of water and put an ottoman under her feet. When the food arrived, I signed for it and wheeled the cart to her side.

"I didn't beat all of them, Dakota," she said.

"So?"

"So…it is not good for my reputation when amateurs draw matches against me." She stabbed some salad onto her fork. "Soon the organizers will stop inviting me."

"I don't think there's any danger of that. They don't want you just because you're a great chess player, they want you because you put asses in the seats."

"They did raise quite a bit of money today," she mused.

"See?"

I switched on the Weather Channel. They were showing the Northeast.

"Hark, weatherwoman! Is that a snowstorm I see heading for Upstate New York?"

"My goodness, it's massive."

"Should be there by the weekend." I rubbed my hands together. "You know what that means."

"No White House tour?"

"It's time to bust Serif out of that bighouse he's in," I said. "But first there's some information I need to get out of Ms. Connolly."

"Spare me the details."

Svetlana ate in silence while I narrowed the TV options to two movies: *Patton* with gruff George C. Scott barking colorful monologues, or *Viva Las Vegas* with redhead Ann-Margret shaking it in tight sweaters. I chose the latter.

The next time I looked up, Svetlana had finished her salad. She had her glasses on and the stack of microfilm printouts on her lap. She tapped the pages with a pencil.

"I don't understand," she said. "Why did you bother with all of this about the art looting? They restituted the painting you said."

"They did, but I want to know more about where it came from."

I poured the two of us some decaf from the cart.

"It'd be great if you could find out who it was restituted to. The record at the National Gallery said the O.B.I.P. Paris, but that was fifty, sixty years ago. The agency is probably defunct by now."

I sipped my coffee and kept an eye on Ann-Margret. Whoever the director was, he had a fetish with women's backsides.

"Maybe you could contact somebody in the French government," I said. "How's your French?"

"*Je parle français parfaitement. Quoi que vous seriez incapable de remarquer la différence,*" she said. "*De plus, je ne suis pas celle qui se trouve hypnotisée par une salope aux cheveux roux.*"

"That sounded like an insult."

"I will make inquiries," she said.

"Good. Now, about the Simplex lock. I borrowed a device that will tell us which buttons are being used. Once I determine which four—and I hope to God it's only four—how will you know the combinations?"

"I already thought of that." She gestured at her laptop on the desk. "I wrote a program. Once we know which buttons, I input them and the program generates a list of possible combinations."

"Now all we need is snow. Did you order that gear for yourself?"

"Yes, and received it." She sipped her coffee while skimming the printouts. "By the way, I'm not wearing that ridiculous snowsuit."

"Oh, yes you are. This is my bailiwick, Ms. Krüsh. We do it my way."

In a thick Russian accent, she said, "You are chauvinist American pig. But you are boss, so I do your way."

"It'll be cute on you," I said. "Hey, look at it this way—we'll match."

"*Zadnitza.*"

Svetlana had called me an ass in Russian before, so it didn't really bother me. When you have a sharp-tongued associate who speaks seven languages, you get used to exotic insults.

I turned back to Ann-Margret. She never insulted me.

40

GET-LUCKY-CITY

Shay and I had just arrived at my place in Millbrook. It was mid-morning. Inside, while she freshened up, I put the bags in the bedroom. After two hours in the car with Shay, my blood sang, and it took five minutes of splashing my face with very cold water before I could breathe again. I got a fire started in the living room fireplace and went looking for her.

"Shay?"

The door from the kitchen to the greenhouse was gaping. I stepped down. Shay was strolling around with her arms crossed.

"The light's awesome out here." She puffed out a breath. "But it's freezing."

"Too expensive to heat."

Outside, the wind blew loose powder across the yard. The greenhouse roof whistled. I shivered.

"Need me to warm you up?" Shay enveloped me in a hug. Once again, her reality-distortion field was operating at full power. I needed to remember why I'd brought her up here.

"How about some hot chocolate?" I said.

"Fun."

We drank them in the sunroom curled up together on the built-in sofa, not talking, just staring at the birds out at the feeder. I was tense about confronting her. After a few minutes, she put down her mug.

"Show me around the castle."

So I did, pausing in each room to tell her a little story about it.

"There's one more room I want to show you." I led her down the hall to the office and pushed the door open.

"Wow," she said.

"My grandfather loved Mark Twain's place in Hartford, especially the billiard room, how Twain kept his desk in there."

She brushed past me and walked the length of the pool table, running her fingers over the felt. She nodded at her lake scene self-portrait on the wall.

"Are you getting hours of viewing pleasure from it?" She winked broadly.

"*Hours.*"

"So, how many women have been in this lair of yours?"

"A couple."

"Bullshit. This place is get-lucky-city. I bet you've got Barry White cued up on the stereo over there."

"Nope, Sinatra."

While her back was to me, I laid the wrapped-up, rescued painting on the pool table.

"Come here, I've got a surprise."

She skipped over.

"Go on," I said, "open it."

With her eyes closed, she tore off the wrapping and threw it aside. When she opened them again, they blinked at the painting.

"So," I said, "were you really in a theater, or did you just dream it up?"

"How did you—"

"It's amazing what people throw out these days."

"You *followed* me?" Her eyes glowed like portholes to a furnace.

"You stole your own painting...from René's gallery." I leaned it against my desk, safe from her wrath. "All along, you've been telling me you don't know him, and I've let you get away with it—"

"Get away—"

"—but today you're coming clean," I said.

"Is that what this sleepover's all about? Getting information?"

"Shay, you're caught. Do yourself a favor and answer my questions. As long as you didn't kill anyone, I can probably help you."

Silent, she snatched a cue stick off the wall. Adrenaline pulsed down my legs; I'd seen what she could do with a hatchet.

She tossed balls onto the pool table. "Got anything to drink in this place?"

"Let's try without it."

"Prick."

With one foot flirtingly off the floor, she lined up on a cluster of balls. She went to slam them and the stick glanced off the cue ball. It dribbled into the side pocket.

"Shit." Her shoulders drooped. She stared at the torn-open painting.

"Look," she said, "when you came around asking about Jean René, I got worried because he had a painting of mine. I didn't want anything he was into biting me in the ass."

"That *would* be a shame. How'd you meet him?"

"It was years ago, when I was at the Sorbonne." She set up the cue ball for a another shot. "Jamal Carter introduced us."

"And?"

"That's it."

"I don't believe you."

Bending over the opposite side of the pool table, Shay tried to create a bridge for the cue stick. I was observing her technique, or lack of it, when her lavender blouse billowed open. She looked up and caught me leering.

"Dakota...would you help me?"

"We're not finished."

"Forget that for a minute. Show me how to do this."

I walked around the table cursing my weakness. As I reached for her stick, she backed into me until I was spooning her. I swallowed.

"First of all, your stance is all wrong." I kicked her feet apart. "And this is how you make a bridge." I spread her fingers on the felt and stroked the fleshy webbing between them. "And this is how you grip the cue."

As I touched the soft inside of her wrist, the stick slid out of her hand. Shay turned around and boosted herself up so she sat on the edge of the table. Parting her knees, she yanked me into her by the belt and jammed her tongue in my mouth. The resolve was draining out of me. Her hair, her smell, her feathery touch—they all conspired to make me lose myself. When we pulled apart, she was gyrating softly on the narrow edge.

"Yeah, nice and sturdy." She unbuttoned and peeled off her blouse, revealing a sheer purple bra. "Your favorite color, see?" She fingered one of the cups.

"Not on the table, Shay. I don't want to bang it out of alignment."

"Baby"—she wriggled out of her jeans—"I want you to bang *me* out of alignment."

Detective or not, when a man hears a line like that, there's only one thing to do.

I swept the balls off the table and pushed her flat on her back.

We were still in the office, but had somehow ended up on the couch, our naked skin sticking to the leather. A small quilt covered very little of us.

"So much for sledding," Shay said.

"We can still go." I checked my watch. "It's only noon."

"But I'm *hungry*." She poked me in the ribs. "Cook me something."

"Sorry, no food. There's a bag of marshmallows out there. That's about it."

Her eyes got big. "Hey...can roast them on the fire?"

"I think we can arrange that."

We showered and dressed and went out to the living room. Shay sat on the hearth wrapped in a blanket while

I fetched the marshmallows and a couple of sticks. When I came back, the phone rang. "Go to town," I said on my way into the office.

Just as I picked up, a chill on the nape of my neck told me Svetlana was on the other end and that the news wasn't good. Her voice was shaky.

"Dakota…something has happened."

"Tell me."

"Lazar and I…we were coming out of the club…two men approached…we started walking. Then three more men jumped out of a car. They shot the other two and drove off. It was terrible…I did not sign on for this."

"Thank God you're all right," I said.

"The men, they were your idea?"

"Mine and your father's. Sure you're okay?"

"Not a scratch. The men are staying in the living room tonight. Lazar is here, too. He was very shaken up."

"A bit more exciting than the Sicilian Defense," I said.

"It seems we have hit a nerve with these people."

"It would appear so."

"We have to get them," she said. "That snowstorm arrives tomorrow night. We go?"

"Affirmative. I'll call when I'm on my way."

"Dakota?"

"Yes?"

"Thank you."

I fiddled with the papers on my desk. "Anything for you, Champ."

We hung up, and I sat paralyzed in my chair, gripping the armrests. A storm of conflicting emotions churned inside my head—rage, affection, disgust and self-loathing—so I couldn't be sure what my real feelings were, except on one subject.

While I had been screwing a suspect on a pool table, Svetlana was almost killed. Not some faceless *painter*—Svetlana. I'd given Shay every chance to come clean, and she kept playing games with me. Well, no more. Today I was getting answers.

41

ANSWERS & QUESTIONS

I stood up, slid the chair under the desk and strode out to the living room. Shay pulled a flaming marshmallow from the fire and blew it out.

"Want one?"

I heaved her up by the hair.

"Dakota, you're hurting me!"

I dragged her to the rocking chair and shoved her into it.

"How do you know Jean René?" I shouted.

"What? I don't kn—"

I slapped her. Hard. She started to sob, and something inside me died. I jerked her chin up. Her cheek glowed where I'd smacked her. Flecks of mascara washed away in copious tears. Coldly, I forged ahead.

"If you ever want my trust, you need to tell me everything you know about René, *right now.* Otherwise, I'm taking you back to the city and dumping you."

She nodded and pulled the blanket around her. I got some tissues from the bathroom, and once her tears were under control, the chair slowly began to rock.

"Jamal introduced us," she said softly. "It was at the Sorbonne. René was looking for painters skilled with oils to do reproductions, and he was paying excellent money. I had pretty much disowned my parents at the time, so it was either that or strip."

Her eyes were still. I sat on the coffee table across from her.

"Go on."

"For the first couple, he worked with us one-on-one. We had to do everything exactly as he said."

"Who's *we*?"

"Me, Jamal, David Birchfield. I'm sure there were others, but—"

"You said you didn't know Birchfield."

She looked away. The firelight danced in her eyes.

"Yeah, I get it," I said. "What about the women?"

"Never met them." She blew her nose and tossed the tissues into the fire.

"Tell me more about the paintings," I said.

"They were European. Mostly 19th and 20th century— Impressionist, Expressionist, a few 17th century Dutch Masters. Top shelf, all of it."

"Did you ever ask who they were for?"

"No," she said. "Jean René always claimed they belonged to rich collectors. See, it's not unusual for people to commission reproductions of their most valuable paintings, then store the original and display the copy. But I'm not stupid...the second I realized he was actually selling *forgeries*, I stopped doing it."

I jabbed the fire with the poker. "What made you realize it?"

"The materials," she said. "Before every copy, René would drop off the canvas and paints you were supposed to use. The canvases were already stretched and mounted on really old wood. Some of them had even been painted on already."

"And you painted over them?"

"Exactly. It's a trick of forgers—use canvases with underpaintings to give the illusion the top paintings are really old. The paints were another thing. They came in these generic containers without labels. René said if I didn't use the exact paints and canvases he gave me, I would be fired."

"Excellent. Keep going."

"Then there was the canvas size," she said. "Every canvas he gave me had the exact same dimensions as the one I was copying."

"How is that unusual if it's a copy?"

She shifted in the chair and continued rocking.

"Okay, when you do reproductions, like if you get permission from the Met to go in and copy a painting, it's pretty standard that the copy needs to be a different size than the original." She rocked faster. "When the second canvases were exact, I remember thinking, 'This is weird, I wonder if they got permission from somebody....' Jean René always covered himself by saying the owner wanted a perfect replica, but I knew he was lying, and as soon as my own work started to sell, I quit."

"How many forgeries did you paint?"

"Only five," she said. "Each one took me about six months, but the money was enough to live on for a year. I stopped doing them three years ago and put it behind me. But when you showed up with Contessina that day, I got worried."

She wiped her eyes with another tissue.

"You said Jamal was dead, and then I heard my movie theater nude was in René's gallery. I knew you were looking into him, so I stole it. I was afraid you'd find out about the forgeries. And when you told me David had been killed, too—forget it, I freaked. That's why I hired you to protect me."

"So nobody was following you?" I said.

"Not at first. That was a lie. But I've had a sixth sense lately, like somebody's been watching me and going in my apartment when I'm not around. Maybe it's the landlord still trying to scare me out."

I took a deep breath tinged with wood smoke and riveted her eyes to mine.

"Did you kill Jean René?"

"No, but…"

"But what?"

"I threatened him once," she said. "It was a couple of years after my last forgery. He came on to me at a show and said if I didn't sleep with him, he was going to tell Contessina what I'd done."

"And?"

"And I put a knife to his neck. But a bunch of people saw me do it."

"Does anybody know about the forgeries?"

"I ended up telling Contessina. She promised if it ever came up, she would protect me."

"And she protected you this time…"

"By lying to you," Shay said.

"What was her relationship to him?"

"They slept together a few times. Other than that, I don't know."

"What about Nadir Serif?"

"Honestly, I've never heard of him."

"And Terrence Young?"

"No."

I kissed her hands and led her to the sofa. "Thank you for telling me the truth."

"I've wanted to ever since you beat up those guys in front of my building." She put her head on my shoulder. "No one's ever stood up for me before. I was dying to tell you, but I was afraid you'd think I was a horrible person."

In the fireplace, the wood hissed and popped. Shay's hair was the same color as the fire and I could smell her mint conditioner.

"I'm sorry I slapped you," I said.

"I deserved it. Dakota, remember that night at my show?"

"The wine bottle? How could I forget?"

"I really didn't come on to that guy. I stopped that stuff the day I first met you. Something told me I shouldn't do anything to screw it up."

I kissed her hair. "Why don't we go in town and get something to eat? We can do some sledding on the way home."

"I don't want to leave yet. I feel so close to you right now." She caressed my arm. "This is gonna sound weird, but—screw it, I'll just say it—you make me want to be better. What would you say if I said I was falling for you?"

"I'd say go ahead and fall. I'll catch you."

For reasons totally within our control, we were delayed getting into Millbrook, but being lightheaded with hunger made our lunch taste better. At Marona's we bought groceries, including hot chocolate for after sledding. Back in the car, Shay gazed at the neighboring horse farms with their gently rolling, fenced-in hills.

"This place must be beautiful in the summer."

"Year-round," I said.

"Too bad I don't do landscapes. I'm just not talented enough."

I turned to her. "Are you kidding? Do you have any idea how many people wish they could do what you do? And you're able to make a living from it."

"Yeah, painting soft-core porn of myself."

"Maybe," I said, "but it takes skill. Just because somebody makes something look easy doesn't mean it's easy. Those things are like photos, for God's sake. They're actually arousing."

"Well, I've been giving it a lot of thought, and I'm not doing them anymore. You woke me up, Dakota."

"Glad to hear it."

"I'm not kidding. I've been lazy about my painting for a long time. But starting now, I'm taking it seriously again."

I glanced at the toboggan jutting out of the trunk and rubbed her leg. "Ready for some sledding?"

"Sure." She hugged my arm, then sat up and pinched my sweater. "What's this?"

"This," I said, "is my British S.A.S. Commando sweater. Note the way the ribbed black merino wool hugs my rugged frame."

"*Please.*"

"It even has elbow patches. You like?"

"You look like a JC Penney model."

"Ah, but you did say *model…*"

She laughed. I took the fork in the road back toward my place. A pair of blanketed horses nuzzled in the field to our right. "Oh, look," Shay said, squeezing my hand. Now that Shay had opened up to me, I felt relieved. It was okay if I had feelings for this woman. Unlike everybody else I'd encountered in this case, she'd told me the truth. With what Shay had told me about the forgeries, my investigation had a fresh angle, new life. She leaned against me, and for a millisecond I was content.

I checked the rear-view: a black SUV and a pickup were back there.

"Shay, did you tell anybody about our trip up here?"

"Just Contessina. Why?"

If you think you're being tailed and want to know for certain, take three right turns. The odds that your tail needs to take the same three turns as you are nil, so if the tail stays, you've got a problem. Casually, I turned into an assisted living center.

"Where are we going?" Shay asked.

"Just checking something."

After three right turns, they were still back there. I had a problem.

"Buckle your seatbelt, Shay."

"What's wrong?"

The pickup swerved, roared up on my left.

"Do it. And keep your head down."

I yanked my own seat belt taut, and the second hers clicked, I put the hammer down on the Cadillac. In any evasive driving situation, the first ten seconds are critical. Tearing down the bumpy, winding road, I put as much distance between them and us as I could. I flew over frost heaves and landed heavily on the shocks. There was alarm in Shay's voice.

"Dakota, what's going on?"

"I have to concentrate, Shay."

When I reached Brush Hill Road, I was confident we would make it. Home was less than a mile away. I ripped down a straightaway. Then, a quarter-mile ahead, another SUV shot up the hill and and blocked the road. Behind me, the pickup banged my rear bumper, trying to pit me.

Off the road, beyond a stand of thin birches, there was a worn tractor path through a field. Straight wasn't an option and neither was stopping. With every second, the gap between us and the roadblock was shrinking. There was only one choice.

"Shay, brace yourself."

42

HUNTED

We crashed through the trees and splashed down in deep snow that blew over the windshield like flour dust. There was a thud beneath the car and then deafening flatulence. The muffler was gone. The car began to stall. Momentum plowed us through and we skidded onto the tractor path. The car oversteered, I corrected, tapped the accelerator, got traction on the packed snow. The path turned and we rumbled across the field toward the woods. I checked the rear-view. The trucks had stopped. A man outside directed them to the field entrance. As we approached the far end of the field I reached over and unbuckled Shay's seat belt.

"All right, the second we stop, you run to the woods."

"But what about—"

"No arguments. I'll be right behind you."

A hundred yards from the trees, I pounded the brakes and swerved the car so it blocked the path.

"Go!"

I grabbed the car keys and my jacket. We hopped out. Shay ran for the woods. Halfway there, she stopped and looked at me.

"Shay, go!"

I went to the trunk. The lid was tied down. I heard the trucks coming in the distance. I fumbled for my knife, slashed the rope, hauled out the toboggan, dropped it flat on the snow. I laid the hard case containing the rifle on the sled. When I reached the tree line, Shay was huddled behind a rock wall, holding her knees and shivering. She'd forgotten her coat.

"It's okay." I helped her up and put my jacket on her. "See that big tree? I want you to take the sled over there. Aim it downhill and wait for me."

"I want to stay with you," she said.

"I'll be right there."

As she trudged away, I pulled out my revolver—a .45 Smith and Wesson with serious knock-down power.

One of the SUVs stopped near my car. Two men got out. I didn't recognize them. Each had a Glock in one hand and a walkie-talkie in the other. The guy on point noticed our footprints and the sled trail. He said something into his radio. Meanwhile, his buddy rummaged through my trunk and pulled out the snowshoes and poles.

Out on the road, two men exited the pickup and disappeared into the woods. The truck pulled into the field. They were trying to surround us.

Back at my car, the man on point followed our tracks. He spotted me, firing as he came. A bullet whanged off the rocks. His buddy started shooting. Crouching behind the wall, I sighted down the barrel, squeezed... and missed. They were too far. I waited until the point man was 50 feet away, galumphing through a drift, then squeezed off another round. It hit him dead center in the chest, flattening him. I fired two shots at his buddy, holstered my gun and slogged through the snow to Shay and the sled.

At the bottom of this hill was an abandoned barn. It was in the middle of a broad field with great visibility in all directions. But to get there—I took in the slope—we had to navigate a minefield of trees and rocks and fallen logs half-buried in snow.

No matter what, this was going to hurt.

"Lie flat on the gun case," I said. "Face down."

She did. I climbed on her back, wrapped my hands around the lead ropes, and kissed her neck.

"You wanted to go sledding."

"Not like this," she said.

"Just hold on tight." I pushed off and we tipped over the edge.

The sled bogged at first, but we quickly picked up speed. Gunfire rang out from the ridge above. Shay screamed. I kept tension on the ropes, and as we neared our first tree, pulled hard to the side. The sled grazed the bark on our way by.

One down, a few thousand to go.

We bounced, then bounced again, then slammed down on what had to be a rock. Shay grunted beneath me. The hill pitched steeper. Branches whizzed by, birds flapped madly out of our path. Snow exploded over us. I buried my face into Shay's neck and squinted ahead. A branch whipped my cheek. When I looked up we were hurtling toward a massive maple. I dragged my leg. The sled was as responsive as an oil tanker.

"Shay, lean!"

She tipped with me. My hands strained on the steering rope. The tree loomed ahead, and just as I prepared to ditch, we jumped off an exposed root. We flew for what felt like minutes. We landed hard and smashed through underbrush until the sled hit a log and we were thrown clear. As I got to my knees, snow ran down my back, under my sweater. Shay was on her side, eerily still. I crouched beside her, brushed snow off her face.

"Can you move?"

Her eyes blinked open. She looked at me with girlish wonder. "You saved us."

"We're not out of the woods yet." I pulled her up. "Literally."

She touched my cheek. "You're bleeding."

"Just a scratch." I looked around. The sled had gone downhill in one direction, the rifle case in another. The rifle was everything. I took Shay's hand. "Come on."

Gradually the ground leveled and the trees thinned. From far up on the hill were the sounds of underbrush snapping and men shouting. They were catching up. We found the gun at the very bottom. Its case was cracked, but the gun was secure.

We emerged from the woods onto a stark white landscape where the only color was the bleached gray of the barn. It sat at the top of a long rise. As we staggered up the hill toward it, I looked behind me. A few hundred yards away, three trucks stopped on the edge of Brush Hill Road. Somebody had consulted a map and determined where we'd come out. These were not amateurs.

Shay was shaking. I put an arm around her and helped her through the deep snow.

Inside the barn, it was dim but not dark. Light from chinks between the boards striped the dirt floor. There was a ladder up to the hayloft. I led Shay to it.

"Up," I said.

She went. At the top I made her hide behind some thick hay bales. I reloaded the revolver.

"Ever fired one of these?"

"Yes."

I didn't ask, just handed it to her.

"Kicks quite a bit. Make sure you grip it tight. Anybody comes up here, you plug 'em."

"Dakota, who are those men?"

"Not sure," I said, "but it's got something to do with those paintings you forged."

I was about to get into position when I noticed a single tear rolling down her cheek. A feeling of protectiveness swelled up inside me, and at that moment I knew Shay was the special someone I'd been searching for. I'd defend her to my last breath.

"Hey"—I cupped her face—"where's my little hatchet girl? You're a fighter, Shay. Why do you think I'm with you?"

She sniffed. "For my hair?"

"Yeah, you got me."

"Kiss me, Dakota. For luck."

I did, finishing by running my fingers through her hair. That part was for me; it's good luck to run your hands through the hair of a redhead.

Shay wrapped herself in my jacket and clutched the pistol. "Ready."

"Good girl."

I crawled over to the corner facing the road and found a spot where the slats were broken out. I flipped the case open, put in earplugs and took out the rifle. I was scared, but with the smooth stainless rifle in my hands now, not as much. Worming on my stomach up to the opening, I settled into a prone shooting position, clicked the bipod into place and peered through the scope.

There were seven of them milling around the trucks 300 yards away, each carrying a pump shotgun. I gulped down some air. If I had any talent for self-deception, now was a good time to break it out. The sun sat low in the sky, faintly glowing through the gray overcast. Another hour of daylight, maybe. And like every other day this winter, it was on the verge of snowing. My phone rang. I didn't recognize the number.

"Is that your *phone?*" Shay said.

I took out an earplug, peered through the scope and picked up. It was the Voice.

"You are in quite a predicament, Mr. Stevens."

"Yeah? You should have seen our bobsled run."

He had to be out there. I scanned the vehicles for movement, but the windows were dark.

"You are trapped and well outnumbered," he said.

"Not as outnumbered as you think." I chambered a round, flicked the safety off. "Hurry up, you're wasting my minutes."

"I told you to stay away. I gave you a way out and you refused. A foolish choice."

"Why are you doing this? Because of a forgery?"

"Goodbye, Mr. Stevens," the Voice said, and hung up.

I shut off the phone and scanned the men. They were restless.

"Was that *them*?" Shay said.

"Shay, I have to focus now. Whatever happens, just stay down."

I put the earplug back in and checked my gun a final time. Since the targets were only 300 yards away, and the rifle fired flat within this range, I left the elevation screw alone. The windage was negligible. With the crosshairs settled on the pack, I waited.

It wasn't long before they headed toward the barn. My brain reeled. Okay, there were seven guys out there with guns and bad haircuts prepared to kill us. Correction, nine guys—two more wobbled out of the woods. The taller one wore my snowshoes, which rankled me. The second guy looked like the one I'd shot up on the hill. He wasn't moving quite as fast, I noticed, but it *was* him. They were wearing bulletproof vests.

Nine guys with shotguns and body armor. Not good. But I had a few advantages, like the high ground, decent cover and a rifle firing 150-grain bullets traveling at 2900 ft/sec, which basically nullified their vests. And they were overconfident, attacking the barn head-on. They kept coming, Gunter and Hans in front. When they fanned out twenty feet apart, I knew they weren't kidding. I tried to take a deep breath, but couldn't. I hated the idea of killing anybody, but if even one of them escaped my line of sight, they would flank us. I'd have to shoot fast.

"Shay, cover your ears."

I aimed at Hans's shoulder, exhaled and fired. The recoil jarred me. I checked the scope again. The shot had spun Hans around and dropped him. One down, eight to go. They stopped and fired their shotguns. At this distance, the few pellets that reached spattered harmlessly against the slats. I ejected the spent shell and loaded a fresh one.

The guy wearing my snowshoes broke away from the pack. He bolted toward the barn in an attempt at a serpentine pattern, but in the deep snow it was tough and he quickly tired. *This'll teach you for stealing my things.* I aimed low and ahead of him, relaxed and squeezed off a round that lasered through his thigh. He screamed and tumbled over face-first, the snow around his leg turning instantly scarlet.

When they were a football field away, Gunter shouted something and they broke into a run. The drifts slowed them, but they were all zigzagging now, making them twice as hard to target.

My elbow points hurt from digging into the wood. I chambered another round. Had to make every shot count. I trained the scope on the end man, who, although the slowest, was almost out of view. I aimed ahead of his next step, waited, fired. The bullet blew out the side of his knee. He toppled over. When he looked up, fine snow caked his face like confectioner's sugar. His cries made the hairs on the back of my neck dance. In the hay behind me, Shay whimpered. The remaining ones stopped and fired. They were closer this time. I covered my head. Something stung my shoulder.

Three men down, and they were still coming. I could fire maybe four more rounds before the gun barrel heated up and became inaccurate. One more flesh wound as a warning, and if they kept coming after that, I would shoot to kill.

The youngest one rushed ahead of the others. Training the crosshairs on his forearm where it held the gunstock, I waited for him to plant his feet, then squeezed off another round. He doubled over, clutching his arm. The shotgun disappeared into the snow.

I yelled out the opening, "The next one who steps this way gets his head blown off!"

Confused, they stopped and looked to Gunter. No one moved. Their frozen breath formed a cloud around their heads. My arm shook from holding the crosshairs steady on Gunter's head. I ached to shoot him. Something told me that letting him go was a mistake.

Picking up their wounded, they retreated across the field, leaving my snowshoes in a patch of red snow. I clutched the rifle until they got in the trucks, and as they drove away, the gun slipped from my hands. I crawled to my feet, went to Shay and threw my arms around her.

"Your shoulder, it's bleeding!" she said. "We have to get you to a hospital."

"Just let me hold you."

We hugged for a long time, until the light faded over the field and sirens echoed across the valley. Then we walked out of the barn together, clinging to each other for support.

43

SNOWSHOES AND LOCKS

Afterwards I was patched up by paramedics and questioned at length by a semi-pal of mine, State Police Detective Lt. Brian Sutherland. He took my revolver and rifle as evidence, but let me keep the shotgun and groceries from the Cadillac, which was towed into Millbrook for repairs. Then he drove us back to my place and posted a cruiser on the property overnight.

"Case they get cute and try another run at you," he said. "Any of 'em turn up at a hospital, we'll get a call. But from what you told me, they won't go anyplace public."

"I owe you, Brian."

"Not doing it for you. Doing it 'cause your girlfriend's friggen hot."

"Well, thanks just the same, you lech."

Since I knew the owner of the garage, the car was repaired by noon the next day. As I drove us back to Manhattan and explained the plan, Shay was sullen.

"I want to come," she said.

"Nope. This is strictly a two-person thing."

"You and *Svetlana*."

"That's right. Unless you happen to know discrete mathematics."

"But I'll be all alone," she said.

"You're staying at my place tonight. There will be three men there watching you. You'll be very safe."

"Okay, if that's the way it has to be." She pivoted in her seat, punched me lightly in the arm. "But you better get these guys *quick*, Dakota. I'm a woman that needs attention."

"Really? I hadn't noticed."

It was late afternoon and the snow had just begun to fall when Svetlana and I parked down the road from Wittenberg View. I put my cell phone in the glove compartment and gestured to Svetlana to do the same.

"Anything that rings," I said.

"What if there's an emergency?"

"There's no reception up here anyway. Besides, if anything happens in there, our little devices aren't going to help us. What's that other thing?"

"A camera. In case we want pictures."

"Like the layout. Clever girl."

"Yes, that is me," she said, "a clever girl."

Outside, we geared up. Svetlana's knapsack contained the computer and some food, and I gave her the binoculars case to carry like a purse. As she fastened her pink-tinted goggles and raised her hood, I noticed that her snowsuit fit much better than mine. It was a one-piece jumpsuit with a matching white belt cinched smartly at the waist.

"Where'd you get your suit?" I asked.

"Same place as yours. You insisted I wear one, so I had mine tailored."

Tailored. I helped her into her snowshoes, then loaded myself up with the SceneScope and a backpack. In it I had the usual survival equipment and my lock-picking set, as well as a complete set of winter clothes for Serif. Strapped to the outside was an extra pair of snowshoes; I just hoped the man was alive and ambulatory. The light was waning as we crossed the road into the trees.

After only 100 yards, my face began to itch from the biting snow. I rubbed my cheeks. When I found my original snowshoe tracks and the huskies' paw prints, they were crusted-over but undisturbed, which meant my first incursion hadn't been discovered. I took a deep breath of relief.

Svetlana adapted surprisingly well to the snowshoes, enabling us to reach the lookout point at the gorge within an hour. She whistled softly over my shoulder.

"Quite the retirement home. Where do I sign up?"

She handed me the binoculars. The storm lowered the visibility, so I couldn't make out details. In the residential clearing, lights shone inside the all-purpose building. The breezeway appeared empty. Sweeping across to the main house, there was smoke coming from one of the chimneys. That was all I could tell. Off to the side, sheltered among the firs, the fenced-in building was lifeless.

I led us along the ridge to my second scouting spot, beneath the balsam firs. While Svetlana snapped photos, I trained the binoculars on the side of the house, checking for motion detector lights. There *was* one, at the corner. This could be a problem. I studied its location relative to the outbuilding. If we moved slowly and kept our distance, we should be able to prevent the light from turning on. I plotted a not-too-steep course down the ridge face. That was the route we'd take.

"I don't want to complain," Svetlana said softly, "but won't we get wet if we keep sitting on this snow?"

"I'm about to fix that."

I opened the saw blade on the Leatherman, cut a mass of fir boughs and dragged them back to our bivouac beneath the tree. In the meantime Svetlana had carved a cozy space out of the snow around the trunk. I laid the boughs in an overlapping pattern until we had a thick, dry carpet beneath us.

"I always knew you had talents," she said. "Can you make a fire with two sticks?"

"Sure, but I find a match is easier."

A snowflake clung to her eyelash. I brushed it off. She gave me a rare warm smile.

"Now?"

"Now, we wait," I said.

As darkness set in, we ate sandwiches, sipped coffee and stared out at the mounting storm. What started as a breeze soon intensified into a swirling gale. Before the light faded completely, I rolled onto my stomach with the binoculars and checked out the scene one more time. The main house was dark, but up on the plateau beyond it, the activity building blazed with light. I still couldn't make out any details. Maybe it was bingo night. There was a vague glow where I remembered the fire tower, but even if somebody was up there, they wouldn't be able to see us through the storm.

It was time. I put the lock-picking set in my pocket and strapped the SceneScope over my shoulder. I checked my pistol, clipped the flashlight to my belt and tapped Svetlana on the arm.

"You have the computer?"

"On my back."

"We're in stealth mode now," I said. "No light or talking till we get to the door."

We strapped into the snowshoes again and headed along the ridge. The snow came in sideways, making it near impossible to navigate the darkness. Twice Svetlana stumbled, but I grabbed her before she fell. We wound through the trees and down the ridge slope to the back of the building.

Paranoid of tripping the motion detector, we moved like sprinters in super-slow-motion. Along the way I spied the burn barrel. The charred canvas flapped in the wind. I gestured to Svetlana to stay put, trudged over and cut off a section.

Half an hour later, we reached the fence. It took me another ten minutes to pick the brass padlock, and we made it to the building door without tripping any searchlights or sirens. We took off our snowshoes and leaned them against the cement steps. Quickly I shone the flashlight around the door, checking for signs of an alarm. All clear.

"I'll do the Master lock first," I said.

We stood cramped together on the narrow stoop. Svetlana cupped the flashlight over the lock. Fortunately it was an older one and the tumblers were worn. I had it off in five minutes.

"Now the fun part."

I popped open the case with the SceneScope, took off my snow goggles and slipped on the safety goggles.

Holding the scope about a foot from the Simplex lock, I put my eye to the viewfinder.

"Turn your back."

Flipping the switch, I saw nothing at first but a green glow on the door handle. I focused the lens and the buttons came into view. They were in a vertical line, 1 through 5.

"Anything?" Svetlana asked.

"Not yet. Don't look."

Since the SceneScope was a reflected ultraviolet system, when I didn't see anything, I angled the scope forward. Tiny black ridges appeared on the buttons. The blood pounded in my ears. Then I moved and the ridges disappeared. I shifted toward Svetlana and they came back again. I counted the buttons with fingerprints on them, and my heart sunk.

"Forget it. Five buttons."

She swore in Russian.

"We can't do over a thousand combinations," I said. "We'd freeze to death first."

As I glanced through the viewfinder one last time, Svetlana bumped my arm.

"Wait a second…" I refocused the scope.

The ridges on the 3 button were only on the edge, as though a finger had grazed it on its way to the 4 button. The other marks were distinct.

"We're in business—one, two, four and five." I put away the SceneScope. "Run your program and let's get started."

Svetlana squatted on the stoop with the laptop on her knees while I stood ready to punch buttons. As she announced each combination, I punched it in and jerked the handle, which, when it was incorrect, reset the buttons for the next attempt.

I would have preferred it if Svetlana's program gave all of the two-number combinations first, then the three-number ones, but it didn't. Instead it gave all of the combinations that began with "1" before moving on to the ones that began with "2" and so on. Also, because two buttons could be pressed at the same time to form a new button, there were confusing ones like "One, two *and* four, five."

The snow blew in at a fierce angle. To protect the computer Svetlana made a canopy with her snowsuit hood, which muffled her voice. My ungloved fingers were frozen, and I had to stop every ten combinations to warm them.

"How many have we done?"

"I don't know," Svetlana said. "Over a hundred. The computer's getting wet, I don't know if—"

"Shhh, hold it."

Dampened by the snow, the sound of barking dogs echoed from the main house. No lights went on, but the woofing continued. I turned back to the lock.

"Okay, let's finish this."

"Dakota, the keys aren't working. I can't scroll down."

I pounded the door. "All right, just read me what you have on the screen, and if those don't work, you'll have to give me the numbers out of your head. You're the Queen of the Endgame. You can do it."

"I think I have the pattern," she said.

We continued, but at half the pace. And now we had those dogs to worry about.

"Serif," I said, "you are going to get such an ass-kicking when I open this door."

"Two, four, five, one," Svetlana said.

I punched the numbers and jerked the handle, expecting it to stop short, but it didn't. The door opened.

"We're in."

"Thank God." Svetlana closed the laptop and stood up. "My legs are frozen."

"Let's grab Serif and get the hell out of here."

"Do it fast and I take you to Denny's," she said.

"Deal."

We brushed each other off and went inside. We were in a small dark room. I wedged the SceneScope case in the door so it wouldn't lock behind us and switched on the flashlight. There was a coat hook and a rubber mat for shoes. Ahead was another door. Not knowing what I'd find on the other side—Serif, a dozen art dealers, or Gunter and a team of mercenaries—I drew my gun before easing it open. Svetlana was right behind me.

My immediate impression, even before I was able to find the light switch, was that the place was big and that it had a distinctly odorless smell, like a museum. I groped along the wall for a switch, found one and hit the lights.

"*Ho-ly...shit...*"

Beside me, Svetlana breathed a similar obscenity.

I felt as if I'd been walking on thin ice ever since this case began, and the ice had just cracked. I was officially in over my head.

44

BREAKTHROUGH

Paintings. Hundreds and hundreds of them, hanging in narrow aisles that stretched the length of the building. A dozen aisles, each four feet wide. Partition walls that went to the ceiling, twelve feet up, were covered by paintings, making them blur into one giant mural of colorful images and gleaming gold leaf.

In the corner there was a thermohygrograph, and against the wall stood a row of giant racks also crammed with paintings. There were at least fifty works in each rack.

"Holy shit," I said.

"Yes, you mentioned that," Svetlana said.

I led us briskly down the first aisle. I didn't recognize any of the paintings, but a few signatures were legible: Degas, Braque and Van Dyck.

"Here's a Renoir," Svetlana said, scanning up and down. "Chagall. Matisse…"

We wound through the aisles, half a football field in length, Svetlana scanning one side, me the other, taking in all of the paintings from floor to ceiling. We had searched only the first three aisles when I stopped at a painting of an angular woman in a turban. I read the signature.

"Sweet Jesus, this is a Picasso."

"Do you think they're real?"

"René and his artists couldn't be *this* prolific," I said. "It took Shay six months to do one and all told she only painted five. At that rate, the guy would need an army of forgers."

Svetlana walked to the end of the corner aisle and took in the entire length and breadth of the place. It was the only time I'd ever seen her flabbergasted.

"This must be worth…tens of millions."

"Tens? More like *hundreds*." As I said it, the enormity of our find struck me. A prickling sensation crept down my head and neck.

"All right," I said, "start taking photos. Set the camera to high-res and get pictures of as many as you can, especially the big boys—Picasso, Matisse, Renoir, et cetera. Fill the camera, and do it fast. We can't afford to get caught here. I'll be watching out front."

I went out to the mud room. I didn't know what to do with my hands, so I just shoved them in my pockets and leaned in the doorway, sucking in the cold air, shaking my head.

This case was a tentacled beast, and my job was to put it back in its cage. But every time I thought I had it contained, another damn tentacle flapped out and mocked me. If Serif wasn't here, *where the hell was he?* Hopefully Abedi had a new lead on his whereabouts. That is, if Serif wasn't already dead. One thing that finally made sense was Serif's desperation when he came to us.

Serif has a supplier of artwork—*this* artwork—someone for whom he acts as a dealer. Since this warehouse was on Terrence Young's property, until I found evidence to the contrary, I'd assume Young owned the artwork. Okay, Young wants to sell a painting. He contacts Serif. Serif takes it and, without Young knowing, has René make a forgery of it. Serif then sells the original to his clients in the Middle East, and peddles the fake to unsuspecting galleries in the Far East under various identities, like Malcolm Azzopardi of Malta.

But when one of the forgeries shows up at Sotheby's, Serif panics. He needs to get it back fast, before the Sheik or Young finds out. To do this, he needs to hire a private detective with no knowledge of art. Somebody like me, who will accept his story and simply recover the painting. And he pays in cash, to hide the transaction.

But what was the connection between these paintings and the deaths of DeAngelis, Carter and Birchfield? René had a strong motive: to shut up anyone who knew about the forgery scheme. But he was dead, too, which hinted at another suspect. Somebody with an equally strong need to cover up the forgeries. *Somebody like Serif.*

Lastly, who was Terrence Young and how he had gotten hold of all this artwork? I was convinced Young was the Voice, and I had a couple of theories about his identity, one more incredible than the other. We'd look into the less bizarre of the two in the morning. Right now, the priority was getting away in one piece.

It was as dark as a cave on a New Moon. The icy snow scratched against the building like sand. Behind me, the door opened and Svetlana came out.

"One hundred twenty-five photos."

"Great. You shut off the lights?"

"No, and I left one of our business cards. Of course I did."

"All right, let's scoot."

I opened the outside door and took one step when headlights cut through the woods on the hill. The thump of doors slamming carried in the wind. I tipped the snowshoes over so they were out of sight, and went back inside and pulled the door closed, leaving a crack to see out.

"What about the outside gate?"

"I closed it when we came in," I said.

"And the lock?"

I pulled it out of my pocket. "Hopefully they won't notice."

"Hopefully? You really know how to put a woman at ease, Dakota."

I had my gun ready and held the door in place with my boot. After five minutes of waiting, I had to look. The motion-activated light on the corner of the house was on, shining a bright beam on our building. The front windows of the main house were lit up, and the shadows told me people were moving around. I didn't see or hear anyone outside.

"Must have tripped the motion detector when they went in," I said. "We'll have to wait for it to shut off."

We stood still for what seemed like eons. The wind howled in the door cracks. When the light finally switched off outside, Svetlana put a mitten on my shoulder.

"You are going to solve this, Dakota Stevens."

My cheeks, which had been cold from standing by the door, flushed hot.

"No, Svetlana Krüsh, *we* are going to solve this." I checked outside again. The light was off. "Okay, no talking until we get back to the tree."

We locked up, retraced our steps to the bivouac and collected the rest of the gear. As I buried the cut fir boughs, neither of us spoke. Somehow we sensed the same thing.

This case had just gotten a lot more complicated.

45

THE MISSING CLIENT

"And you're sure that's her maiden name?" I asked.

We were in the conference room back at the office, Svetlana on her laptop with the LCD projector aimed at the whiteboard, Shay leaning back in her chair with her feet on the table, munching a bagel as she talked.

"Positive," Shay said. "I've seen those medals in her office a thousand times. Lieutenant Peter Fulcinetti, right? Her father was from Genoa, came to the U.S. just before WWII. Ended up fighting for us, and after the war the Army kept him around to translate. Met Contessina's mother in Florence, I think, and Contessina was born in like '63 or '64. Her father died in '69, I'm pretty sure. Unexploded land mine or something."

The whiteboard showed a WWII veterans' registry website with the dates and basic information on Lieutenant Fulcinetti's U.S. Army record. Svetlana nodded.

"According to this, the dates she mentions are correct."

"And he was never stationed in France or Germany," I said.

"No."

"And there were no American GIs named Terrence P. Young in the European theater?"

"There was one—middle initial 'J'— in the Pacific, but he was killed at Okinawa. Of course, Young could be an alias."

"Maybe," I said, "but there's nothing else to suggest that."

Shay dusted her hands and sat up. "I don't get how this helps you. What does Contessina's dead father have to do with anything?"

I collapsed into a chair. I was grouchy and stiff from overwork and lack of sleep.

"First of all, we know that our Terrence Young is not her father because her father is dead. And since Central Europe was where most of the art looting took place and Fulcinetti wasn't stationed there, we can be pretty confident that he wasn't involved in its theft. So much for the first theory."

"Where does this leave us?" Svetlana asked.

"We follow the paintings," I said, "figure out where and how Young acquired them. I called Ms. Zellars at the National Gallery and set up an appointment."

"Isn't that risky?" Svetlana said. "How do we know we can trust her?"

"I just said I had some photos of paintings for her to look at."

The office phone rang. I hit the speakerphone button. It was James the doorman.

"You're on speaker, James. What's up?"

"Remember those cats I told you about? Secret Service types, picked up Serif's stuff?"

"Yeah?"

"They're back. Just went upstairs."

I grabbed my coat. "Delay them, will you?"

"How?"

"You're a Marine, man. Improvise, adapt, overcome. I'm on my way." I hung up. "Coming, ladies?"

They grabbed their coats. The car was parked right outside, and in the thin late-morning traffic we were able to zip up to Serif's building on Park Avenue in fifteen minutes. Oleksander's men followed in the BMW. I double-parked a couple of cars behind an idling taxi. James was standing under the awning when two men came out carrying suitcases. He pointed at them as they got in the cab. I waved back and followed the vehicle.

The taxi headed down Park. I maintained a two-car buffer, which wasn't easy because the driver kept weaving in and out of traffic and accelerating to make the lights. Shay leaned forward between the seats.

"I'm jealous," she said. "You two having adventures like this all the time."

Svetlana stared straight ahead at the cab.

"Yes, it is incredible fun with Dakota. Death threats, fist fights, dead bodies—"

"High-speed chases," Shay said, "and shootouts. Don't forget the shootouts."

"But"—Svetlana glanced my way—"every so often he shows his cleverness and solves a case."

"Please," I said, "keep talking about me in third person. I love it."

The cab crossed Park Avenue and pulled up in front of the Waldorf–Astoria. I idled a couple cars back. A doorman tried to help the men with their suitcases and got shoved aside.

"I knew Serif couldn't have gone very far." I turned to Svetlana. "You'll have to do this. Meet you at the Lexington entrance."

She gave me a quizzical look, which changed to a smirk when she remembered why. Without a word she got out and vanished through the revolving doors. One of her guards went after her. As I pulled away from the curb to loop around the block, Shay hugged me over the seat back.

"Why is she doing your dirty work?"

"Hotel security," I said. "We had a tiff last year. I was banned from the place."

On our third time around the block, Svetlana emerged from the Lexington Avenue doors with her guard close behind. She hopped in.

"Room 2549."

"Did you see Serif?"

"No, but I heard him," she said. "They left the door open, and as I was walking by he was scolding them for forgetting his cufflinks."

"At least he's got his priorities straight." I phoned Abedi. He picked up immediately.

"Ah, Dakota Stevens," he said. "You have news?"

"Yeah, but I'm going to need your help."

I explained the situation as I cruised down Lexington.

"We need to lure him out of there somehow," I said. "*Without* his bodyguards."

"Bodyguards? He is scared of something," Abedi said. "He does not know I am looking for him, correct?"

"Far as I know."

"Then it is easy. I will call and say I heard through the grapevine he was at the Waldorf, and that the Sheik would like to invite him to a party at his apartment in Trump Tower."

"What about the bodyguards?"

"I will tell him the Sheik's people are handling security, and have a car waiting for him at seven o'clock."

"And so he gets in the car, and—*surprise*—we confront him."

"I think it will work," Abedi said, "but we will need some bait to ensure he comes."

"What do you suggest?"

"He uses escort services quite often. He has a weakness for pale blondes. Shall I call a service?"

I glanced at Shay in the rear-view. "No, but we'll need a blonde wig."

At seven o'clock, Abedi, Svetlana and I were waiting in a stretch limo at the main entrance of the Waldorf. Shay, who was supposed to meet Serif at the bar and lead him out to us, had been inside for half an hour. I was beginning to worry when Serif finally emerged from the entrance with Shay on his arm. She got in the limo, then Serif climbed in. He had a smug expression on his lips as he sat down across from me, but as soon as he recognized us, his face fell. The door slammed shut.

"What...what are you doing here?" He looked around the cab. "*Yahya?*"

"Serif," I said, "if you say one word that isn't an answer to a question, I *will* punch you in the face. Got me?"

"I don't have to take this."

As he dove for the door handle, I grabbed his necktie and jerked him toward me so his nose and my fist collided. He yelped. It was barely a punch, but the blood didn't know that. It ran down his lip.

"My nose, you broke it!"

"Why does everybody say that?" I said. "Relax, it's not broken."

Svetlana passed him a handful of cocktail napkins. Abedi rapped on the glass divider and the car began to move.

"Okay, Serif, here's the deal." I leaned into his space. "I know why you're hiding. I know all about your forgery scheme with Jean René, and how you've been double-dipping with the Sheiks and the Far East crowd. What I don't know, and what you're going to tell me, is your connection to Terrence Young, and why you killed those painters."

"Painters? What painters?"

This time I slapped him—a real smacker that resounded in the crowded limo.

"Ow! What was that for?"

"*That* was for abandoning your cat." I gestured to Abedi. "I believe you know each other."

"The Sheik is displeased," Abedi said. "It appears some of the paintings you sold him are not genuine."

"That is not true," Serif said. "Yes, I sold some forgeries, but only to the Asian infidels."

Svetlana and I rolled our eyes at each other.

"May I have a drink?" Serif said.

"Me too," Shay said.

She removed the wig and tossed it on the seat. At the sight of her red hair, Serif frowned. Abedi poured Jack Daniel's into two highballs with ice. Shay tapped my leg with her heel.

"It's not Old Grand-Dad, but it'll do."

Abedi said, "I am waiting for an explanation."

Serif quaffed the liquor in two swallows and threw his head back so he was staring at the ceiling. The napkins were saturated, but he continued to hold them under his nose.

"All right, Serif," I said. "Who was your supplier of originals? Terrence Young?"

He lowered his head and spoke softly.

"Every few months we would meet to discuss the sheiks' shopping lists and the paintings he was selling. Terrence kept a catalog of them—photos, numbered, the whole bit. There were hundreds of them."

"You're talking in past tense, but this was going on until just recently, right?"

"Yes."

"Okay," I said, "so where did *Young* get the paintings?"

"I don't know. I got the sense that somebody had stolen them, and then he stole them from that person. Anyway, he wasn't worried about being caught."

"Why not?" Svetlana said.

"The one time I expressed concern, he said..." Serif stared out at the traffic. "He said there were people in high places who wouldn't let the truth get out. He also warned me not to cheat him because he had connections in the art community."

"Who?" I asked.

"He didn't say, and I didn't press the matter. I think he was bluffing."

"Does he go by anything besides Terrence? Maybe one of his guards slipped up and called him by another name?"

"Never," Serif said.

"Now, about those painters," I said.

"I never knew the painters. Jean René handled that end of things. *He* probably killed them. When I told him about the copy showing up at Sotheby's, he said, 'Something will have to be done about that.'"

"René's dead by the way," I said.

"I know."

"Who do you think killed René?"

Serif removed the napkins from his nose. "Must have been Terrence's men. Sadistic bastards, the lot of them."

"How about a tall, lean guy? Chestnut hair, cleft chin?

"That's Christian, his son. He's the worst."

"So they're why you hired protection," I said.

"Yes. The night I hired you, after they broke into your office, I decided it would be safest for everyone involved if I went into hiding. That's when I checked into the Waldorf."

"How selfless of you," I said. "You know, Serif, your greed has gotten a lot of people killed. Including DeAngelis."

No clever rejoinder. No response at all. As the limo wended its way across town, Abedi phoned somebody and spoke in Arabic. Serif looked out the window.

"Can I go back to my apartment yet?"

"Sure," I said, "if you want to be killed."

"But you work for me," he said testily.

"Nope. Svetlana and I are off the case, now that we've found your painting."

"You did? Where is it?"

Svetlana produced a manila envelope from her purse and dumped the contents into Serif's lap—the charred big head.

"Sadly," she said, "they burned the rest."

"But…the money I paid you."

"Yes, it's covered our expenses nicely," I said. "And now you're going to pay us the balance. We held up our end."

"But I can't stay in hiding forever," he huffed.

I shrugged. "Young and his people will probably whack you."

Serif's face turned as white as a blank canvas.

"Or," I said, "you can help us nail Young and the killers, and I might be able to convince the authorities to go easier on you. But there's something else you'll have to make good on first."

I nodded to Abedi.

"To regain the Sheik's confidence," Abedi said, "you will pay him, in cash, the eight hundred thousand he paid for the painting."

"But the Sheik has the original, I swear it."

"It is a matter of trust. You will do it, or the Sheik will inform everyone in the region about you, which I promise will cause you far greater problems."

After a long pause, he nodded minutely. Shay grabbed the whiskey bottle, refilled Serif's glass and her own.

"You know what?" she said. "You're fucked."

When the car pulled up at Trump Tower, three dark-skinned, sturdy-looking men were waiting by the revolving doors. Abedi got out and beckoned Serif to join him. Serif's eyes darted to Svetlana and me, then Abedi.

"Aren't they coming?" he said.

Abedi shook his head. "Mr. Stevens's work here is done. Besides, the Sheik is very eager to speak with you." He leaned into the car and shook my hand. "Thank you, Dakota. I will make sure this one pays what he owes you."

"Thanks."

Abedi shut the door and rapped on the roof. As the limo pulled away, I felt a sudden twinge of regret for having punched him. Abedi, that is. Serif deserved what he got.

46

MR. YOUNG

Our first morning back in D.C., I went alone to the National Gallery Library. Using Svetlana's photos from the storage building, Ms. Zellars and I compared them to the photos of paintings from the Munich Central Collecting Point. It was a tedious process, especially since mine were color and the microfilm versions were black and white.

After three hours we had found only seven matches: one small Renoir, one Degas drawing, a landscape by Courbet, two portraits by Marie Laurencin, and two country scenes by Paul Cirou. My groan shook the quiet stacks. Ms. Zellars patted my shoulder.

"This kind of research takes time, Mr. Stevens. Have you any idea what you've got here?"

"A lot of valuable paintings?"

"Uh, *yeah*." She held out the stack of color prints and shuffled through them. "Vermeer. Rubens. Degas. Valasquez. Goya. Palma Vecchio. Renoir. Matisse. Picasso. Rembrandt. *Rembrandt*, for God's sake. This is huge!"

"So…if we find these paintings on the microfilms… that means they were recovered?"

"Correct." She removed the first roll.

"And restituted?"

"We are about to find that out."

She had written down the property card numbers for the seven matched paintings, and it took another hour to find the individual records. According to the microfilmed property cards, as of 1951, when the Munich Central Collecting point ceased restitutions, all seven of the paintings had been returned to their rightful owners or descendants.

Then how the hell did some guy in the Catskills end up with them?

My second theory was looking increasingly plausible. Ms. Zellars took off her glasses.

"Did you contact the French government about that first painting?" she asked.

"My associate did. They said they never received it."

"Interesting."

"Yeah, and I bet if we contacted the O.B.I.P. and the other claimants about these seven, we'd get a similar report. But first, I need somebody to *find* all of them. Somebody I can trust."

"I see," she said. "Dump it on the librarian, is that it?"

"No." I lowered my voice. "Since it's becoming clear these are all stolen, *I* need to focus on finding out the identity of the person who has them. If you could handle this end of things, you'd be doing me a huge favor."

"And what do I get?"

"Part of the reward, if there is any. That, and virtue."

"*Virtue?* Well, that settles it." She grinned.

I handed her the sheaf of photos and didn't let go. "We have to keep this secret."

"Okay," she said, wagging a finger, "but you owe me."

We shook on it, and I slipped on my coat.

"Oh, two women might drop by looking for me. Tell them I went to the World War Two Memorial, would you?"

"*Two* women?"

I shrugged and walked the gauntlet of wispy-haired scholars to the exit.

Out on the Mall, the wind blew snow over the gravel paths. No one was following me today; it was too damn cold. The only signs of life were clumps of tourists scuttling between buses and the Air & Space Museum. I hiked, head down, toward the Washington Monument.

The cold helped me think, and at the moment I was thinking about all of those paintings. It seemed impossible that one person could get his hands on so many. And to think, what we found were the *leftovers*—after years of black market sales to the Sheiks. How many had Young started with? And more importantly, how had he gotten them in the first place?

I circled around the Monument and saw the WWII Memorial in the frozen distance. Hopefully Svetlana and Shay got my message to meet me there.

Shay. The woman had hit me like a fire truck. True, she was no saint, but then neither was I. Wallflowers didn't suit me anyway; they wore me out with their constant need for reassurance. One thing Shay wasn't lacking was confidence. Or talent. Or beauty, for sure. Ever since she opened up to me, I had begun to see her differently. I thought about my lair on the Upper West Side, where she could stroll around in nothing but an Oxford shirt and paint happily in the northeast bedroom. On weekends we'd go to Millbrook. I smiled in the bitter wind. That settled it. When this case was over, I'd ask her to live with me. Now all I had to do was solve it.

The case. Once Ms. Zellars found all of the photos and property cards, I suspected we'd discover a pattern: that the paintings had been recovered and restituted, but the alleged recipients had never received them. The thief was probably aided by someone involved in the restitution process—at Munich or one of the other collecting points. But he needed access. He needed to have been in a position to steal a lot of artwork undetected.

From the OSS Art Looting Investigation Report, I knew there was only one organization that had had that kind of access during the war, and as far-fetched as it seemed, it was the best explanation. Like Sherlock Holmes said, *"Once you eliminate the impossible, whatever remains, no matter how improbable, must be the truth."*

I crossed 17th Street and walked down into the Memorial. The fifty-six pillars representing each of the states and territories encircled the courtyard. I strolled around the reflecting pool, past the field of 4,000 stars, and found the Maine pillar on the Atlantic side. I took off my glove and pressed my hand to the icy granite.

Footsteps echoed in the courtyard. I spun around. Svetlana and Shay came down the steps carrying shopping bags. Two of Oleksander's men stopped at the Memorial entrance. We shared a nod.

"What are you doing here, sweetie?" Shay said. "It's freezing."

"Yes, Dakota," Svetlana said, "we could have met back at the hotel."

"I needed to think."

"About?" Svetlana said.

I told them what Ms. Zellars had found out, and I shared my theory that the thief was somebody with access, and that the organization with the most access during the war was the *Einsatzstab Reichsleiter Rosenberg*. The *Einsatzstab's* mandate, I explained, was the systematic acquisition of artwork and cultural treasures for Hermann Goering's private collection, as well as Hitler's planned museum in Linz, Austria. When I finished, Shay and Svetlana were stunned.

"Ladies," I said, "I think Terrence Young is a fugitive Nazi."

47

Detective Work Sucks

The good news was, the National Archives in nearby College Park held the largest collection of Nazi records from before and during the war.

The bad news was, armed only with a copy of Young's driver's license photo, we had potentially 70,000 microfilms to review.

During this case, I'd been whacked on the head, hit with a hammer and shot at, but none of that bothered me as much as the tedium that lay ahead of us. As Svetlana and I crossed the parking lot, I couldn't help being a little surly.

"I assume they have *Einsatzstab* records," I said.

"Collections and personnel."

"And they're all in German?"

"Mostly."

"How is your German by the way?"

"*Mein Deutsch ist hervorragend, aber Sie würden den Untershied sowieso nicht merken.*"

"Why does everything in German sound like scolding? What did you just say?"

"I said, 'My German is excellent, not that you would know the difference.'"

I paused at the revolving doors.

"Is there a cafeteria at least?" I asked.

She ignored me and went inside.

The facility was modern and brightly lit, more like a Silicon Valley office than a sterile Federal building. It gave me the feeling that if we wanted to find Young's true identity, we'd come to the right place.

However, before we could compare photos of German military staff to Young's driver's license, Svetlana had to find *Einsatzstab* personnel records. Since "Young" was certainly an alias, we needed a list of staff who would be about his age today. In the meantime, I would check out the records of U.S. agencies involved in the art recovery and restitution. Svetlana handed me a notebook and pen from her Gucci bag.

"Enjoy."

"Bite me," I said.

She strode gracefully to the elevator, where a young academic held the door for her. The gesture made me think of Shay, who had wisely gone to the National Gallery with the bodyguards instead of tagging along with me. I wished we could have spent the afternoon together, looking at art and making out in the museum stairwell, but I sensed I was ten pieces away from solving a 1,500-piece jigsaw puzzle and I wasn't stopping for anything. In the textual documents department, I requested a thick packet of declassified OSS material about the art looting. I took a study carrel in the back and got to work.

I was operating under the hypothesis that an inside person—someone in the U.S. military or OSS—had aided Young by signing off on paintings as having been restituted. Otherwise, it seemed impossible that so many paintings could show up decades later in the Catskills.

For two hours I pored over the material for clues. There were dozens of names of OSS, military and MFA&A personnel, but none appeared on documents related to restitution. In fact, anytime I found something dealing specifically with restitution or one of the collecting points, the names were blacked out. When I returned the documents to the archive technician, I asked if there were other copies.

"You've got the originals," he said.

"What about microfilm?"

"Just pictures of the same stuff."

"Why so many blackouts?" I showed him the pages. He nodded as he flipped through them.

"Actually, these aren't bad. You oughta see the JFK assassination stuff. Every other *word* is blacked out in those things." He sighed, tucked the papers away. "Sometimes I think they do it 'cause the person's still alive when they declassify it. Other times it's to protect somebody's reputation. Who knows, really?"

"Thanks for the help," I said.

"What I'm here for."

After an egg salad sandwich in the cafeteria my mood improved, and I went upstairs and meandered through the aisles looking for Svetlana. I found her all the way in the back, scanning a yellowed, typewritten page. Two file boxes, their tops hinged open, sat on the shelf above the study carrel. I leaned over the side and knocked.

"Hello, *Fräulein*."

"Good, you're here." Svetlana put up her glasses, rubbed her eyes. "I have read through all available staff lists of the *Einsatzstab* and have found seventy-nine possible matches for Terrence Young."

She handed me her notebook. In her precise and elegant handwriting she had noted each person's name, section, military branch, rank and specialty, as well as his age in 1941—when the *Einsatzstab* was created.

"Great work, Svetlana," I said.

"You will notice," she said, "the ones I picked out were all thirty-five or younger in 1941. It is unlikely anyone over one hundred is still alive."

"True. What about pictures?"

"For those we go to microfilms upstairs," Svetlana said. "They are organized by branch or administrative function, and there should be photos."

"All we have to do is find these seventy-nine guys?"

"There are over a thousand rolls of microfilm just for personnel records."

"Ugh."

Svetlana stretched, checked her watch. "But now, they are about to close. We start tomorrow."

When the doors opened the next morning, Shay, Svetlana and I went straight to the microfilm research room, where a technician showed us an index to the films. The records were organized by section of the German government or military branch, then by the person's last name. We took seats at three adjoining readers, and when the first cart of films arrived, we went to work.

As each one's microfilmed personnel record appeared onscreen, we checked the picture against Young's license photo. Often the pictures were difficult to make out, and some records had no photos at all. There were also a few microfilms missing. Despite working non-stop, by five o'clock we'd eliminated only 19 names. Shay, unaccustomed to long stretches of left-brain activity, kept wandering off. Even Svetlana looked beat.

"Let's call it a day," I said.

"I want crab cakes," Svetlana said.

"Fine. We'll hit Annapolis for a nice dinner and come back fresh tomorrow."

The next day was more of the same: requesting microfilms from the technician, loading them onto the readers, spinning through and missing the record, spinning back and missing it again, at last finding the record, comparing the picture, discovering it didn't match and starting over again. We broke for lunch, but the respite didn't rejuvenate us. At day's end, after three days' work and half-blind from staring at fuzzy images of German documents, we had eliminated only 41 of the 79 names. Exhausted, we went to bed without supper.

The next morning, while stuck in traffic on our way to College Park, I made an observation.

"Fucking Nazis."

From the back seat, Shay slapped me on the arm.

"Remember how I said I was jealous of you two and your adventures?"

"Yes?" Svetlana said.

"I take it back. Detective work sucks."

That morning, I found myself sneaking away every chance I got. Searching the microfilms was even more discouraging than the Simplex lock. In that case, I knew if we kept at it, the lock was guaranteed to open; in this case, there were no guarantees—we were doing it on the basis of a theory, and a shaky one at that. My chest felt constricted. I put away another non-matching microfilm and went outside for air.

The sky was overcast and still. I paced in front of the building. What if this was the end of the line? What if my theory was right, but I couldn't prove it? And why was I bothering anyway? We'd found the painting and Serif was going to pay us, so what was the point?

The point, I told myself, was that, Nazi or not, this guy had attacked me and threatened Svetlana, and I couldn't have him free to take a crack at us at a later date. Besides, after all the work Svetlana and I had invested in this case, we deserved to know the truth. What was Young selling the paintings for? Were the murders committed to cover up something else? Whatever the questions, at this point I wanted answers.

I did 20 pushups, inhaled the brisk air and went back inside. As I stepped off the elevator, Shay bounced down the hall.

"She found him! She found him!"

We ran back to Svetlana's reader. She waved at the screen.

"Allow me to introduce *Oberleutnant* Hartmann Grüber," she said. "Luftwaffe Special Adjutant to the *Einsatzstab* for Reichsmarschall Goering."

"Damn," I said. "We probably should have started with Goering's staff."

"The records were not organized that way."

"I know, sour grapes. Nice work, Svetlana."

Shay pointed at the screen. "*Oberleutnant?*"

"First Lieutenant," Svetlana said.

"Let's have a look," I said.

We huddled around the reader and compared the enlarged black and white photo on the screen to the copy of Young's license. The similarities were astounding. At 22 years old, Grüber had more hair and tighter skin, but even sixty years later, his pale, sharp eyes and hooked nose were unmistakable.

"Amazing," I said. "I bet if we ran these two pictures through one of those identity verification programs, we'd find they're the same guy. Print out a few copies, note what roll you got it from and let's get out of here."

"As you wish," Svetlana said.

Shay massaged my shoulders. "So, what's next?"

"We call in the cavalry," I said.

48

THE CAREER MAN

Craig Hanson and I had been friends since Quantico. A dedicated career man, Hanson was now the Albany Division Special Agent in Charge. A clock ticked on the office wall as he stared across his desk at Svetlana and me.

"A Nazi," he said. "In the Catskills."

"We didn't believe it either," I said.

"In a nursing home? He a patient or what?"

"Retirement home," Svetlana said.

"We believe he's the owner," I said. "The Young alias appears on the land records."

"And the artwork," Hanson said. "You're positive it was stolen?"

I looked at Svetlana.

"I contacted the French government," she said.

"Svetlana speaks French," I added.

"According to them," she continued, "they never received the paintings that were recorded as having been returned."

Hanson flipped through photos of the paintings. "And the rest of these?"

"An expert at the National Gallery is ninety percent certain they're stolen," I said. "Remember, the hundred twenty-five you see there are just the beginning. I'd say there's close to a thousand paintings in there. If you count sketches and small pieces."

"Jesus," Hanson said. "Are you sure?"

"It seems far-fetched," Svetlana said, crossing her legs, "but it is not. Only a few years ago, there were over a hundred thousand pieces of artwork still missing from the World War Two era. For one individual to have so much in his possession is not unrealistic. Particularly somebody like Hartmann Grüber, who had total access. He was one of the officers in charge of the acquisition."

Hanson stood up and went to the window. During the summer, the view from his office was of a broad green meadow where deer came out of the woods to graze. Now, in the dead of an Upstate New York winter, there was only endless white.

"Can you believe this winter?" He stood with his hands in his pockets. "Worst I've ever seen."

"Pretty bad," I said. "Listen, there's a lot more to this. What do you think so far?"

Hanson sat on a credenza. "I think I don't have any legally obtained evidence. And this Young? No record, nothing. Just an old guy in a retirement home."

"You saw the two photos. One of Grüber, the other of Young. It's him."

"It might be him." Hanson picked up the stack of photo proofs. "I've also seen a lot of photos of paintings that *might* be stolen, and said photos were obtained illegally."

I shrugged. "I have fewer limitations than I used to."

"That's for sure," he said. "But…what you're showing me is pretty compelling, and…"

"Yeah?"

"If you're right about this—a Nazi, stolen art and a possible connection to terrorism—well, we don't get many cases like this up here."

"How long to put something together?"

"Tell you what," Hanson said. "I'm pretty friendly with the U.S. Attorney for the New York Northern District. I'll speak with her, talk up the Nazi and terrorism angles. If she goes for it, we can have warrants in a couple of days."

"I want in on the arrest," I said.

"No way. You know the Bureau's policy."

"You'll have to make an exception. I've worked too hard on this. Besides, I know the layout."

"All right, but we're not going in gangbusters. This guy may be a Nazi, but he's an elderly one and I don't want him or the other residents having a stroke. Just me and you, and we ought to have somebody from OSI."

"*OSI?*" Svetlana said. "This I have not seen."

"Office of Special Investigations," Hanson said. "Tiny unit in the Justice Department. Created in the late seventies to track down fugitive Nazis in America. They've managed to get something like a hundred war criminals deported."

"It's a good idea," I said. "Lend it legitimacy. Just make sure he brings a gun. Young won't be overjoyed to see me. I had to shoot a couple of his men."

"Dead?"

"No, just wounded."

"Obviously we'll have backup, but I don't think OSI guys carry."

Hanson got up from the credenza and paced around. I knew him well enough to know when he was hooked.

"Now," he said, "what about this Nadir Serif? We'll want to speak with him about the Middle East connection."

"You and Marty Paulsen," I said.

"CIA Deputy for Ops?"

"Yup. We met at one of Svetlana's chess tournaments recently."

Hanson raised an eyebrow at her. "You play?"

"A little."

"Hey"—he snapped his fingers at her—"anyone ever told you, you look a lot like that woman in—"

"The Victoria's Secret ads?" Her eyelashes fluttered.

"Yeah."

"I get that occasionally."

Svetlana was being modest; at least once a month around Manhattan, some pervert would approach her, asking for an autograph.

"Anyway," Hanson said, "what's Paulsen want with Serif?"

"They've been monitoring Serif's dealings with one of the Sheik's underlings—guy named Abedi," I said. "When Abedi came stateside, they handed off to the Bureau."

"Shit, you mean somebody in Washington already knows about this?"

"Just about Serif and Abedi. You're the only one who knows about Grüber and the art."

"We've got to move fast then," Hanson said. "Day after tomorrow, we go in."

49

A Soupçon of Romance

We were in my apartment bedroom, Shay and I, snug beneath a down comforter as the early morning sun slanted into the room. A fierce north wind rattled the windows. Seconds later the radiator tinked to life, in reply to the wind's growl.

"Ah, heat." Shay turned on her side to face me. She gathered her hair in one thick rope and pulled it under her neck. "You have no idea how nice it is not to wake up shivering."

"So long as it doesn't affect your work," I said. "But the second your painting goes downhill, no more heat for you."

She kissed me. "You know what would be great right now? Coffee."

"Yeah, coffee would be nice."

She made puppy-dog eyes.

"All right…" I jumped out of bed and threw on my bathrobe. Before I could leave, Shay tossed off the covers, wriggled, then snapped them back.

"A reminder of what awaits you." She laughed.

"You won't be laughing in an hour."

She smiled wickedly. "Coffee first. Chop-chop."

I brewed the coffee, but had pastries delivered from the bakery downstairs. When everything was ready, I put it all on a bed tray and carried it in.

"Your breakfast, my little strumpet."

She was sitting up against the headboard reading a book on tornadoes. As I placed the tray across her legs, she gestured at my other books.

"Tornadoes, Antarctica, the Loch Ness Monster, *Bigfoot?*" She tossed the book on the nightstand. "What's your damage?"

"They're things I've always been curious about." I slipped back into bed and grabbed my coffee and a scone. "Couple years ago, I was scheduled to go to Oklahoma and tool around with storm chasers, but—"

"Let me guess, you got a case."

"Yeah," I said. "A Hollywood producer with deep pockets. Svetlana insisted we take it."

"And Bigfoot?" She sipped her coffee.

"I always wanted to solve one great mystery, something involving nature maybe."

"Well, they haven't caught Bigfoot yet, have they?"

"No."

"Then cheer up, sweetie"—she mussed my hair—"there's still hope."

I fed her some scone and the crumbs tumbled into the bed. A few settled on her chest, which I promptly vacuumed up with my mouth.

"You ass," she said. "You're letting them fall on purpose. Is this what living with you is going to be like? Crumbs in bed?"

"No, much better."

"Tell me." She put the tray on the floor and sat up in the bed.

"Well," I said, "you'll paint every day, and cut back on your drinking—"

"Boo…hiss…"

"And when I come to your shows, the only person you'll make out with is *me*."

"I can live with that," she said. "Go on."

I drank some coffee and stared out the window.

"Upstate we'll build you a studio, and when you get on a roll with a project, we'll stay up there. In the early spring, we'll tap the maples for syrup. In the summer, I'll take you horseback riding—my neighbor owns a farm—and in the fall, we'll go on long drives to see the foliage. And sometime, I'll take you up to Maine and we'll eat lobster and swim in the quarries, like when I was a kid."

Shay was smiling with her eyes closed. It was the closest to adorable I'd ever seen her. I stroked her hair. Long and glossy, it gleamed in the light from the window. She rubbed my arm.

"So, what are we doing today?"

"Besides shagging until we have to claw our way outside for air?" I kissed her neck. "I thought we'd go shopping for the apartment. Right now it's very me. It should be *us*."

"Let's go rent a van and pick up my stuff!"

"Uh-uh. Not until the case is over."

She pouted. "When?"

"We're arresting Grüber in the morning. I go up tonight."

"Don't go, Dakota. I have a bad feeling." She touched my cheek.

"It's almost over, and the second it is, you'll get all my attention. I was thinking we might take a vacation together…"

"Really? Where?"

"You pick," I said. "Just someplace warm, where we don't have to get dressed. The most I want to see on you is a bikini."

"Mmm. If that." She grinned.

The radiator hissed. We finished the scone and fed each other Danish. Shay pinched a piece in her incisors and made me kiss her to get it.

"So," she said, "now that I know your freaky secret ambition, you want to hear mine?"

"Absolutely."

Her face relaxed as she gazed at the ceiling. She seemed to be recalling a pleasant journey.

"I want to do one superb painting," she said. "Just one. A landscape so peaceful, people would give anything to live there. An abstract so unique, it inspires people to create. A painting that gives sick people hope. *That's* what I want to do, more than anything in the world." She flopped on her side. "Do you think I can?" Tears welled up in her eyes.

"Shay, I know you can. And I'll do anything to help you." I held her face and wiped her tears away with my thumbs. "Why couldn't we have met years ago?"

"Shhh." She pressed a finger to my lips, and we kissed like it was the first time for both of us.

50

WITTENBERG VIEW, DAWN

It was eight o'clock and the woods along the driveway of Wittenberg View glowed with the fading vestiges of dawn. The packed snow squeaked under our feet as we marched down the drive, and in the icy stillness I was sure the sound carried for miles.

While Hanson and I walked abreast, our eyes habitually scanning our surroundings, Joshua Weinberg, the OSI agent, walked a few yards ahead, itching to capture a Nazi. He was a shade over five feet tall, and the ink on his law degree was still wet, but he strode with steely purpose, his arms swinging stiffly at his sides. The tension in his face said it all: he took this personally.

"Hey, Weinberg," Hanson said. "Slow down."

As we caught up to him, I patted him on the shoulder. "Take it easy, Grüber's not going anywhere. And you can you slap the cuffs on him. Right, Hanson?"

"Long as you read him his Miranda," Hanson said.

I walked alongside Weinberg. "How many of these have you done anyway?"

"This is my first."

The driveway switchbacked down through the trees, and we crunched along in silence for a while. Hanson unzipped his coat, a reflex from years of Bureau arrests. Weinberg coughed.

"My grandfather is a survivor of Auschwitz. When you grow up hearing the stories, you can't help wanting to see them all suffer."

"Grüber didn't have anything to do with the camps did he?" I asked.

"No," Weinberg said, "but we believe he was SS, and he's wanted for war crimes. He himself shot at least two dozen museum officials, gallery owners and art collectors. And the *Einsatzstab* thugs under his command are believed to have killed many more. Grüber is not just a thief who happened to work for Goering."

"I never said he was, kid. His people almost killed me, remember?"

"Okay," Hanson said, "how do we take him without giving the others heart attacks?"

"He's probably still asleep," I said. "Let's try the main house first. If he's not there, he should be up in the community building."

The driveway straightened out, and at the end of the dark canopy of firs was the parking area. This time, besides the fleet of black SUVs, a dozen large moving trucks were crammed into the clearing.

"Moving trucks?" Hanson said. "How the hell did they get up here? What's going on you think?"

"Not sure," I said.

As we drew closer, I saw chains on the tires, and I knew. Grüber had been tipped off, and the trucks were for hauling off the art. But a dozen trucks? It was excessive, even for all those paintings. There were his personal possessions, but…unless…the residents were coming with him. But why?

"Look at him, will you?" Hanson gestured at Weinberg, who had marched far ahead. He was almost out of the parking area.

"Craig, we've got a problem," I said. "Call him back."

"What's up?"

"I'll explain in a minute."

Hanson cupped his mouth and yelled in a loud whisper.

"Weinberg, get back here!"

He didn't hear us, and as we jogged across the parking lot after him, he disappeared behind one of the trucks. I pulled my gun, jacked a round into the chamber and sprinted after him. By the time I rounded the corner of the last truck, Weinberg was halfway up the stairs to the community building. He was reaching into his jacket for the warrant.

At this point, stealth wasn't a priority. We needed to get out of here.

"Weinberg, stop!" I yelled.

He reached the top and shrank out of sight, and for a couple of heartbeats I thought I had made a mistake. Then the shots rang out. Dozens—from automatic weapons.

Instinctively I dropped to a prone position, Hanson right beside me. Weinberg staggered back into view, his shirt soaked in blood, his face as white as the snow around him. He collapsed. The crumpled warrant slipped out of his hand and fluttered down the stairs.

A fiery sunrise silhouetted the plateau above, and into this infernal backdrop walked a line of men in winter garb, with MP40 submachine guns slung over their shoulders. There were at least twenty of them, their backs straight and proud, but as they drew closer, their slight unsteadiness and their wrinkled faces said they were old men.

They were Nazis.

51

A Sound Like Ripping Cloth

Every muscle in my body tightened at once. The men drew closer to the stairs. Hanson said something and tugged on my arm, but I was frozen with disbelief. Before I had a chance to process what was happening, a potato-masher grenade sailed down and plopped into the snow ten feet away. We covered our heads, but nothing happened.

"Dud," I said.

"Let's move, Stevens!"

We ran. Staccato gunfire broke out behind us. We dove between two trucks.

I peeked around the rear bumper. They were coming down the stairs. Over and over they yelled, "*Wir sterben, bevor wir zurück gehen! Wir sterben, bevor wir zurück gehen!*"

"What the hell are they saying?"

"Something about 'We'll die before we go.' Who cares? Let's get the hell out of here." Hanson pulled out his two-way: "There's dozens of them. Call for backup. We're coming your way."

We leaned out to make sure the driveway was clear and five more emerged from the woods, blocking our exit. Hanson turned and looked at the house.

"We're fucked. Look."

On the top floor of the main house, a row of windows opened and riflemen appeared. Hanson and I had maybe 50 rounds of ammunition between us. We were in no position to shoot our way out. We took cover in the wheel well. Hanson checked his gun.

"A nice little arrest, you said. One measly old Nazi, you said."

Chips of fiberglass from the truck roof sprayed into the air. In the distance I heard the cause: a machine gun. But not just any machine gun. Shooting 1,200 rounds per minute, it was one of the deadliest and most fearsome weapons ever made.

"What is *that*?" Hanson said.

"That," I shouted, "is an MG42! *Now* we're fucked."

The gun continued to fire. Splinters flew as we crawled all the way under the truck. I couldn't believe I was hearing the same vicious sound that had terrified my Uncle Henry. It was like a snare drum being played inhumanly fast. At the end of each salvo, the gun stopped for a moment, allowing me to place the echo.

"It's coming from the tower," I said.

"Where I'd put it," Hanson said.

"Let's just hope he cooks the barrel."

Between bursts, there were shouts in German from the house. Out in the parking area, five sets of boots ran our way. They were bunched together. I fired at the group and hit three of them in the legs. Hanson covered our rear. The MG42 continued to fire, then suddenly stopped. A loudspeaker on the tower blared. It was the Voice.

"Mr. Stevens," he said. "It is unfortunate that it should come to this. These, you have surely guessed by now, are my compatriots. Your government calls us fugitives. But we did only what we were ordered to during the war."

I wanted to yell back that the "superior orders defense" didn't work so well at Nuremberg.

"For over forty years, we lived here in peace," the Voice said. "You destroyed that in a month."

My brain ticked through places we could hide—the storage building, the house, the ridge—but we couldn't run anywhere; they had us pinned down.

"All you have succeeded in doing," the Voice said, "is to force us to leave. But as I told you before, we have great resources at our disposal, and there are others who will follow in our footsteps."

His last words gripped my spine and rattled me. I looked at Hanson. Even in the bitter cold, his brow was perspiring. The longer we stayed under here, the worse our chances. "It is time to end this charade…," the Voice said. I tried to turn and banged my head on the undercarriage. *The trucks.* I nudged Hanson. "We're getting out of here." I wormed out, got up in a crouch and tried the door. It was open. I crawled in with Hanson right on my heels. The keys were in the ignition. "Gotta love that German efficiency," Hanson said.

As the engine roared to life, I dropped it in "Drive" and floored it, aiming for the mouth of the driveway. A pack of men jumped down from the snowbank, leveled machine guns at us. We ducked. The windshield shattered. Some glass got under my jacket. Glimpsing the fire tower access road on my left, I cranked the wheel hard and gunned it. The shooting was behind us now. We sat up. Freezing wind poured through the wrecked windshield.

"Where are you going?" Hanson pointed behind us. "The driveway's back there."

"I'm taking out that gun."

"Stevens, this is—"

"An MG42, Hanson?" I said. "It'll cut your guys into confetti."

The chains rattled in the wheel wells. After a breath, Hanson slapped a fresh clip in his gun.

"Let's do it."

The fire tower just peeked above the treetops. Ahead the road turned a corner and went straight toward the tower across a hundred yards of open ground.

"Get ready!"

We rounded the turn. Noting the tower's position at the end of the straightaway, I aimed for the footings and ducked below the dashboard. The shooting started. I crouched on the floor, keeping the wheel steady. The side windows blew out, then a tire. The truck reeled. Bits of seat cushion and plastic flew around the cab. The sound of the MG42, now like ripping cloth, grew louder until the truck lurched and slammed into something with a tremendous gong. The truck flipped on its side. Hanson and I were dumped against the door.

The gunfire had stopped, and so had we.

"You okay?" I asked.

Hanson rubbed his head. "Dammit, I thought I was *done* with field work."

Grabbing the far seat belt, I hauled myself up through the window. The truck had rammed the left footing, but the tower hadn't collapsed as I'd hoped. Although listing 20° or so, it appeared solid. Hanson climbed out of the window. We looked up at the tower.

"So much for that," he said.

"It had to knock him on his ass," I said. "I'm going up there."

"Make it quick. I'm down to my last clip, and you know his pals'll be up here any minute."

I jumped off the truck and waded through a deep drift to the tower ladder. With my gun in one hand I clambered up as fast as I could, and when I reached the hole in the floor, I raised my free hand through and waved. Nothing happened. I stuck my head through the opening. Hartmann Grüber lay against the far wall, his head of white hair dripping blood. Beside him, also dazed, was his son, Christian—a.k.a. Gunter. I held my gun on them as their eyes focused.

"Gentlemen," I said, peeking out of the hole, "hope you don't mind my popping in like this."

I climbed inside and spread my feet for balance. The thick stench of gunpowder made me cough. A table, chairs and TV had been thrown against the opposite wall, where the two men lay. The windows were shattered, the cold wind rushing in. The MG42 teetered on the sill. "Watch out, Hanson!" I shouted and shoved it out.

Grüber barked at his son in German. With visible strain, Christian got to his feet.

"Look, Christian," I said, "I'm sure you're tough, and I know Dad's watching and all, but I can shoot a lot faster than—"

His leg whipped out in a perfect crescent kick, sending my gun out the window.

"Well, *that* was embarrassing," I said. "Any chance of a do-over?"

His limbs were a blur as he launched forward, driving a side kick into my hip, slamming me against the far wall. I slid down until I was sitting. I'd be lying if I said it didn't hurt. Across from me, Grüber laughed.

"Kill him. With your bare hands."

As Christian moved in, I pretended to be knocked out. I needed him closer and off-balance. I waited, and just as he lifted his foot again, I uncoiled from the floor and punched him square in the solar plexus with all 200 pounds of me behind it. His face froze in mid-breath and he tumbled backwards and banged against the window frame.

The entire tower groaned. Like a chorus of angry ghosts, a thousand pieces of metal screeched at once. It began to tip. I scrambled for the opening, got my feet on the ladder and frantically lowered myself. A hand appeared in the opening and slipped away. The tower continued to fall as I raced down, sliding down every other rung—60 feet, then 50, then level with the trees. Twenty feet from the ground, I jumped into the arms of a balsam fir, the feathery limbs snapping as I fell, until I landed flat on my back in deep powdery snow.

The wind was knocked out of me, but I was able to sit up. With one final moan the tower plummeted toward the cliff, until the observation hut sheared off and crashed down the mountainside. When I looked around,

Hanson was in the road with the MG42. He shook his head.

"You always were subtle, Stevens."

The platoon of old men that a few minutes ago had ruthlessly shot Weinberg now stood slump-shouldered and sobbing, their proud posture deflated, their weapons dangling from feeble hands. Decades of running and hiding had finally caught up with them. Hanson leveled his gun at them. One of the Nazis dropped his rifle. And then another.

52

THE SUMMATION FROM HELL

"You really stepped in it with this one, buddy," Hanson said.

We were in Grüber's office, poring over boxes of files. It was surreal. I still couldn't believe that a missing painting had led to this: the discovery of a Nazi hideout in the Catskills. While state police combed the ravine for the bodies of Grüber and Christian, the eighty-nine residents of Wittenberg View—mostly SS, along with a few South American domestics and private nurses—were shuttled to the Albany Field Office for identification and interrogation. A handful of bedridden men were taken to the hospital and placed under suicide watch, and, sadly, Agent Weinberg's body had been bagged and taken to Albany for an inquest.

The paintings were carted off to the Field Office. Soon an FBI team would pack up the entire compound, and in a couple of days you'd doubt anyone had lived here. I wandered around, taking in the framed photographs on the bookcase. There were black and whites of a young Grüber in uniform with other soldiers, Grüber with a woman and children, and a color photo of him with a little girl. Were it not for the damning files, at first glance this could have been the office of any successful retiree. There were no Nazi flags on the walls, no signed copies of *Mein Kampf* on the shelves. I was admiring a Matisse sketch when Hanson pulled something out of a desk drawer.

"Hey, catch."

He tossed it to me. It was a knife in its scabbard. The handle was black and textured, with an enameled red and white diamond and swastika in the center. I was holding a Hitler Youth Knife. And an early model at that, with the motto *"Blut und Ehre!"* etched on the blade.

"Keep it," Hanson said.

"But it's evidence."

Hanson peered down the hall. Nobody was around.

"We've got more than enough," he said. "You've earned it."

"Thanks." I slipped it in my jacket pocket.

An agent appeared at the door. "Sir?"

She was a fresh-faced, all-American brunette. She stood at attention with her hands behind her back.

"Yes, Agent Olson?" Hanson said.

"There's something you should see."

"The crematorium? Already have."

"No, sir. Something else."

"We're busy, Miss Olson. What is it?"

"I can't describe it, sir. It's downstairs."

Hanson and I followed her down the hall to a spiral staircase. We clanked down for a long time and turned a corner at the bottom. She led us down a long cinderblock passage. The ceiling was low, and we had to duck our heads. We were under the hillside someplace. At a pair of ornate wooden doors, Agent Olson stopped. Fluorescent lights hummed.

"A bomb shelter?" Hanson said.

She averted her eyes and opened the door. Hanson led the way. Ten feet inside, he stopped and gaped.

It was a vast room with a high ceiling. At the far end a Nazi flag hung over an altar. Built into the wall around the perimeter was a continuous Lucite case with artifacts inside. It reminded me of an exhibition at the Smithsonian. I went closer. Behind the Plexiglas were dozens of black cubbies, each containing a neatly folded uniform with a hat or cap on top, medals, pictures, a plaque with an inscription in German, and an urn. The plaque stated the person's name, rank, unit, and dates of birth and death. A few had second urns and photos of women. I looked around the room. There were at least 100 occupied cubbies and an equal number of empty ones.

"It's a mausoleum," I said.

Hanson shook his head. "How many fugitives did Grüber sneak out, I wonder."

I could feel the ghosts hovering around us. Hanson turned to Agent Olson, who remained at the entrance.

"Olson, write down the names and make sure the crime scene guys photograph this place thoroughly before they dismantle it. I want the U.S. Attorney to see this." He tapped me on the arm. "Which reminds me, we need to get back and prepare for tomorrow's debriefing."

"You can handle it," I said.

"I know I can. But *you* uncovered this mess, so you're going to do most of the talking."

We were at the FBI Albany Field Office outlining the case for Margaret Fox, U.S. Attorney for the Northern District of New York. The debriefing session was about to begin. Svetlana was here, along with Hanson, a few of his agents, members of Ms. Fox's legal entourage and a stenographer. Ms. Fox, a sharp, silver-haired woman with eyes almost as piercing as Svetlana's, looked at me from across the table.

"Mr. Stevens," she said, "before the break, you detailed your and Miss Krüsh's involvement in the case. The steps you took to uncover the paintings and their looted status, and to determine Mr. Grüber's real identity are commendable. They show great ingenuity and persistence. However, at this point I would like to know more about some background items, items that may have bearing on any prosecutions or extraditions of the remaining residents of Wittenberg View. Please tell me about the following…"

Fox's assistant handed her a legal pad. The attorney ticked through the items with a pen.

"One, how did Mr. Grüber acquire the paintings in the first place? Two, what became of the proceeds from the sale of said paintings? And three, what elements of *your* case—involving Serif, DeAngelis, René or the dead artists—do you consider unresolved? I have a video conference with the Attorney General later this afternoon, so brevity would be appreciated."

"Yes, ma'am." I took a drink of water. "Let me start with the history."

I nodded to Svetlana, who with Agent Olson had created a simple PowerPoint presentation. The first slide was a side-by-side comparison of Terrence Young's driver's license photo with Hartmann Grüber's *Luftwaffe* personnel record.

"First," I said, "Terrence Young, the owner/operator of Wittenberg View, was actually Hartmann Grüber. In 1941, Grüber was an *Oberleutnant*, or First Lieutenant, fighter pilot in the Luftwaffe. During the Battle of Britain, he suffered a serious leg injury and was reassigned to the Luftwaffe General Staff.

"Around this time, the German High Command created a special section for the systematic collection of artwork, focusing on prominent Jewish citizens and other collectors, as well as dealers, galleries and museums—primarily in France. This group, the *Einsatzstab Reichsleiter Rosenberg*, was headed by Alfred Rosenberg. Do we have a picture, Svetlana?"

"Of course." A moment later Rosenberg appeared on the screen.

"Besides developing the *Einsatzstab*," I said, "Rosenberg was the Nazi party's chief ideologist and racial theorist, the man largely responsible for the party's anti-Semitism propaganda.

"Back to Grüber," I said. "In late '41, he was appointed Special Adjutant to the *Einsatzstab* for Reichsmarschall Goering. Hermann Goering, as I'm sure most of you know, was a gluttonous art collector. Because of Goering's personal interest in the *Einsatzstab's* activities, he provided Luftwaffe resources—planes, trains and trucks—for the transport of all seized artwork.

"As Senior Collections Officer, Grüber was placed in charge of the physical collection of art. In effect, he was Goering's eyes and ears, making sure the *Einsatzstab* didn't cheat Goering out of the most valuable pieces. He supervised the pickup and transport to a number of warehouses—most importantly, the *Einsatzstab's* headquarters, the *Jeu de Paume* in Paris."

"*Jeu de Paume?*" Hanson said.

Svetlana sat up from her computer.

"The principal staging location for displaying captured works," she said. "It was set up like a large gallery. Goering, one of his representatives, or one of Hitler's representatives would visit and choose pieces for their respective collections."

Up on the screen, a series of slides showed Hitler and Goering "shopping" for art. In one picture, Grüber was just visible among the general staff.

"Between 1940 and 1944," I said, "approximately twenty-two thousand pieces of art went through the *Jeu de Paume* alone. And those were just the cataloged works. You see, all this time Grüber was in a perfect position to withhold paintings *before* they could be recorded."

"In other words," one of the lawyers said, "the stuff *fell off the truck?*"

Everyone chuckled.

"In a sense, yes," I continued. "Grüber took the ones he wanted and stashed them around France. Who knows exactly how many paintings he skimmed, but it wouldn't surprise me if the final number was in the thousands. Based on OSI documents"—one of the FBI agents passed out booklets—"it's clear that Grüber was more than a simple courier. He was charged with acquiring collections by any means necessary. Seizing them, purchasing them for a fraction of their real value, or in some cases, murdering the owners. According to the late Agent Weinberg, Grüber killed at least two dozen collectors and museum officials himself. So, besides all of the art theft, he was wanted for war crimes."

"Interesting," Fox said. "Please continue."

Svetlana, in blasé repose, gave me an encouraging half-smile. I stood in front of the projector screen.

"This is where it gets tricky. When looking into the paintings, we consulted the records of the MFA&A—the U.S. agency responsible for recovering and restituting the stolen artwork. In 1951, all of Grüber's paintings were listed as having been returned to their rightful owners."

I nodded to Svetlana.

"I have spoken to an agency in the French government," she said. "So far, at least fifty paintings listed as returned were never received by them."

"Which means," I said, "Grüber had someone on the inside. This person was probably an American, either somebody in the OSS's Art Looting Investigation Unit, the MFA&A, or an Allied soldier with access. Grüber must have bribed this person into signing off on his skimmed paintings and helping him smuggle them out of Europe. I believe this same person aided Grüber in smuggling out Nazi war criminals and hiding them in the United States."

"But you have no idea who this person is?" Fox said.

"No, ma'am, I don't."

She frowned. "Something you haven't addressed, Mr. Stevens, is how Grüber managed to keep himself and a camp full of Nazis hidden for so long. The Catskills are hardly the Andes."

I turned to Svetlana. "Do you have the Google Earth picture?"

Five seconds later it appeared on the screen. I pointed at landmarks as I spoke.

"Here's the compound. Bungalows, community building, chalet—which served as Grüber's residence—swimming pool and a crematorium—Hanson and I discovered that this morning. Auto repair shop, generator shed, art storage building, not to mention the bunker we found beneath the main building. Besides a firing range and arsenal, we found years of food and water down there."

"None of this explains how they remained hidden," Fox said.

"In a way it does," I said. "For one thing, they were all military men, and many of them were highly skilled. According to work logs, each man had specific duties on the compound to reduce dependency on outside help. But this"—I waved my hand over the surrounding woods—"was their ace in the hole. It's all old growth forest, managed by the Catskill Forest Preserve. As you can see, it surrounds Wittenberg View. According to the deed, it's closed to settlement and recreation, and the only people allowed up there are select DEC officials and residents of Wittenberg View. My sense is that Grüber had a powerful associate behind the scenes to make all of this happen and keep it hidden."

"But this is just a theory," Fox said.

"Afraid so." I took my seat again. "The next topic is the money. Hanson is the one to tell you about it."

Agent Olson passed out copies of a spreadsheet. Hanson took one and stood up.

"First off," he said, "it appears Grüber used a major portion of the art proceeds to fund his fugitive-smuggling operation. Mind you, this is based on preliminary information, but it looks like he was bringing them in from all over."

He pointed at a series of tables and charts on the screen.

"Germany, Austria, Brazil, Paraguay, Bolivia and Argentina," he said. "Between 1948—when Grüber first settled in the U.S.—and 1991—when he closed Wittenberg to new fugitives—he brought in 183 Nazis, almost all SS and Luftwaffe. Here's the breakdown: 3 generals, 8 colonels, 12 majors, 21 captains, 51 lieutenants and 88 enlisted men. More than half of them are already dead, as confirmed by the mausoleum found on the property."

Fox scribbled on her legal pad. "And the money?"

"The Bureau's forensic accountants are working on it," Hanson said. "Grüber was a meticulous record-keeper, which helps. His computer and ledger show large deposits into accounts in the Caymans. I've already contacted State about freezing them."

"Good," Fox said.

"But, we found something much more disturbing than the accounts themselves."

"I can do without the suspense, Agent Hanson."

"Grüber was supporting Neo-Nazi and anti-Semitic groups."

"How many groups?"

"At least twenty. And we're talking *a lot* of money."

Fox's team stared at each other in disbelief.

"Names?" Fox said.

"They run the gamut," Hanson said. "Everything from the National Alliance here in the U.S., to foreign ones like the São Paolo Skinheads in Brazil and Neo-Nazi 'schools' in Paraguay. He's also been depositing money into private accounts, so I'm confident we'll find more fugitive Nazis at the end of the money trail."

Hanson took a deep breath and continued.

"Grüber was also supporting groups engaged in historical revisionism and Holocaust denial," he said. "The Institute of Historical Review, Jew Watch, and authors of denial literature like David Zündel in Germany. There are a few historians and archivists in the U.S. government that we'll be investigating as well. It's possible these individuals were paid to sabotage historical records in an effort to deny the Holocaust. It seems Grüber was patient. He wasn't interested in an immediate Nazi rebirth. He was content for this to take generations."

"Jesus," one of the lawyers said.

Hanson drank some water. "Finally, it's possible Grüber's money has aided Muslim extremist groups like Al-Qaeda."

"*What?*" another lawyer said.

Hanson gave a grim nod. "We've known for a long time that the common ground between Neo-Nazis and Muslim extremists is Holocaust denial," he said. "Our friends at the Agency have video of meetings between Hamas and Neo-Nazi groups. It's for real."

Ms. Fox took off her reading glasses and dangled them from pinched fingers. There was a vacuum of silence in the room. We were all thinking about the awful scenarios that might grow out of what we'd uncovered.

"The idea of these groups receiving funding is disturbing," Fox said, "but we may be able to include them in conspiracy charges. We'll also pursue charges against those involved in the sale and forgery of the looted artwork. Mr. Stevens, perhaps you could give us a verbal flowchart of the scheme?"

"Sure," I said. "Using the stock of artwork that Grüber looted, Mr. Serif and other dealers sold pieces on the black market, mainly to wealthy sheiks in the Middle East. This arrangement was successful until Mr. Serif decided to double-dip.

"Working with a master forger named Jean René, Serif had forgeries made of Grüber's originals, and using antique typewriters, paper and rubber stamps, Serif created false provenances for the fakes, which were more likely to come under scrutiny. Then, Serif sold the originals to his Middle Eastern customers, and dumped the fakes on galleries in the Far East, never expecting the two would cross paths. And they didn't until one of the forgeries showed up at Sotheby's, which started this whole mess."

"Excellent." Fox looked at Hanson. "I will need diagrams showing all of this."

"No problem," Hanson said.

"Before we finish, Ms. Fox," I said, "you asked what aspects of our case are still unresolved. While the circumstantial evidence points to Grüber's men killing DeAngelis, we don't know for certain who killed René and his two subcontracted artists. It's possible René killed the artists himself, and then someone else killed him, but we can't be sure. The other unresolved point, as I've mentioned, is who Grüber's confederate was."

"And what of the artwork?" Fox said.

"Being off-loaded downstairs as we speak," Hanson said. "We'll work with Stevens's contact at the National Gallery Library to track down the rightful owners for restitution after trial."

Hanson wagged a pencil at Svetlana and me. "Seems some of these Holocaust claims organizations have rewards. Any of the paintings show up on their lists, I'll make sure they know who found the stuff."

"We won't hold our breath," I said, "but if anything comes of it, tell them to contact Svetlana. She handles the money."

Ms. Fox and her entourage stood up. "Very good, Agent Hanson," Fox said. "And as for you—Mr. Stevens, Ms. Krüsh—excellent work. Rest up. We may need you to testify at trial in a few months."

Svetlana and I looked at each other. "We can't wait," I said.

53

WHEN TRAINING TAKES OVER

Shay and I were meeting at her place, then going out to dinner to celebrate. From Albany I drove straight to her apartment and bounded up the stairs two at a time. Her door was unlocked and I went right in. The lights were on. Soft jazz saxophone played on the stereo.

"Shay?"

An acrid smell hung in the air. Matches? Candles? I walked slowly into the apartment.

When faced with something it doesn't want to see, the mind is very good at playing tricks. Across the room, Shay was slumped against the wall, staring up at a canvas. From a distance it looked as though she was simply getting a different perspective on her work. I wanted to say something, hoping a word from me would snap her out of her trance, but I was afraid to shatter the illusion that she was daydreaming. I forced myself to walk forward.

She lay against the wall with her legs stretched in front of her. Her overalls were dark with blood down the bib and belly. Her hand, still clutching a paintbrush, lay on the floor in a puddle of blood. Another paintbrush—a thin one from her hair—jutted out of her neck, and more blood covered her throat. The hair on that side of her neck was matted and stuck to her skin. I reached out to touch her but couldn't bring myself to do it. Shay was dead, her eyes glazed over and fixed in the direction of the last thing she saw…her canvas.

The strength went out of my legs. For maybe an hour I was frozen in a penitent position, forcing myself to breathe. The stereo, locked in a sadistically endless loop, played the same melancholy saxophone over and over. There would be no sharing of my apartment with Shay. No strolling Central Park in the fall, no making eyes at each other across crowded rooms. No weekends in Millbrook. No more fights, no more laughter. Nothing.

A chill went down my back, like I was entered by her spirit. Immediately I knew what I had to do. *Find who did this and make him suffer.* I'd smash the person's teeth out with a hammer. I'd crush his windpipe with my heel and watch him suffocate to death. I'd devote every scintilla of training and intelligence to catching him and making his last experience on Earth one continuous scream.

When I tried to stand, my legs were numb. I fell down. I sat on the floor for a minute, welcoming the prickly sensation as the circulation returned, then got to my feet and shut off the stereo. I walked over to Shay and closed her eyes. And as I touched her icy forehead, something delicate inside me broke.

I didn't have any gloves, but I didn't care. I got down on all fours and scrutinized the floors a square foot at a time, starting with the area around Shay's body. Miniscule drops of dried paint, in every imaginable color, stippled the Linoleum. There were a million tiny pieces of debris: insect husks, beer caps, bits of monofilament from clothing price tags, and desiccated grains of fried rice. Finally, after an hour of methodical crawling, I hit pay dirt: a tiny sprig of balsam fir, the needles still green and tender. Although possibly a coincidence, the one place where I'd seen balsam firs lately was Wittenberg. And since this sprig was fresh and in a part of the room where I hadn't been before, it most likely came from someone else's clothing. I left the twig, crept three feet, and found clue number two.

Ten feet from Shay's body, covered by a fallen canvas, was her hatchet, the blade streaked with blood. I left it alone and rose to my knees. I could picture Shay throwing it at her killer just before she was shot. Judging from the tight, regular pattern of the droplets, the person stood in shock before moving. I got back down and followed the drops. The spatter pattern suggested the person ran for the door. Following the drops into the kitchen area, I spied something wedged under the refrigerator. For several seconds, I stared at it.

It was my gun. The one Gunter took from me the night of my abduction.

The killer was one of Grüber's people.

I didn't even think about taking it, not for one second. It was registered to me, which meant that when they removed the 9mm bullet from Shay's body, they'd check for people close to her who had 9mm handguns, and I would be at the top of the list. There was already a report on file with the state police that the gun had been stolen, and when the medical examiner established time of death, it would be clear that I couldn't have done it; a dozen people had seen me upstate, over three hours away, for two days.

I picked up the blood trail again. A blood-soaked dishtowel lay in the sink. Shay had seriously wounded her killer, which pleased me. After lingering at the sink, the drops were off again, but they appeared to return to the body. This made no sense. Then I realized what had happened: the bastard went back to stab Shay in the throat with the paintbrush. I gritted my teeth. The blood trail went into the bathroom.

There, the killer had paused at the sink, which, too, was bloody, and in doing so, had allowed a puddle of blood to collect on the Linoleum. And right in the center of the puddle was the semicircular impression of a woman's heel.

The fir sprig suggested the killer had come from Wittenberg View, and the gun convinced me of it, but this new piece of evidence threw me. The mark wasn't big enough to be from the heel of a man's boot, and even if Gunter or one of his men had been clever enough to wear a woman's shoes to confuse matters, they couldn't have done it because Gunter was dead and we'd arrested the others. So it had to be a woman. One of the South American domestics? Or somebody else?

I thought of the photographs in Grüber's office. There were several of him with a wife and children, and at least one of the children was a girl. I needed to see those pictures again. But first, there was something I had to pick up. I left without looking back.

Driving up to Millbrook, despite a seething desire to speed, I took my time. As I cruised along with the windows down, letting the bitter air shock me into wakefulness, I tried to forget how I'd last seen Shay. I wanted to remember her as vivacious and beautiful, not lifeless and mutilated.

When I reached my place, I left the car running and ran inside. I grabbed some latex gloves and a glass cutter from the lab and went downstairs to my bedroom closet to fetch my other gun. I unwrapped the oil-soaked cloth.

It was a Smith & Wesson .45 Colt revolver that had once belonged to my paternal grandfather, a charming scoundrel named Al. It was the gun he'd used as a bootlegger, the gun he'd allegedly shot two pirates into the Atlantic with, the gun that was unregistered and untraceable. I opened the cylinder. Six brass casings glinted back at me. I snapped it shut.

As soon as I caught up with this woman, she was going to get all six bullets right in the chest.

54

DOWN THE RABBIT HOLE
(IT'S APROPOS, TRUST ME)

It was seven o'clock and two below zero when I parked in the dead-end outside Wittenberg View. While the compound was sure to be empty, I couldn't afford to be seen. I snowshoed in and paused on the ridge overlooking the compound. No smoke from the chimneys today. No rattling from snowblowers. The very air rang with silence. Time for a simple B&E with no frills. Grab those family photos and get out. I headed down the ridge for the main house.

At the deck, I leaned the snowshoes against the railing and readied the glass cutter. I was about to start cutting the sliding glass door when I noticed it was open a crack. I nudged it and crept inside. The place was cold and dim and vaguely dead. Nothing but Grüber's armchair in front of the fireplace. I went to the office.

Except for the desk and an empty power strip that lay on the floor like a dead snake, the room was empty. The filing cabinets, books, artwork, and most importantly, the photographs, were all gone. I knew Hanson's team was efficient, but this was ridiculous—everything carted away within a day of the arrest. Hopefully they'd left me *some* clue to the woman's identity.

I rifled through the desk drawers. Not even a paper clip. Knowing how thorough the evidence collection teams were, I was lucky to still have a floor to stand on. All I could do was wander around and see what, if anything, was left.

I had just started down the hall when I heard a muffled clunk, emanating from the walls. Holding the gun at my side, I padded down the hallway, checking a bedroom, then another bedroom, then a TV room, then a game room. There it was again. The noise was coming from someplace deep under the house.

I crept down the spiral staircase. When I reached the bottom, I heard the noise again, louder this time. A person, not a machine, was making the sound and the person was frustrated. My chest flushed under the heavy jacket. My ears strained to pick up a voice, or voices. If Bureau personnel were making that racket, there would be at least two of them. As I eased along the corridor, it became clear the noise was coming from the mausoleum. The doors were open. I still hadn't heard any talk. In a low crouch, I swung inside with my gun aimed ahead of me. The Nazi flag was gone, the Lucite cases empty. Fluorescent lights flickered in the bare room.

I turned to go, and there it was again. In the far corner, the floor of the display case was hinged open. Now instead of a clunking, there was the sound of something being dragged. I crept over with the gun aimed at the hole. It was a 3' by 3' opening, and the rungs of a ladder showed at the top. How far that ladder descended, I had no idea. I felt in my pockets for the flashlight. It was in my other coat.

If ever a situation called for a grenade, this was it. I didn't know if the person down there was friend or foe. If I went down without announcing myself, and they were agents, I might get shot. And if I *did* announce myself and they were bad guys, I might get shot. The hole sneered at me. I considered jumping straight down, but I couldn't see the bottom, and if it was more than eight feet, I could break my legs. *The answer to all of this was down there.* Gun in hand, I secured my feet on the ladder and started down, unsure of who or what I'd find at the bottom.

55

THE BITCH

I'd descended six feet when a piece of wood clonked me on the side of the head. I fell the rest of the way, whacking my chin on the ladder and landing on my knees on cement. The gun skittered away. My kneecaps screamed like they'd been run through with red-hot swords. The room spun. A single light bulb glared from the ceiling, but my eyes hadn't adjusted yet and everything was a gray blur. From back in the shadows there was the inimitable click of a gun hammer. I looked with a start. A figure came into focus. She was sitting atop a steamer trunk with her legs crossed, pointing my revolver at me.

She was Devon Trevelyan.

"Dakota Stevens," she said, "how sweet of you to drop in. Don't mind me. Just picking up a few things."

At her feet, two canvas duffel bags brimmed with loot. Mixed in with wads of cash were hints of gold and gems. She tapped a duffel with her boot.

"Father always said, if there was one thing he learned from the Jews it was to keep some portable wealth handy, in case one needs to leave in a hurry."

"Your *father*?"

"Yes, Hartmann Grüber." She raised her chin. "And my mother was the youngest daughter of *Waffen SS* Colonel Dietz."

"Now *there's* a heritage to be proud of," I said. "You realize your father's dead, right? Along with your brother."

Her eyes flashed and for a second I braced for a bullet that never came.

"Half-brother," she said brusquely. "Regrettable. But I warned father about doing business with Serif. Anyway, not my problem anymore."

Painfully, I got to my feet and steadied myself against the wall.

"You killed Shay." My words sounded hollow in the cement room.

"Sorry, love, couldn't have loose ends lying about." She hopped off the steamer trunk. She was favoring her left arm. "Now, as convenient as it would be to shoot you in this ready-made tomb, you will notice that I have limited use of one arm. So, be a dear and help me with these bags."

"Shay got you good. I saw the blood."

"The bitch only nicked me," she said. "Move."

The idea of helping her filled my throat with bile, yet I needed to buy time until I could wrest my gun away from her. She stepped aside as I cinched the bags tight and lifted them up one at a time. They were dense.

"Now it all makes sense." I slung the straps over my shoulders. "The imperfect British accent. The multiple languages. The fact that you didn't panic the night your brother and his goons abducted me. The attempt to take me off the scent by mentioning the Quedlinburg Hoard.

The 'connections in the art community' your father warned Serif about. The color photo upstairs of the little girl. It was all there."

When I turned around, she was outside of the hole, looking down with the gun aimed at my head. I took each rung deliberately, trying to balance the load.

"Let me guess how it went," I said. "Your mother dies when you're young, so father sends you off to England to boarding school." I went up a rung. "By the time you finish university, you're able to return to the states with a decent British accent, fluency in foreign languages—including German—and knowledge of art."

I climbed a few rungs. "With monies from the looted art, your father is able to buy your position at the museum. You become his eyes and ears, using your connections and insider knowledge to deflect any suspicions. But when you found out Serif was double-dipping, you had to put an end to it." I paused to catch my breath. "How am I doing so far?"

"Admirably," she said.

"You wanted Serif eliminated," I said, "but your father said no. He needed Serif's Middle East buyers, and keeping him as a middleman enabled your father to stay in the background."

At the top, I pushed the bags out one at a time, then pulled myself up. Devon backed away, steadying the pistol on my chest. The hammer was still cocked. I picked up the bags again and led the way down the low passageway to the spiral stairs.

"As for your boss," I said, "when DeAngelis told you about the painting, and how he suspected forgery, you decided he had to go. You needed to clean up the situation before it got out of hand. So, you had Christian and his boys try to nab Serif and run over Svetlana and me, but they failed. And when they killed DeAngelis, they botched that, too."

We plodded up the stairs. I was sweating from the exertion and from the thought of a .45 slug aimed at my spine.

"David was your fault," she said. "I might have let him go were it not for you."

"Sure, keep telling yourself that," I said. "So at that point, you took over. You found Jean René's loft, and while he was in China, you got the identities of his forgers…" The spiral stairs kept going. The duffel straps dug into my shoulders. My knees throbbed. "…And you killed two of them—Carter and Birchfield. To implicate René, you left a news clipping, and to convince me that Contessina was involved, you planted the bogus appointment card."

"Which you most willingly bought," Devon said.

"Not for long," I said. "Anyway, when René returned from his latest trip to Shanghai, you picked him up somewhere, went back to his loft, killed him and put him on ice. Christian must have helped you there. You even tried to implicate Shay using hairs from a red wig. *You* were the woman I saw coming out of René's building that night, not Shay."

Devon was behind me as we crossed the great room. At the stone fireplace, I stopped and took the duffel straps off my shoulders.

"Easy," she said.

"Just getting a better grip. The damn things weigh a ton."

I balanced the duffels on my shoulders with my palms flat underneath. I needed to make my move soon.

"You tried going after Shay next," I said, "but with me hanging around, it was impossible to get close."

"A temporary nuisance," she said.

I bristled. "So what were you left with? A last-ditch attempt to throw me off the scent—that crap about the Quedlinburg Hoard and how I'd never find the painting. And when *that* doesn't work, your father's mercenaries come after us and get their asses handed to them."

She went to the sliding glass door, flung it open and stepped back. I led the way.

"Nasty, the cold, isn't it?" she said. "It's summer where I'm headed. Too bad you can't accompany me."

"Where, Argentina? What are you going to do, run one of your father's Nazi schools?"

"You realize, of course, that you accomplished nothing." The wind rustled the fir trees. "Too many things are already in motion."

We reached the stairs that led to the parking lot. This was my last chance. I started up.

"You know what I think? I think you're just pissed off that I chose her over you."

"*Please*, that mutt? Do you really—"

Pivoting on my heels, I heaved the right duffel at her like a giant shot put, so hard that I slipped backward and landed on my ass. It struck her square in the chest. The gun went off and clattered down the stairs. I dropped the second duffel to grab her, but before I could, she rolled clear. I glanced around for the gun, couldn't find it and when I looked again, she was scrambling up the hill.

She was unbelievably fast. Remembering that whetstone body of hers, I followed her up the stairs and into the woods. Devon bounded through the snowdrifts like a whitetail doe. Just as I would glimpse her, she'd disappear behind another fir tree. I was losing her.

I staggered down the hill, using her footprints for purchase. I broke out of the trees and she was 50 yards ahead of me, racing across the frozen pond. But just as I was getting my second wind, she began to tire. The gap between us narrowed—50 yards, then 20, then an arm's length away, my entire being fixated on grabbing that pretty Aryan neck and choking her to death.

I sprang for her, my fingers hooking the hood of her jacket. And as I pulled her down, the ice cracked beneath us.

56

HYPOTHERMIA

The water hit me with a shock, instantly sucking the heat from my body, the cold so intense it burned. I gasped, scrabbled to grab hold of something, anything. Devon surfaced, gurgled, flailed in the slushy water. She clawed at the edge of the hole, pulled in snow with every thrash of her arms. Digging my elbows into the packed snow around the rim, I started to haul myself up. Devon gouged her nails into my neck. She clutched my jacket collar, dragged me back in. Splashing back into the freezing water, I felt my limbs slowing down, seizing up. My body had only a couple minutes of struggle left.

Devon had attached herself to me, her legs locked around my hips, her good arm choking my neck. I threw an elbow and connected with her ribs. She yelped and loosened her grip. I got my head above water. We faced each other.

Her eyes were wide and crazed. She made strange, primal grunting noises as she snatched at my face and hair. She grabbed my ears and pulled me under again. As the water frothed around me, my mind became very clear, very still. The noise of our struggle was gone. I remembered the thing in my pocket.

With fumbling hands I pulled the Hitler Youth knife from its scabbard and plunged it into her side. She let out a watery scream and released her grip. Still holding the knife, I swung my arm out of the hole, rammed the point into the ice and pulled. I couldn't feel my arms and wasn't sure they were working until I was out of the water.

Flat on the snowy ice, I rolled away from the hole and lay on my back, hyperventilating and coughing at the same time. Something tugged at my feet. Devon, her face an icy blue that matched her eyes, was almost out of the water, kicking frantically. I was about to help her, in fact started to reach for her, when she smiled. In that instant I thought of Shay, of her beauty and talent, of how she must have suffered when she died. I snatched the knife from the ice.

"Goodbye, *Fräulein*."

I stabbed Devon where her chest and throat met. She tried to scream, but instead a catlike hiss came from her throat. The look of disbelief on her face morphed into horror, perhaps as she realized where she was headed. With one final burst of strength, she grabbed my boot by the shoelace and pulled. It came untied. She slid into the hole, then floated for a moment, before slowly sinking and drifting under the ice.

I stared at the blood-stained ice for I don't know how long. My teeth were chattering so hard they ached. I shook my head. My hair was frozen stiff. Suddenly I realized something…I might be out of the water, but I was far from safe. If I didn't get warm immediately, I could die of hypothermia.

I was still clutching the knife. Trembling with cold and adrenaline, I wiped the blade on my pant leg and stuck it in its scabbard. I crawled off the ice and creaked to my feet. Following the ragged trail we'd left behind, I staggered back toward the house.

When I reached the driveway, a man grabbed me and helped me down the stairs.

"I've got you, Mr. Stevens," he said.

When we got inside, another man was sitting in a chair in front of a fire. The man helping me stripped off my clothes as someone else wrapped me in a blanket. They took me to the fire and sat me down on the warm hearth.

"Did he do it?" the man in the chair asked.

"Yeah, with a knife."

I looked up and there was Deputy Director Marty Paulsen of the CIA, sitting in the chair, sipping a cup of tea.

"So, you got rid of her," he said. "Excellent."

I blinked for a few seconds, too stunned and too cold to speak. I was shaking uncontrollably, but wide awake. This was a good sign. One of the agents handed me a mug of tea. I sipped it and shivered.

"Relax," Paulsen said, "I'm good at keeping secrets. Besides, you did me a favor."

I thought about this as the fire sputtered and popped. And then I had it—the last piece of the puzzle.

"The inside man," I said. "Of course…the OSS… forerunner of the CIA. The blacked out names…your *father* was in the OSS…*he* was the one who helped Grüber."

"An arrangement that was supposed to end when my father died," Paulsen said. "But Grüber wouldn't let go, and I wasn't about to let that scum destroy my father's legacy. There was also my own reputation to consider."

"But now…" I suddenly remembered that nobody knew I was up here. "What now? You eliminate me?"

"I don't see why," Paulsen said. "You know my secret, and I know you killed a woman. Besides, your talents could prove useful someday. We might even be able to help each other."

His words nauseated me. I thought of Faust, of Daniel Webster, of deals made with Satan. Paulsen reached into his coat, pulled out my grandfather's gun. He pointed it at me for a moment before tossing it on the rug.

"Nice weapon," he said. "But unless I'm mistaken, that isn't standard government issue."

I didn't say anything. One of the agents came in from outside.

"Got them, sir." He handed Paulsen a thick folder of aging documents. "They were in the duffels."

The Deputy Director flipped through the papers, nodded and tossed them on the fire. We watched them burn until there was no trace of them. I pulled the blanket tighter.

"You're a long way from D.C.," I said.

"Information sharing, my boy," Paulsen said. "Came up to talk with Hanson—he may very well become the new Bureau Deputy thanks to you—and while in the neighborhood, I thought I'd do a bit of tidying up. Turns out you did it for me."

Two agents appeared at the sliding glass door. They had sunglasses on and were carrying the duffel bags.

"Ready, sir."

Paulsen stood up, put a hand on my shoulder.

"I'm sorry about Miss Connolly, son," he said. "I'll be in touch. And when I contact you, don't say no."

With that, Paulsen and his agents walked out. I listened to their footsteps on the deck until they faded away and I was left with only the crackling of the fire.

57

A Prayer That Would Go Unanswered

A month after I was cleared of Shay's murder, Svetlana came to my apartment, forced me to shower, shave and dress, then drove us out of the city. I asked her where she was taking me, but for the entire hour ride she didn't say a word. We were on the Saw Mill Parkway heading north, and I had no idea where we were going until she exited at Chappaqua. And when she turned into the cemetery, I knew.

"No, Svetlana."

She cut the engine, unzipped her jacket, and dropped the keys down her sweater.

"Mature," I said.

"Yes, and so is hiding in your apartment from the rest of the world."

"I'm not hiding. I've been nursing my wounds. Regrouping."

"Ah," she said.

"Look, I'm not ready for this, okay?"

Outside, water dripped off the trees and crawled down the windshield.

"Dakota, it wasn't your fault," she said. "She was involved in the forgery scam long before you met her.

She was self-destructive, and there was no way you could have saved her. If it wasn't some unknown killer, it would have been the alcohol or some violent drama."

Svetlana was right, but I didn't say anything. I just stared at the water drops, carving rivulets down the side window.

"You need to make peace with this woman," she said, "so we can help the police find her killer."

I hadn't told Svetlana about Devon and was unsure if I ever would. What happened between Devon and me was personal. Then Svetlana did something she'd never done before: she took my hands in hers.

"Please do this for me," she said. "It saddens me to see you this way. I need to see the old Dakota again, the cocky and charming Dakota who talked me into doing this nonsense. Three years ago, do you recall where we first met?"

"Harvard Square, in front of the Au Bon Pain," I said.

"Good, go find him. Go find *that* Dakota." She squeezed my hands and let go. "We need him. The phone has been ringing off the hook."

"Really?"

"Yes, it seems we are becoming moderately famous," she said. "Or I should say *you* are becoming moderately famous, as I already have fans."

"I've missed your modesty," I said.

"Abedi brought Serif to the office the other day." She adjusted the rear-view and primped her hair in it. "He paid us the balance, then Abedi punched him and left. Serif will be prosecuted, Ms. Fox said, and the owners of the originals are going after Serif and his clients to get their paintings back. Serif is finished."

"Good."

"And…a lawyer from the Holocaust Assets Recovery Administration came by and offered us a lump settlement. He said the rewards for all of the paintings individually would be astronomical, but that if we insisted on the full amount for every work, we could be in court for years trying to collect."

I groaned. "Did you tell him we didn't do this for the money?"

"I told him we did not wish to cause either the HARA or the owners of the paintings any trouble, and he wrote us a check on the spot."

I shifted in my seat. "How much?"

She shook her head. "I don't want you to get a swelled ego. Let us say it is more than enough to see us through the slow times or when clients don't pay."

"Well, do whatever it is you do with the money."

"Invest in shoes?"

I smiled faintly and opened the door.

"Wait." She reached behind the seat and pulled a bouquet of lilies from a paper bag. She handed them to me.

"I don't even know where it is," I said.

"A hundred feet down on your left. It's a lovely spot, under a dogwood. She loved them."

"How do you…never mind." I patted her arm and stepped out into the wet. I closed the door.

And then I set off, down the muddy lane, to do something we all find ourselves doing in life, the lucky ones just not as often. Alone, with nothing but the squish of my footsteps to keep me company, I wondered what I was going to say, and I hoped, no I prayed, that this was the last time I would have to do this for a person I cared about.

It was a prayer that would go unanswered.

ABOUT THE NOVEL

While this is a work of fiction, it is also the product of wondering "what if" in relation to a number of historical facts. In a famous 1964 *Playboy* interview, the brilliant Vladimir Nabokov had this to say about the mysterious process by which he began to assemble a work of fiction:

"All I know is that at a very early stage of the novel's development I get this urge to garner bits of straw and fluff...After the first shock of recognition—a sudden sense of 'this is what I'm going to write'—the novel starts to breed by itself..."

For me, the "bits of straw and fluff" were these:

1. The alleged fraud committed by art dealer Ely Sakhai, by which he commissioned forgeries of masterworks, then sold the originals and the forgeries to collectors on opposite sides of the globe.
2. Even after 60 years (since the end of WWII), tens of thousands of works of art were still missing; yet, previously lost works were being discovered with regularity.
3. Hermann Goering, a gluttonous art collector, siphoned off considerable Luftwaffe resources to

support an organization called the *Einsatzstab Reichsleiter Rosenberg*—a group dedicated to plundering art and cultural artifacts from Nazi-controlled territories.

There were several other bits of straw and fluff that contributed to the novel's coalescing, including the Monuments Men, the Munich Central Collecting Point, and the Quedlinburg Hoard; however, once I became curious, it was really the articles and government records themselves that prodded me—including a National Archives microfilm roll of the Einsatzstab's own records, for which I found myself using Google's Babel Fish translator almost daily.

I found this to be a fascinating subject, and hopefully you do, too. To that end, I invite you to visit the Dakota Stevens website and read PDFs of some of the government reports and other documents I consulted in writing the book. Since the page is password-protected, only purchasers of the book, like you, will have access to this information. The password is "zugzwang" (without the quotes). You can find all of this at www.dakotastevens. com.

About the Author

Chris Orcutt has written professionally for over 20 years as a fiction writer, journalist, scriptwriter, playwright, technical writer and speechwriter.

Orcutt is the creator of the critically acclaimed Dakota Stevens Mystery Series, including *A Real Piece of Work* (#1), *The Rich Are Different* (#2) and *A Truth Stranger Than Fiction* (#3). Orcutt's short story collection, *The Man, The Myth, The Legend*, was voted by IndieReader as one of the best books of 2013. And his modern pastoral novel *One Hundred Miles from Manhattan* (an IndieReader Best Book for 2014) prompted *Kirkus Reviews* to favorably compare Orcutt to Pulitzer Prize-winning author John Cheever.

As a newspaper reporter Orcutt received a New York Press Association award, and while an adjunct lecturer in writing for the City University of New York, he received the Distinguished Teaching Award.

If you would like to contact Chris, you can email him at corcutt007@yahoo.com or tweet him @chrisorcutt. For more information about Orcutt and his writing, or to follow his blog, visit his website: www.orcutt.net.

EXCERPT FROM *THE RICH ARE DIFFERENT*

Book 2 in the Dakota Stevens Mystery Series,
The Rich Are Different, is also available.

It was a steamy Sunday morning on July 4 weekend and I was being kidnapped.

Okay, not kidnapped exactly. After all, I hadn't been forced at gunpoint and the car I was riding in was a Bentley. Its tangy leather seats and walnut trim made it tough to claim I'd been taken entirely against my will. Besides, people who owned vehicles this nice didn't kidnap, they summoned.

Svetlana sat with her legs crossed, waggling one foot. Her laptop rested on a fold-down table. She was playing chess. Without a game or reading material, all I could do was take in the scenery.

We were on the Long Island Expressway, creeping through a construction zone. A workman sweated on a jackhammer outside, but the Bentley's thick body blocked out the noise so it was barely audible above the A/C washing over my face. Now I knew why the very rich were so aloof: Money insulated them from all things unpleasant. Things like going to a detective's office.

Vivian Vaillancourt, the enigmatic heiress who wanted our help, had refused to come to us. Instead she sent her three-ton luxury tank and her niece: a college-aged girl in Daisy Dukes and a rhinestone "DIOR" T-shirt. Delilah was a decent chauffeur, if a bit lead-footed, and as we reached the end of the construction zone, the big car surged forward, plastering Svetlana and me against the seats.

"Finally!" Delilah said.

Svetlana gave me a look. I leaned into her shoulder and spoke softly.

"So, what is this case about? She must have given you some idea."

"I only spoke to her assistant," Svetlana said. "It is an interview."

"Damn it, Svetlana, you dragged me out here for an *interview*? I'm not even sure I'm ready for this yet."

She touched my arm. "That was a once-in-a-lifetime case. This one won't be like that."

"I don't want to talk about it," I said.

"I know," she said. "But I have to say, it is nice to see you shaved for a change."

"Thanks. I was sick of the Robinson Crusoe look anyway."

We exited the expressway and minutes later glided into a tunnel of stately oaks. Pristine golf courses glistened. This was Sands Point. I rolled down the window and drank in the salt air from the Sound. Driveway gates whooshed by.

"I wonder which place is Daisy's," I said.

"Who?" Delilah's hair flounced on her shoulders. She was a blonde with brunette streaks or vice-versa.

"You know—Daisy Buchanan, from *The Great Gatsby*." I rolled up the window. "Fitzgerald used Sands Point as his model for Daisy's East Egg. Gatsby lived across the water on West Egg. Poor guy spent all his time staring at a light on Daisy's dock."

"Daisy Buchanan, hmm." She glanced over the seat back. The car drifted. "I'm sure I would've met her."

"She must have moved," I said. "My mistake."

I thought every American high schooler had to read that novel. Even Svetlana, a defected Soviet, knew who I was talking about. She smiled faintly and pushed a tuft of hair behind her ear.

At a towering iron gate with a "V" crest, we motored up a gravel drive, curved through a gauntlet of sculpted trees, and ground to a stop in front of a white Italianate mansion with a red tile roof. As I helped Svetlana out of the car, at least two dozen windows glared back at us in the bright sunlight. How many rooms? Twenty? Fifty? The manor's sweeping wings alone made my country retreat look like a tarpaper shack.

When I snapped out of my trance, the Bentley was gone. Still beside me was Svetlana, clutching her Gucci bag. We went to the door and rang. No one answered. As I rang again, the distinctive boom of a shotgun echoed from behind the house.

"What the hell is that?" I said.

Svetlana batted her eyes. "A gun perhaps?"

I sneered waggishly at her and strode across a gleaming lawn in the direction of the gunshots. The thick grass was like walking on memory foam. In the meantime the gun went off again: a blast, a brief silence, then another blast. Sounded like a double-barrel...

CPSIA information can be obtained at www.ICGtesting.com
Printed in the USA
LVOW07s1829250815

451486LV00010B/313/P